Of Faith Under Fire

previously The Diary of Narcissa Dunn

Elaine Violette

Critic's Comment

"The blending of historical fiction, paranormal, and romance genre gives depth to the story line and will grab your attention and your heart. The plot spins a web of lies, deceit, and a complex relationship between a young girl and her father... The story hits exactly the right tone and rhythm for a true page turner. I normally can sense what is coming next, but pleasantly not in this one. Violette made me fall in love with the character, Olivia, as she embarks on this epic and paranormal quest that will change her life forever."

~Shirley Webb, Author

"Elaine Violette has done an incredible job transporting the reader back to a time when women were judged by their standing, class, and what type of wife they would become. ...thought-provoking...harsh historical truths served up with love, lust, betrayal, and a ghost who is determined to see justice done."

~Readers Favorite

Of Faith Under Fire
Elaine Violette
ISBN: 978-0-9966821-9-0

Dedication

This book is dedicated to my husband Drew, my children
Roland Jr., Kevin, and Kristin, who bring joy to my days;
to my precious son, David, who left too soon and lives in my heart always.
To my grandchildren who keep me young, and to my students who
represent so many wonderfully diverse cultures and races.
It's been an honor to care for and serve all of you

CHAPTER ONE

Spring 1826

HMMM HMM HMMM hmm

A smile played on Olivia's lips but faded as her eyelids fluttered and she became fully awake. Startled, she lifted her head and glanced around her bedroom. "A dream...only a dream," she mumbled, sinking back into her pillow. She closed her eyes, hoping to recapture a vision of the mysterious woman humming a tune as sweet as a lullaby, but the memory flickered and disappeared into the world of dreams.

Tossing back her covers, she sat up, disturbing her cat who had been taking a long stretch at the foot of the bed. "It appears we've slept too long this morning, Speckles." With a yawn, Olivia smoothed a hand over the cat's gray and white spotted coat until a rapping on her door caused Speckles to jump from the bed and scoot under it.

"Livie, you best get your bottom out of bed before

your father gets back from the barn. He been gone over an hour. You know it take him half the time it takes you to get ready for church."

Being Sunday, Olivia wasn't surprised at the intrusion or the maid's scolding words clearly heard through the closed door. "I'm awake, Lovena. Be down shortly."

"You need to get some food in you before sittin' through one more of your daddy's long sermons. Get a move on."

"I'll be dressed and ready." Olivia called out with a yawn as she swept her thick, nearly black curls from her face and touched her feet to the cold wood floor. As she made up her bed and fluffed her pillow, she heard the customary sound of the housemaid's heavy shoes clomping down the stairs.

A spark of recollection from the strange dream returned as she poured water from her pitcher into a small basin. She'd sensed a deep sadness in the woman. *Maybe there's someone in our church who needs prayers.* She tried to recall the woman's features but she'd remained in shadows just as in previous dreams.

"Who is she?" Olivia wondered aloud as she immersed her hands into the cold water. Splashing her face helped her snap out of the remnants of a poor night's sleep and the lingering dream.

When she finished washing, she dressed quickly. The sun's reflection on her mirror as she brushed through her hair reminded her of her lateness. She tied the thick unruly curls back with a ribbon. After taking one last look in the mirror, she stepped into her shoes, laced them quickly and hurried downstairs.

Her father, the town's Congregational minister, refused to listen to any excuse for being late for church. He liked to greet his congregation as they walked through the meetinghouse doors. Olivia never minded the hours spent at church. Her father's sermons were always well prepared and even though his messages were ones she'd listened to at the dinner table many times, she didn't mind hearing them again. He still had a great booming voice, though he'd grown grayer and paunchier in the last few years.

When she entered the small breakfast room, her father was dressed in his Sunday suit with his worn Bible beside him. He lifted his eyes to his daughter, his expression sending a disapproving message at her late arrival. Lovena gave her a knowing glance as she set down a basket of warm biscuits to add to the thick slices of country bacon and scrambled eggs she'd already served.

"I won't be able to fit into my trousers, Lovena, if you keep serving these hearty meals. You make enough for ten," Reverend Fuller said as he reached for a biscuit.

"Who knows who gonna stop in any time mornin' or night? Young Mr. Tapley don't seem to think he needs an invite anymore," Lovena said, shaking her scarf-wrapped head that concealed her gray nappy hair.

"William has become part of the family over the past few months. I am impressed with him," he countered. "He takes his studies seriously and seeks my guidance, though I doubt I am the reason for his frequent visits." Raising a brow, he smiled at Olivia who sat opposite him.

Olivia took a large bite of a buttered biscuit hoping to avoid another discussion of William's merits. Her father was especially pleased William not only came from a well-respected family in town, but he'd be ordained in a couple of months. Since her father planned to retire soon, he appeared to have his eyes on William as his successor to the pulpit.

"He is an honorable young man, Olivia, and he'll

make a decent living as a minister." He paused to take a sip of tea. "I believe he'll ask me for your hand soon."

Olivia could no longer ignore her father's piercing gaze over the lip of his cup. Marriage was far from her mind. Only a year and a few months had passed since her mother's death. "I look forward to spending more time with you before I think of marriage."

"I appreciate the sentiment but you are of an age to consider your future. William's twenty-five. He wants to be settled down before taking on the responsibilities of a congregation. You could hardly do better than with a man of the cloth." Winking at his daughter, he lifted his Bible and held it to his chest as he so often did when he was preaching.

Olivia pursed her lips rather than be drawn into his attempt at humor. She might agree if she fell in love with someone as Godly as her father. She knew William was much admired by other girls in town, but she felt no passion in his presence. True, nineteen was a marriageable age but she wasn't ready for such a commitment. Apart from her church duties, she looked forward to helping at the local school in the fall. Picking up a bacon slice, she bit into it, hoping her father would resume his own breakfast.

"Lovena, will you be going over to Reverend Baylor's house later?" the minister asked, rising from his chair and pushing it into place.

"Not 'till later today."

"I understand his parlor may be getting too small for your church meetings."

"We sure is cozy in there. Reverend Baylor's been talkin' about startin' a fund to build a Baptist church but, Lordy, I be dead before that come about."

"No need to think so dismally. The Lord provides. Olivia, you'll need your cloak today," he said, addressing her without turning around. "There's a chill in the air. I'll be waiting on the porch. Don't dally."

Olivia stared at her father's back as he walked out the kitchen door that led onto the side porch. Standing now, she accepted the cloak and bonnet Lovena held out to her. She didn't miss the sympathetic look on the maid's round face.

BENJAMIN STOOD LOOKING up at the Fuller's old barn and its adjacent structure. His instructions were to tear down the section that once housed servants and farmhands and use the wood not yet rotted to repair the barn. Uncle Sylvester bartered Ben's labor to the church during the slow months in return for wood, nails, and other commodities needed to run his shop. Since the weather improved daily, it wasn't a bad part time job, though he preferred working in his uncle's carpentry shop.

His uncle expected him to take over the business someday and had put a hammer in Ben's hand as soon as he was old enough to hold one. Now as his apprentice, Ben was learning every aspect of the carpentry trade. Uncle Sylvester, or Uncle Syl as he called him, taught him about the different types of wood and how to carve and smooth each piece to perfection. It was as if the wood axed from tree trunks came alive again under his uncle's master hand. Ben wanted to do the same. Being covered with splinters and sawdust in the morning and cleaning up for an afternoon of polishing wood to a satin finish was a great day's work but in late winter and early spring, business was slow. Except for staining a piece of furniture or making a coffin when needed, new jobs had been sparse.

Walking through the open barn doors, Ben gazed around the enclosed area one last time before preparing to leave for the day. The smooth hand-hewn timbers and post and beam structure of the barn impressed him. It had been built well to withstand New England winters. Removing some old boards and patching up the roof would keep it sturdy for a few more years.

The barn was no longer used to house cattle or large farming equipment but areas needed cleaning up and re-structuring to meet Reverend Fuller's expectations. The minister wanted the barn renovated as a carriage house, keeping a couple of stalls for the horses and bartering off unneeded farm tools and machinery. Tools for planting and harvesting, horse and carriage needs, as well as bins to feed the horses and chickens would be cleaned up and refurbished.

The minister was a fair man, though he wasn't too pleased Ben had chosen to evaluate the job this morning rather than attend the long hours in church. He at least understood Ben's hours might not be regular, especially if one of his uncle's jobs needed his immediate attention. Simply overseeing his week's accomplishments and not carrying out heavy work on the Lord's Day seemed to appease Reverend Fuller. Ben much preferred walking the fields on a Sunday morning or riding to Snipsic Lake, the "Snip", as most called it. He liked to toss in a line and talk to God on his own terms.

Watching Olivia Fuller leave for church this morning with her father was the highlight of Ben's morning. Her striking beauty and a willowy figure caused his breath to catch. Today she was wrapped in a deep purple cape and wore an ivory-colored bonnet, her thick black curls spilling down her back. Would he have an opportunity to talk to her one of these days? Even a simple 'good morning' would do. He might recognize a disagreeable manner that would cause him to release her from his thoughts. He hoped so since now that her father hired him, he needed to keep his mind on his work and not on the minister's daughter.

How many years had he admired her from a distance? He doubted she ever noticed him though they were in the same school room for a time. He'd been a scrawny kid wearing trousers with holes worn into the knees and attended school only when he wasn't needed for farm work. Olivia, on the other hand, was always well dressed and perfectly groomed. Fortunately, Ben's uncle was his best teacher and what he didn't learn in class, Uncle Syl made sure he learned at home.

Why was he wasting his time thinking about Miss Fuller? The news circulating around town rumored she was practically engaged to Will Tapley who wasn't one of Ben's favorite people.

He walked outside and decided to do a last check of the small adjoining rooms. From his observation of the inner barn wall, the attached section appeared to be barely tacked on with few crudely tapered iron nails and was most likely built quickly out of necessity rather than from careful planning.

A door to the right of the larger barn doors led into a dank, narrow hall that ran the length of the side of the barn. As he walked down the hallway, he took a quick glance into each of the three small rooms. It was obvious the old living quarters hadn't been occupied for years and no one took the time to clean them out from their previous tenants.

Entering the last room, he looked about, grimacing. Two sets of bunks with moldy mattresses stained with dirt and rodent feces were left to decay. What appeared to be rags or old blankets were heaped in a corner. The middle room was smaller and in similar condition, except it held one cot with a shredded mattress hanging half off the bed. The mattress' filthy stuffing was pulled out and strewn about the floor. A couple of empty drawers were heaped on top of each other without a chest to contain them. As in the other room, long, crudely made nails were hammered into a wall and must have served as a place to hang work clothes or coats. Both of the rooms' side windows exposed cracked panes covered in cobwebs and dead insects.

When he walked into the front room, he noted the larger window that looked out at the main house a few hundred feet away. A moldy candle, its holder caked with dead spiders, sat on the window sill. Pressed against the front wall was a small cot with rusted springs and a filthy mattress in the same rotting condition as the others. A broken drawer lay on the floor. In a corner, an old wooden rocker sat with cobwebs snarled about its vertical rungs. Crumpled on its seat, lay a moth-eaten wool blanket. As he looked up and studied the support beams above, a creaking noise caused him to shoot a glance toward the rocking chair. It moved slightly, then stilled. Had a mouse skittered by?

Enough for today, he decided.

He wasn't looking forward to working through the cobwebs and filth before tearing this whole section down, but it had to be done. Once it was razed, he'd set aside salvageable boards and use them to repair the barn, a more constructive job that would give him some sense of accomplishment.

Relieved to be back outside, he breathed in the fresh spring air and brushed off cobwebs clinging to his sleeves and pants. Tomorrow he'd start shoveling out the side rooms. Taking a last look around, he returned to the barn, pushed the large doors closed and bolted them.

"You keep walkin' 'round the barn, Benjamin, like you been doin' and you gonna get dizzy."

Ben turned to see Lovena, the Fullers' housemaid, smiling at him, her arms crossed under her full aproned bosom. He tipped his worn cap and returned the smile.

"The Reverend Fuller and his daughter are off to church. They left behind a table full of food I ain't about to waste. Come in for some nice warm biscuits and my strawberry preserves before you figure out what you gonna do with that ramshackle barn."

"I am obliged ma'am. I've heard you're one of the best cooks in town. I'm not about to say no."

"Well, come on then."

Ben walked with her toward the farmhouse.

"I been telling the reverend those horses are gonna have the roof fallin' in on them if he don't get that old barn fixed. With the wind and rain goin' through there in the coldest months, it ain't fit for an old raccoon to live in, never mind those two fine horses he got in there."

"No doubt he heard you. He hired me to whip it back into shape though I can't promise much. I'll close up the holes as best I can."

"He says you gonna rip out those old rooms."

"Those are my instructions, ma'am."

"You call me Lovena, like everybody else."

When they reached the house, he followed her up the side porch steps and into the kitchen. Once inside, she signaled him to take a seat in the breakfast room.

"I'll be right back with some tea. You help yourself."

Ben took a biscuit from a basket on the table and scooped jam on it as he looked around the small area sectioned off from the larger kitchen and painted beige. Except for a side board, the room held just the wood table and four chairs. An open doorway led to a larger dining room. From his vantage point, it appeared more elegant, with beige and dark blue striped wallpaper. An ornate gold mirror on the wall reflected a dark wood dining table beyond it with a vase of spring flowers set in the center. His observations were interrupted when Lovena walked in carrying a tray with a teapot and cups.

"Before the missus moved into the back room behind the kitchen, I lived in those drafty rooms you be tearing down," she said, setting the tray down on the table. "Mrs. Fuller wanted me nearer to the kitchen so I didn't waste no time gettin' busy. She was one bossy lady, always…" She stopped, slapping a hand to her cheek. "Listen to me goin' on. Good Lord, I shouldn't be talkin' against the dead. Anyways, I think those rooms are haunted. You be careful. Those damp walls have frightenin' stories to tell. I don't go near 'em, no way, no more." Lovena rubbed goose bumps appearing on her heavy brown arms. "No way, I say. You be careful."

As Lovena poured his tea, Ben raised a brow at her superstition. The house had been built by Reverend Fuller's father in the early 1700's, he'd been told. Ben guessed the barn and adjoining quarters were slightly newer but not by much. He enjoyed learning about the history of the older homes and their designs. More were being built in town in the Georgian style with Federal and Greek revival features. His uncle enjoyed teaching him the specific characteristics of each house along the main road. Ben hoped to build his own one day so he carefully noted the features that interested him most.

Though the town was mostly farm land, some of the

older homes held interesting histories. Despite slavery being outlawed in the late 1700s in Connecticut, a few landowners still enslaved domestics and towns kept a blind eye. This house remained in the family and being a religious one, Ben wasn't about to believe some disgruntled spirit, slave or free, chose those rundown rooms to haunt.

LOVENA LOOKED THE young man over as he reached for another biscuit. He was tall, slim, and broad shouldered with a light complexion, reddened by the sun. A sprinkle of freckles crossed the bridge of his nose. Muscled arms caused the material on his faded flannel sleeves to pull taut when he creased his elbows. She guessed he was in his early twenties.

Good lookin' boy and polite, she thought, returning to the kitchen to finish cleaning up from breakfast, *not like that uppity, pasty-faced Will Tapley who don't give a nod or a thank you though he shows up for dinner more times than I can count. He ain't the one for my Olivia. Not with those thin lips and bushy eyebrows. They meet like squirrels' tails touchin' when he's listenin' to the reverend talk religion.*

Not that her opinion mattered, though she'd been

with the family for close to thirty years. She figured she'd gone past fifty but she had no birth certificate to prove it. Her bones told her she was old. What did matter was being here. She'd been with Olivia since she was born and the girl needed her, especially with Mrs. Fuller gone.

The minister's time was taken up by church business and Olivia was expected to serve the church just as her mother had done, taking part in Bible studies, working with the choir and playing the organ, not to mention her home chores. Olivia could only do so much and the minister could ill afford to hire another maid.

My sweet Livie, she thought, remembering the day the child had come running into the kitchen and saw Lovena leaning over a pail of water with blood dripping from a cut finger.

Lovena, you're bleeding!

No harm done chile. I just got sloppy slicin' up peppers.

Your blood...it's the same color as mine when I fell on the stones outside.

We is all the same on the inside, honey. Our hearts the same too. Don't you forget chile, we is all the same in God's eyes.

She hid a grin with her palm as she recalled how little Livie's eyes widened and the child reached up and gave Lovena the biggest hug a little girl could give. She was the one who gave the child hugs. Her mother was stern and tended toward coldness with strict expectations for her daughter. She loved the child, the maid knew, but she was hard on her, always expecting her to behave perfectly, especially in front of others. Her father had bowed to his wife's wishes concerning the child. Only Lovena would allow her to play like a little one should when the reverend and his missus weren't about.

"Thank you, ma'am, for your hospitality."

Lovena pulled herself from her daydreaming, realizing she'd gone off into the past and forgot about the young man who now stood by the back-door cap in hand.

"My name's Lovena, Benjamin, and you remember what I said about those rooms."

"I'll keep it in mind and if I run into any spirits, I promise to send them packing."

"Go on, now." She shooed him off with the striped dish towel she held in her hand.

Grinning, Ben tipped his cap and left.

Such a nice young man. Been well brought up by his uncle. As he disappeared down the side porch steps, Lovena's expression grew grim. She peered through the window at the old red barn with its quartered-off spaces built to house the help. She thought of the heartbreak that once lived in those drafty rooms and a shiver coursed through her.

WHEN BEN ARRIVED the next afternoon, this time with a horse hitched to a wagon, he was surprised to see Olivia sitting in front of an easel on the back lawn. He brought the wagon to a halt in front of the barn. Jumping down, he stood wavering between walking over to introduce himself or getting to work and avoiding her.

He didn't have to think for long. She caught his eye and waved.

"It's now or never," he muttered, pushing his hands into his trouser pockets. He strode over and removed his hat. "Good day, Miss Fuller. My name's Benjamin Pratt. Folks call me Ben."

Olivia chuckled. "I know who you are, though it is true we have never been properly introduced. Father told me you would be working here."

Ben was surprised she'd noticed his presence at all.

"I'll be here most afternoons for a while. I work with my uncle mornings."

"Carpentry, I understand." She looked up at him with an arm across her forehead to block the sun's glare.

He nodded. So, she knew more about him than he'd expected.

"Do you design and carve furniture or just build it?"

Ben laughed.

"Is my question amusing? Perhaps I offended. I see carpentry as an admirable trade."

"No offense taken. I build furniture and I suppose I have a knack for wood carving." He shrugged his shoulders and gave her a teasing grin. "My uncle is gifted in creating traditional European designs. He enjoys passing on his knowledge. Most customers seem to prefer a plainer style and it's less expensive."

Olivia smiled at him. She looked too pretty. The cotton ruffle of her bonnet framed her face and emphasized her dark brown eyes. Her voice was as pleasant as her expression. His admiration nearly caused him to take in the sound without absorbing her words.

"Fine carpentry is certainly an art and admired when furniture is well made. My mother took great pride in pieces brought from England by my grandparents."

He nodded, pleased she appreciated the trade. "They're lasting legacies of fine craftsmen from past eras. I have no desire to do anything else." He drew his eyes to her painting. "You're talented. The flowers look alive as if I could touch them; even feel the softness of those petals."

"Thank you." For a moment, she held his gaze.

"Well, I'd better get busy or your father may complain to my uncle that I am loafing on the job."

"It's nice to meet you."

"Enjoy the sunshine, Miss Fuller."

"Olivia."

He nodded, hoping he didn't appear like a sick-in-love school boy. He walked toward the barn, pulling his cap back on. *Olivia*, he thought. *She's not simply beautiful. She's intelligent and observant and her voice...* He pulled at the latch on the barn door, walked in and forked his hand through his hair. He blew out a breath to temper his body's heated reaction to a simple conversation. "The rooms, focus on those gloomy rooms."

LATER THAT AFTERNOON Olivia stood over the wash stand in her bedroom and rinsed paint stains from her fingers. Wringing out the wet cloth, she rubbed a blue smudge of paint from one cheek and wondered if it had been there during her chat with Benjamin Pratt. His hazel eyes seemed to take in every feature of her face and hair. She was accustomed to compliments about her looks and it often embarrassed her, but somehow his manner and gaze said more and it pleased her.

She liked the way his straight, sandy-colored hair hung over his forehead and how he brushed it back with his long fingers. His hands revealed strength and hard work. Yet when he talked about his trade, he gave his uncle credit rather than boasting about his own skill. He stood at least six feet with broad shoulders and a slim waist. Though she'd seen him in town and remembered his name called at school, she couldn't recall his presence. Many of the young men in town near to her own age behaved immaturely and carried on inane conversations. Ben was articulate and obviously goal oriented.

Handsome too.

Ben. Nice name. It suited him.

She dried her hands on a towel and placed it on its hook. She had a meeting at church with the choir after dinner and still had chores to do. Better to get on with her day and stifle her imaginings and the giddiness that gave her pause.

She should be thinking about William. After all, her father expected her to marry him. William treated her courteously and he was every bit a gentleman, but he had never looked at her the way Ben did this afternoon. She walked to the window that faced the side yard. Ben's wagon was filled with the rubble he'd removed from the old rooms. He had worked steadily without taking a break.

The afternoon had grown chillier and she would have usually put away her paints and returned to her chores earlier. Instead, she'd stayed out longer, enjoying Ben's occasional gaze in her direction. Wrapping her arms around her waist, she smiled.

No, William never made her feel this way.

She fingered the edge of the lace curtain and mused about both men. She and William had interesting conversations, mostly about church matters, Bible readings, or her father's sermons. Occasionally, he discussed the town business that went on in the meetinghouse where the selectmen and other town officials met. Even her father often ignored her questions about town issues as if it were a man's domain and should be of little concern to her.

Over the past few weeks, William had been coming to the house more often, at first on Sundays for dinner at her father's invitations. Now it was two or three times a week. He'd come with them to church suppers and over the past month, he'd been finding more time to be alone with her. Since the weather was improving, they walked occasionally in the evening and he'd wrapped her arm in his.

Two weeks earlier, he'd kissed her for the first time, a light kiss on the cheek after an evening walk. This past Friday he'd grown bolder and kissed her on the lips, his hands gripping her shoulders. When he released her, he gave her a brief smile before opening the door to the house and ushering her in with his open palm. The kiss was forgettable, a brush of his lips on hers. She remembered the grip on her shoulders more than the kiss. The encounter and her reaction surprised her, but she'd since given it little thought. He was her first beau and she hardly knew what to expect from a kiss. In time, would she find his kisses more enjoyable?

When her father greeted them, William's smile grew brighter and more engaging than the one he'd given her under the porch light. The two men strode off to her father's study. Naturally he would appreciate her father's attention. He'd be ordained soon and her father was his mentor.

She'd dreamed of courtship and thought it would be more romantic and less perfunctory. William was proper, as he should be, but the only other word that came to mind thinking of him, was *dutiful*. Maybe she was being unrealistic. Her life had consisted of rules and order and spiritual duties. She felt guilty for her desire for a more sensual experience. Her father would be shocked at her thoughts.

A movement outside caught her eye. Ben had jumped up onto the wagon filled to bursting with rubble. She watched him pull at the reins and lead the horse and wagon down the drive to the street until he disappeared. Turning away from the window, she smiled, and wondered what time he would arrive tomorrow.

CHAPTER TWO

"I AM SORRY YOU missed Olivia, William. She's off to a meeting with the Sunday school teachers," Reverend Fuller said as he led the young man into the parlor.

"I had hoped to see her, but I really stopped in to see you. I wanted to tell you how much I enjoyed your sermon on Sunday."

"Glad to hear. Someday your sermons may far surpass mine. Come, sit." The minister waved him to a seat while he took his own.

"You give me a great deal to aspire to in my service to the Lord," William said, as he took the offered seat and placed his hat beside him. "I won't take too much of your time. I have much study to prepare for my final exams."

"Your diligence is admirable." Reverend Fuller relaxed back in his chair and clasped his hands in his lap. He looked his pupil over, pleased that he always dressed impeccably and gave an aura of confidence and competence. "Lovena is working in the kitchen garden. When she returns, I'll have her put on tea."

"Please, no need." William lifted a hand in polite refusal. "Your maid has been in your service for some time?"

"She served my father for many years before his death."

"Olivia seems especially close to her. I've seen them often together chatting away."

"My wife Etta depended a great deal on Lovena, especially when Etta's illness grew worse. Previous limitations were put aside when her aid lessened our burden. Her devotion to both my wife and daughter has earned her a place in the family. Olivia and I are quite fond of her."

"Understandable." William straightened in his chair and pulled at the cuffs of his coat.

"Is it? Your expression tells me otherwise." He allowed a few seconds to pass as he observed his guest who appeared suddenly uncomfortable. "Is it because we treat her as family or is it her...color that disturbs you?" A new fear entered his heart as he asked the question.

"Forgive me if I appeared concerned. As you say, your maid has been a blessing to you and your family. I respect your reasoning. My family holds specific expectation for our hired help. I suppose I've grown accustomed to their way of thinking. And, please don't entertain the thought that I am a bigot. I do admit the lot of the Negro troubles me."

"As it does for many of us. What are your thoughts on the growing anti-slavery movements and the racial divides?"

William seemed surprised at the question and appeared to be searching for a response.

"Perhaps I can help you to voice your opinion. I have no problem sharing mine. Despite the Gradual Abolition Act of 1784, some Connecticut families still keep slaves. I find it outrageous. When will we have total emancipation? Many families with indentured servants treat them little better than slaves." The minister sighed, shaking his head. "The stories I've heard of their confinements are atrocious. I see any form of slavery as ungodly."

"You must admit those who believe slavery is necessary in their states have compelling arguments. Unlike here in the East, their economy depends on slave labor. Even more compelling are arguments concerning the welfare of these poor creatures. Too many are unable to care for themselves."

The reverend picked up his pipe resting on the table nearby and added tobacco. He needed a few moments to digest William's unsatisfactory reply. Once his pipe was lit, he turned his eyes back to his guest. "Those arguments don't stand up to the Word of God. Enslavement defies all that is holy, despite pious reasoning."

"Indeed," William conceded, "but what of the colored in service to us in our homes or as farm laborers? Most have a limited education. Some have questionable and unknown backgrounds. Many have suffered through want of provisions and moral guidance, particularly those who have come up from the South. Is it not our godly duty to use constraint in our desire to free them from *all* encumbrances? Scientific studies have surfaced concerning differences in physiology among races. We can't just toss aside learned men who have studied the Negro problem. I admit I struggle with the findings."

Reverend Fuller took a long, hard look at his protégé but remained silent and let William continue.

"Some of these freed slaves and indentured servants have begun to demand special treatment. When they're refused, they run off. Have you read *The Courant* this week? Notices for runaways are increasing daily."

"I have it right here. I haven't had the chance to look at it yet." He picked up the paper from his side table while his mind and his own personal needs tried to compensate for his student's unsettling views.

"Do you mind?" William held out a hand and accepted the paper.

The minister watched as William scanned the first page before pointing out a notice. He began reading. "Gideon Wolcott has by rebellion left my house and business; this is to warn all persons against harboring, trusting or employing him." There was more. An indented boy named Westley ran away, and another, George Franklin. "Moon, dark complexion, dark eyes.…" William paused, his eyes on the print. "His owner offers a half cent reward. They not only rebel against authority to those they owe their livelihoods, but they remove themselves from a source of protection. I fear it is our laxity in allowing too much freedom to those who are unable to take responsibility for their own lives."

The minister puffed his pipe, searching for an appropriate reply. He needed to believe the best of this young man and he didn't like his thinking. "William, God's word teaches us to treat others with the same kindness as we ourselves desire. 'There is neither Jew nor Greek, there is neither bond nor free, there is neither male nor female: for ye are all one in Christ Jesus. Galatians 3:18.'"

"True, but what of Hebrews? 'Obey them that have the rule over you, and submit yourselves: for they watch for your souls, as they that must give account, that they may do it with joy, and not with grief.' Shall we not be held responsible for those who are under our supervision and need our guidance?"

William sat back in a posture of overconfidence not missed by the pastor. He remembered his own youthful arrogance when his interpretation of the Bible carried little understanding of the Spirit or experiences of life. Better to address the young man's initial inquiry of a servant's place rather than argue doctrine today. "I believe you're concerned I may not be placing enough restrictions on my maid."

William's brow lifted at the change of direction in the conversation. "I only meant to question Olivia's attachment to your maid."

"I shall be held accountable for my flock. Not for

how heavy my hand is over my housekeeper. Lovena demonstrates obedience while at the same time nurtures my daughter, especially now that her mother has passed. My obligations to the church demand much of my time. I have no problem with Olivia's closeness to her. Perhaps, it might be relevant for all of us to look at our servants and their contributions more deeply and through the eyes of the soul."

"Yes, of course." William's lips twitched. "I wonder... have you read about the more recent accomplishments of *The American Colonization Society*? They haven't given up on their endeavors to establish more colonies in Africa. I've read they're thriving."

"Do you mean to say you agree with their declarations that Negroes should be removed to these colonies?"

"Many of those who have left have become missionaries and spread the gospel to pagans. It seems a worthy enterprise."

"We have colored families in our own community who live as godly citizens, even own land and work their farms."

"Yes, but are they not the exception?" William asked

rhetorically, a hint of arrogance in the rise of his chin. "Their good fortune does not diminish the prejudice that abounds. Despite views against the bitterness of slavery, it's still a common belief most free Negroes have received little literary, moral, or religious instruction. Because of this, too many seek immediate gratification without intelligent thought." He held up *The Courant*'s front-page news, "And, unfortunately, they cause a lack of trust in the race. No matter how much I may disagree with the world view, I can't deny what I see and hear. Prejudice abounds. In these new colonies, Negroes are encouraged to govern themselves and take responsibility without discrimination. I only state that the society's aim has moral and ethical value as well as providing a safe refuge for them."

The reverend rubbed his beard with enough intensity to cause his cheeks to redden. With more mentoring, he hoped to change William's radical views. "Ah, I hear Lovena rummaging around the kitchen, and isn't that Olivia's voice?" he asked, relieved at the interruption.

William looked toward the doorway just as Olivia ran into the room laughing with the maid close behind her. She stopped abruptly when she saw their visitor, nearly causing Lovena to trip over her.

William stood, his brow creased.

"William," Olivia raised a sticky finger to her lips. "I didn't know you were here."

Lovena heaved an audible sigh. "Forgive me, Reverend. I just frosted a cake and found Livie with her finger in the frostin'."

Olivia licked her finger. "And so good."

"You best not let sugar ruin your dinner," the maid scolded.

William eyed his mentor. "Livie?"

"Lovena, how long to dinner?" the minister said, ignoring the questioning remark.

"Half-hour at most. Will Mr. Tapley be stayin'?" She directed her question to Reverend Fuller, rather than to their guest whose attentions had diverted to Olivia.

"Not today. Are you certain we can't offer you a cup of tea, William?"

"No, thank you. I must be leaving soon. Olivia," he paused, staring at the maid who remained standing nearby.

With a lift of her chin, Lovena turned and left the room.

"Olivia, may I take you for a carriage ride this week? Tomorrow evening, perhaps?"

She hesitated before looking toward her father who nodded his approval.

"Tomorrow then." She gave him a compliant smile.

As the two young people shared pleasantries, Reverend Fuller's thoughts remained on the previous discussion. William would gain a greater tolerance for differences, the minister decided, once he and Olivia were married and he took over church responsibilities. He had to believe that, and they *would* marry. Pushing his concerns aside, he retrieved the newspaper that had been set aside and perused it.

After Olivia left the room, William returned to his seat just as the minister noticed an interesting article. "I see an instructor has been hired at the new school for the instruction of Latin and Greek. The article says there's room for thirty students, both boys and girls. I'll have to tell Olivia when she returns. She has her heart set on teaching."

"She desires to teach school? I would think with her duties at church and her house chores, she'd have little time left," William said, reaching for the hat he'd set aside on a nearby chair.

"I agree she has much to do but she looks toward the future and hopes to have a classroom of her own someday. Some mornings she helps out at the school house when she's not over busy with chores or her church work."

"She has never mentioned it to me. I…had something else in mind."

"Yes?" The minister leaned forward.

"I hadn't planned on bringing this up today." William cleared his throat. "You must know how much I admire your daughter."

The minister gave a slow nod, his chest tightening with expectation.

"As God has called me to the ministry, I believe he's also calling me to take a wife, sooner than later." William hesitated, taking in a deep breath. "Olivia would be a blessing to me as my wife and helpmate." He paused and gripped the hat he held more tightly. "I pray you might accept me as your future son-in-law."

"You are asking for my daughter's hand in marriage?"

William's pale complexion colored. "I see I have done an awkward job of it."

"It's Olivia you will need to convince, but you have my blessing." He hoped his clamped mouthed expression had concealed the surge of relief swelling within him.

"Thank you, sir. Thank you." William exhaled too loudly, the rim of the hat growing misshapen in his grip.

"Is there anything else?"

"No, I must be on my way." He stood, wearing a broad smile. "As always, I appreciate our enlightening discussion."

The minister rose from his chair and held out his hand.

William shook it vigorously.

"I feel assured you will soon be a member of the family."

William beamed before letting himself out.

Reverend Fuller sank back into his chair, rubbing his chest. Each time his deepest fear surfaced, the discomfort in his chest returned. He hoped once Olivia and William were married, he'd be free of the paralyzing fear that woke him at night and created imaginings in his mind too terrible to think about in the light of day.

I hold rose petals in my hands. They soft like your skin.
I bring one flower in every day while they still alive.

CHAPTER THREE

"LOVENA WHAT'S WRONG?" Olivia asked when she walked into the kitchen the next afternoon. The maid was chopping angrily at raw chicken parts on the long, heavy wooden work table that stood in front of the hearth.

With the meat cleaver still raised in her hand, Lovena looked down at the cut-up chunks of raw meat and bones she'd massacred. She let out a deep sigh before resting the knife on the table with a thud.

"You looked as if you were trying to kill an already dead fowl."

Lovena washed her hands in the water bucket nearby and wiped them. Rather than answering Olivia, she raised her eyes to the ceiling, anger creasing her jaw line.

Olivia understood Lovena had some words to say to God and they weren't praiseworthy at the moment. She was accustomed to their maid praying, questioning, and sometimes arguing with the Lord.

"Is God on your bad side today?"

"I just don't understand all the needless sufferin' sometimes, 'specially with the little ones."

"Come sit with me." Olivia took the maid's arm and led her to the small alcove away from the hearth where a small table and chairs served as their breakfast room. It was far enough away from the hearth but close enough to receive its warmth. Once they were seated, she waited patiently for the maid to unburden herself. Usually Olivia was the one complaining, questioning, or seeking advice from Lovena.

"Guessin' you didn't help out at the school this mornin'."

"I had too much to do at the Meeting House. I plan to help Mrs. Peabody tomorrow. What's happened?

Little Jason, you know, Sally Mae's boy? He was takin' a short cut through the woods to get to the school house this mornin'. Three bigger boys came on him, shovin' him around, callin' him *nigger* and *slave boy* and other names I ain't gonna repeat. They had him on the ground and was kickin' and spittin' on 'im. If it weren't for the Olson's dog comin' through the woods and growlin' at 'em, they might a knocked him unconscious. Mr. Olson let his dog loose when he heard Jason screamin'. He saw the boys run off toward Rockville and found poor Jason whimperin' on the ground. He carried him back home to his momma and she cleaned him up best she could and put him to bed."

"The poor child. He can't be more than five or six."

"He's seven but small for his age. I was out sweepin' the steps and seen Sally Mae marchin' down the road with a bag'a groceries. She looked ready to kill anyone in her path. I asked her what she so riled out about. She told me what happen, tears rollin' down her cheeks. Got so choked up, she could barely talk. I got her to sit on the porch for a few minutes until she calmed down. She says Mrs. Harper showed some concern but expected Sally Mae to finish her chores regardless. That woman coulda let her stay with her boy this mornin' instead of sending her off on errands."

Olivia wasn't surprised at Mrs. Harper's demands. She was one of the wealthier church members. Few homes in the area had live-in maids. The Fullers were fortunate to still have Lovena but she was considered a part of the family and gave more than she received. Mrs. Harper was not a favorite on church committees because of her rigid expectations. No doubt her inflexibility was even greater with her household help.

"Those boys who beat him up weren't much older than him. No doubt they learnin' their bigotry from their parents," Lovena muttered. "Sally Mae says people's attitudes here toward the colored ain't no different than in the South. They just hide it more. It ain't ever gonna change." Lovena looked up at the ceiling again. "Lord, some things I just don't understand."

Olivia shook her head. What could she say? Sally Mae wasn't far off in her thinking. Racist comments were common even from church elders who professed Godly virtues.

"Gettin' beat up by white boys makes me fear little Jason's gonna grow up with a hatin' heart, like so many other colored children. It ain't the first time colored ones at the school been picked on. This time was just worse than others."

Olivia knew it to be true. Only five Negro children attended the school, two of them children of maids. The other three belonged to two Negro families who either owned or rented farms. She'd observed the dynamics in the school room. The colored children stayed to themselves and were seldom included in social conversations by the white students. The truth was separation of races was an accepted part of life in their community despite her father preaching otherwise

Olivia was pulled from her thoughts when Lovena pressed her hands to the table and pushed up from the chair, ready to return to her chores.

"Have you told my father of the incident?"

"No. He looked like he got enough on his mind. He closed himself off in his study as soon as he came home from his church duties. Said he needed to finish up Sunday's sermon. He's been in there all afternoon."

"I'll talk to him. "Perhaps, Father and I can visit Sally Mae tonight and pray with her and her son."

"Might help loosen up some'a the bitterness settlin' in her heart. Might help little Jason too. Well, I best get this mess I made on the counter cleaned up and start dinner. You go on now. I've taken up enough time." Lovena started to turn away, but turned back. "Ain't Mr. Tapley comin' this evenin'?

Olivia brought a hand to her lips. She'd totally forgotten about William's invitation to take her for a carriage ride. It was too late to make excuses but her heart felt heavy after hearing about young Jason. Another thought created turmoil, one she preferred not to address, her lack of interest in seeing William again.

"Thank you for reminding me," she said sheepishly. If only she could feel a greater sense of pleasure at William's visit. No doubt her father is going to be pleased.

"The young man outside's been makin' a lot of noise. He got right to work the minute he showed up and ain't stopped since."

Olivia's face brightened. "Benjamin?"

"Who else be tuggin' old beds and ripped up mattresses out of those dark and gloomy rooms?"

Olivia quietly offered up a prayer of forgiveness for her sin of omission. She'd stopped her cleaning upstairs a few times to look out the window, hoping to see when he arrived. Not wanting to appear anxious, she'd stayed upstairs biding her time while trying to think up a good excuse to talk to him. Realizing she was being silly, she'd come down to see if Lovena needed her to work in the garden or bring in some clothes from the line. Ordinarily, she would think nothing of going outdoors simply to enjoy the nice spring weather. Instead, she felt oddly shy about seeing him again.

"Livie, go on out and see if he'd like a nice cold drink."

Olivia's eyes darted toward the maid. She wondered if Lovena sensed her reticence. The maid smiled at her, a knowing smile. *Am I that obvious,* Olivia wondered.

"I need to tell Father about Jason."

"I suppose once I clean up this mess, I could take a pitcher of lemonade to him," Lovena said, lowering her eyes.

"Oh, no, I'd be happy to." She hoped she didn't appear too eager. "I'll be back in a few minutes."

"Bettin' you will," Lovena murmured under her breath.

"What?"

"Nothin'. Go on. I'll make the lemonade."

WILLIAM KEPT THE horses at a steady pace that evening as he led them along the narrow country road bordered by maple trees on both sides. Wrapping her scarf more tightly about her shoulders, Olivia sat next to him, quietly gazing at sheep grazing in a nearby field.

"Are you cold? How careless of me. I should have brought a carriage blanket."

"The evening air is growing only slightly cooler."

"No excuses for my lack of thought. I admit my total focus has been on my studies."

"Are you anxious about your exams?"

"Not at all. I feel quite confident, but it would be negligent of me if I didn't spend the last few weeks reviewing all the material."

Olivia wasn't surprised at his response. William always appeared self-assured. "No doubt you will do well."

"My professors have been complementary. In fact, I've received *exemplary* remarks on my theological arguments."

"You must be pleased."

"Quite. Enough about my studies. How was your day? You seem distant this evening."

Olivia realized she hadn't been able to conceal her melancholy. "I heard some upsetting news today."

William slowed the carriage and pulled to the side next to a small pond. "Tell me. I may be able to help."

"There is little anyone can do. She went on to tell him about young Jason. "My father and I plan to visit him and his mother tomorrow. All we can do is offer some kind words and pray with them. Children can be so cruel."

"Yes, violence never solves anything."

"There was nothing to be solved. The boys who

attacked him were acting out the hatred and intolerance in our society."

"Yes, yes, I agree. Much needs to be done, though opinions differ on the solution. I am sure they'll appreciate your visit." He wore a pacifying expression. "Let's not spend our brief time together on such dismal talk." He patted her hand. "Once my exams are over, I hope to spend more time with you, Olivia."

She didn't respond. Did he believe it was what she hoped to hear? She looked toward the pond, feeling even more uncomfortable. She'd received William's first attentions months ago with anticipation, but the more time spent together had lessened her attraction to him.

"I realize I have been inattentive lately. I hope you're not angry with me."

Olivia heard anxiety in his voice. She was being a poor companion. She smiled. "Not at all. I would expect you to be devoted to your studies. Father places much faith you'll pass your exams with the highest marks. He has said often that you are a dedicated student."

"And what do you say?"

"I don't know what you mean." Olivia swallowed.

William reached up a hand and turned her face

toward his. "Don't you?" When she said nothing, he drew her closer and brought his lips down to hers.

She allowed the kiss, willing herself to respond. She placed a hand on his shoulder and pressed her lips to his. To her surprise, he stiffened. She'd wanted to find out if she could feel some passion or desire if she participated, but he appeared to be almost affronted.

"Forgive me for my impulsiveness, my dear. I pride myself on my self-control." He turned away and tugged at the reins, leading the horses back onto the road. "I must respect your virtue," he continued, not looking at her. "I also should not keep you out too late. Your father may become concerned."

Olivia was too stunned to respond. He had kissed her first and now he acted as if she had behaved improperly. She was relieved when he turned onto the stone path of the parsonage. William drew the carriage to a stop and stepped down. He came around to her side and reached out his hand to help her down. She accepted it but when he turned to lead her inside, she pulled away.

"Thank you for the ride. You needn't walk me inside."

William nodded. He smiled and appeared oblivious to her curtness. "After my session with your father later this week, I look forward to spending another evening with you." He kissed her forehead.

"Good night," Olivia said without acknowledging his future visit.

She hurried up the side porch steps and entered the house without turning around to see him drive off. She needed time alone. Her feelings for William had not grown and couldn't. In truth, her thoughts had been on a carpenter. Would the initial feelings Ben aroused in her diminish as well in time? With William, there was no doubt anymore. She felt only emptiness.

OLIVIA LAY IN her bed a few days later in a half dreamy state between sleeping and waking. Suddenly awareness stilled her breath and her eyes shot open. She touched her cheek, the one the woman in her dream had smoothed with her palm. Drawing her body up into a sitting position, she scanned her bedroom but no one was there.

"What are these dreams all about?" she sighed, more frustrated than ever. She'd remembered only bits and pieces on previous nights, but this time the woman's touch was as real as if she'd been physically present. In earlier dreams, the woman sat alone in a dim corner of a room, rocking in an old, weathered chair, a loosely knitted shawl wrapped about slim shoulders. She could never make out her face, but she remembered her humming as the rocker creaked back and forth.

Yesterday morning she'd awakened with a sense of foreboding and dreamt of a shadowy figure near the woman. Olivia had sensed her fear as if it were her own. This morning it was as if the woman had been comforting her. She remembered the texture of the woman's palm on her cheek, slightly rough like working hands but warm and soothing.

"Oh!" Olivia pressed her elbows into her mattress and raised her head from her pillow. The woman had murmured a name. *Rosie or Rosalee.* Olivia sagged back and closed her eyes as she tried to recover every detail, but the dream was fading away.

Could it be more than a dream? A spirit? She'd heard of houses that were said to be haunted, even an old uninhabited farmhouse on one of the back roads in town. No one wanted to buy it and youths would often dare friends to enter it. She never took the stories seriously.

She sat up and pushed her quilt aside. She must talk to Lovena. She'd never taken her maid's superstitions seriously and often teased her about some of her silly notions. Now she wanted to tell her about the dreams. She swung her legs to the floor in such haste, Speckles jumped from the bed and scuttled into a corner, glaring up at her with golden eyes. Olivia walked over, bent down, and rubbed the cat's fur. "Did you see her, Speck? Do you think she might have lived here once, in this room?" Her thoughts went to her grandparents who had passed before she was born.

"I've read of spirits dwelling in old homes. I doubt father would believe such things. The dead go to heaven or hell, he'd say, depending on their deeds, good or evil. But who really knows what secrets an old house can hold? What do you think, Speckles? She appears to be a kind spirit, does she not?" Olivia grinned at her imaginings. "No doubt they are only dreams, still..." The lingering and odd sense of something more remained with her.

Speckles purred and rubbed against Olivia's bended knees until the cat eyed something. She scurried toward a straw basket left on a chair and clawed at a strand of yarn hanging from it until the basket fell to the ground. Snagging the yarn, she rolled over on her back and groped the strand with her front paws, only to have it dislodge and her quest begin again.

Olivia laughed at the cat's antics. "So, you believe I'm being foolish too, my furry friend." She walked over and lifted the basket, replacing the balls of green yarn that had rolled out.

She and Lovena had spent hours the week before at the fire pit, boiling yellow rod and sage, to dye the yarn. Olivia had already begun a shawl she planned to give as a gift to an elderly church member who could no longer attend meetings. Speckles had managed to unravel some of her work. She wound the remaining strand the cat had unwound and after cutting off a piece of the snarled yarn for the cat's play, she placed the basket on her chest of drawers. With Speckles pawing at the piece left behind, Olivia went to her washstand, bathed and dressed.

When she entered the kitchen, Lovena was lifting cookies off a tray. "You're baking early this morning."

"It's not early, Livie. It be after seven."

"Olivia stretched her arms above her head and yawned. "I am surprised you didn't come and pound at my door."

"I thought about it while I was feedin' the chickens, drainin' the wash, scrubbin' away and thinkin' the princess is gettin' her beauty sleep," Lovena chided as she poured Olivia a cup of tea and carried a plate of bread and cheese to the breakfast table.

"I'm sorry. I'll catch up with my chores." She yawned again, covering her mouth.

"You got mendin' to do and you can hang out the wash. It's one pretty day out there."

Olivia picked up a piece of cheese and munched on it. "Where's Father?"

"He went over to the meetin' house. 'Doin' the Lord's work' as he always says."

"Why do I even ask?" Olivia breathed in the smell of molasses. "Mmm, I think I shall eat a dozen cookies today."

"And ruin that nice figure? I think the man workin' out in the barn would appreciate `em though. I'll put some in a basket and you can bring it out to Benjamin after lunch."

Olivia suppressed the spark of pleasure coursing through her. Benjamin must have arrived early today. She walked to the window and looked out. "If I didn't know better, Lovena, I would think you have a fancy for him," she said, flippantly.

The maid's hearty laughter filled the kitchen. "My

flirtin' days were over a long time ago but not yours, missy."

"Father would not like to hear you say that. You know he expects me to marry William."

Lovena twisted her lips into a scowl. "You too young to think'a marryin' him and he too busy thinkin' 'bout the pulpit if you ask me." Lovena stopped her chatting when Olivia covered her mouth in another yawn. "For a girl who slept an extra hour, you seem awful tired."

"Maybe I had too much rest, or it could have been my dream."

"Dreams can make a muddle of commonsense. You wanna talk about it? I can sit for a few minutes before bakin' another batch."

Olivia nodded. Carrying her teacup, she walked over to the table and sat down.

Lovena joined her. "Drink your tea before it gets cold and tell me about it."

After taking a sip, Olivia stared into the cup rubbing a finger around the rim. She could tell her about the dream, but the feelings they stirred up were indescribable.

"They began a few days ago." She went on to tell as many details as she could remember including this morning's occurrence. Still staring into her teacup, she paused, wishing she could find the right words to describe the vividness of the woman's presence. "She was so real, Lovena. It was as if she were watching over me while I slept. Her touch was gentle, comforting. I know I've teased you about your superstitions but could we have a spirit floating about?" She looked up at Lovena and expected laughter or a retort. Instead, the maid stared at her open mouthed.

"You think I'm being irrational. No doubt they are only dreams. Could thinking about the woman be causing the re-occurrence? Though, this morning I heard her whisper a name."

Lovena's eyes widened, her shoulders no longer slouched forward. "What she say?"

Olivia wrinkled her forehead. The maid's tone held anguish rather than curiosity and Olivia swore she saw fear in her expression. "*Rosalee*. I think that was it. Yes, I'm sure of it. Rosalee. I don't know anyone by that name." She reached out and rested her hand on Lovena's as it gripped the table edge. "What is it? Is the name familiar to you? You were here when my grandfather was alive. Was someone living here by that name?"

The maid didn't answer but sat still as stone.

"Lovena?" The maid's expression was trancelike. "You believe it's a spirit too? I didn't mean to frighten you. If it is truly a spirit, she is a kindly one. I admit it's a bit upsetting having a ghost roaming about." Olivia's hand hugged her chin as she rested an elbow on the table. "I can't believe I'm saying this," she murmured more to herself. "Father has often said, 'mysteries abound'. I didn't think I could accept such a thing. I should at least pray for her in case it's not just a dream. She may be a lost soul."

The maid appeared to snap out of her trance. She rose from her seat and walked back to the work table.

Olivia followed her, confused by her silence. "Perhaps, I'm simply letting my imagination take flight."

"You don't need to be afraid'a her." Lovena mumbled. "She meanin' no harm."

"What are you saying? Has she visited you too?"

Lovena reached for the cookie batter and began scooping spoonfuls onto a cookie sheet. "It don't hurt to pray. Now I got work to do." She gave a long sigh, as if regretting her abrupt reply. "Livie, dreams, they strange things and got meanin' all their own. Let it rest and get on with your chores. I got to deal with these cookies. The basket'a mendin' gettin' bigger and I can only do so much."

"Thank you for listening," Olivia said hesitantly. She walked from the room, stopping at the threshold. "Benjamin Pratt is going to love those cookies."

WHEN OLIVIA WAS out of sight, Lovena pressed trembling hands against the hardwood work table. "It's Narcissa, for sure," she whispered before clamping a hand to her mouth. *Death can't hold secrets that need to be told.*

Her thoughts returned to the day she'd walked into Narcissa's empty room after her death. She'd felt her presence as if the girl's spirit clung to everything, as if the room were alive and breathing. She'd raced out as fast as her legs could carry her.

She ain't never been gone. Her old room bein' torn down and she got no place else to go.

"What smells so good in here?" Reverend Fuller asked as he walked in from the porch and hung his hat on a wall peg.

Lovena pushed away her fearful thoughts. "Bakin' molasses cookies."

"Ah, my favorite. William is coming at five for a mentoring session. He'll enjoy them too. Where's Olivia?"

"She's gone upstairs, should be doin' some mendin'."

He reached for a warm cookie. Taking a bite, he smacked his lips and gave Lovena a grin of approval. "Please remind Olivia of William's visit. No doubt he plans to spend time with her after our session." Munching on the cookie, he walked through the kitchen toward the hall. "Have a good morning," he called back. "I'll be in my study."

Lovena frowned once he was gone. "If Livie cared for Tapley at all, she'd need no remindin'," she muttered under her breath. Her thoughts returned to Olivia's admission. "Narcissa, what you got in store? The reverend be actin' like everythin' gonna turn out fine for Olivia, but I got chills runnin' up and down my spine."

She continued to mutter as she set the final batch of cookies to baking. She washed and dried dishes and stacked them with a louder than normal clatter. With gritted teeth, she tossed silverware piece by piece in the drawer.

"It's happenin', no doubt in my mind." She snapped her lips together when she realized she'd spoken aloud again. *Those shabby rooms in that ol' barn ain't keepin' her no more now that Ben be tearin' 'em down.* She pushed the silver drawer shut and tossed aside the towel. Pulling out a kitchen stool, she sat down heavily. With eyes closed, she pictured her young helper who died almost two decades earlier. Narcissa Dunn was no more than a scrawny child when she first came to work for the Fullers. As the years went by she'd become a beauty, tall, slim, skin like dark honey, curvy in all the right places. Mostly, she remembered her dark eyes, bright and innocent--beautiful eyes, until they lost their light. "Barely passed her eighteenth birthday, poor chile." Her mind returned to their conversation on the last day of Narcissa's innocence. It was a sunny day and one that remained as lucid to Lovena as if it had been yesterday.

"YOU BEST GET your eyes off that stable boy and finish weedin' or you gonna be lookin' for another job."

Narcissa groaned at Lovena who was pumping water from the well. "I'm near done and it gettin' to be suppertime anyways." Her gaze remained on Jimmy as he unloaded bales of hay from an old wagon and stacked them in front of the barn. "Speakin' of flirtin', Lovena, I saw the peddler yesterday on the porch lookin' you up and down. He been showin' up almos' every week but you keep sendin' him off."

"Stop your foolish talk. He hopin' he gonna make a sale. The missus don't need no more tin. We could use another cast iron pot and he ain't got none."

"I think he's sweet on you."

"I ain't interested. I'm in no mood to be caterin' to a man." Lovena settled the overflowing water bucket on the ground and lifted an empty one to the well.

"Except for the reverend," Narcissa teased, tugging at another weed in the garden.

"Reverend Mr. Fuller took pity on you when your aunt died, not the missus. And if you don't stop oglin' his stable boy, that wife'a his may be givin' you the boot. You need to start actin' like a grown woman and not a giddy girl."

Narcissa sat back on her haunches between the rows of lettuce and wiped sweat off her brow. "I am a grown woman and Jimmy sure seems to be noticin'."

Lovena stopped pumping and glared at her young helper. "Are you blushin' under that honey-colored skin 'o yours? You got it bad. I'm warnin' you, the missus won't put up with nothin' but a good day's work. She don't have the reverend's soft heart."

"Aw, she younger 'en you and she act like a cranky old biddy."

"You shush now. She just bitter for what life brought her, that's all. You do your work and she won't bother you none."

Narcissa gave a resigned shrug and lifted herself off the ground, brushing dirt from her long cotton apron. "I need to dump these weeds."

"Go on. When you all done, come help me bring the laundry in from the line. We'll have our supper and you can go do all the dreamin' you want back in your room."

"Yes, ma'am. You need some help with those buckets?"

"No, thanks for offerin'. I've had heavier burdens than these to carry. Get rid of them weeds and wash your hands before you be helpin' me fold sheets."

LOVENA FORCED HER mind back to the present. How often had she relived that ordinary conversation? Thoughts of Mrs. Fuller and her selfishness and cruelty toward Narcissa caused her nose to flare. *Nobody could be happy if she weren't. What she did to that poor girl…* She sucked in a deep moan, her hand pressed to her chest. *Narcissa, she wants her due.* A chill ran through her again just as it did when she'd roamed the servant quarters after the girl's death. *Narcissa don't wanna be quiet no more. She be dead but she ain't never had peace, no way. What she want with Livie?*

Just then Olivia walked in the room, mending over her arm. Brushing away her dire thoughts, she looked the girl over. "You've changed. You goin` somewhere? That dress looks too pretty to work in."

"I won't ruin it. I haven't worn it yet this spring and the weather is so nice. I'm going to sit in the parlor and finish my mending."

Lovena saw the way Olivia's expression turned sheepish. In fact, the past couple of days she'd noticed a change in the girl. No doubt, the carpenter working on the barn was the reason. She saw them from the back window on more than one afternoon this week talking and laughing together. It had been awhile since she'd seen her so animated. Lovena knew full well what was happening. She wanted to be happy for Livie but worry crowded in, snapping off the pleasure as quick as snipping the tail off a string bean.

"I'm gonna get the basket of cookies ready for Benjamin," Lovena said as Olivia began to walk off. "You have plenty of time to get some chores done before he takes a break."

"Yes, the cookies. I nearly forgot."

Lovena rolled her eyes as the girl escaped the kitchen. "Lordy, the girl's got it bad. If her daddy sees, he gonna be none too happy."

Who they gonna believe? I hurt inside like I'm split in two...

CHAPTER FOUR

BEN STOOD OVER the two piles of old wood, one pile for burning; the other salvageable to repair the barn. Only half of the front room remained, and he hoped to have it torn down by the end of the day. He bent down to pull more nails out of one of the slats when he heard the squeak of the screen door. Looking across the lawn, he saw Olivia step off the side porch and walk his way. He raised himself up to his full six-foot height, thumbed his trouser pockets, and watched her. The late April breeze caused her long skirt to mold to her slender legs. The ribbons on her bonnet tossed about as she walked toward him, a small basket swinging on her arm. He could never get enough of watching her.

He knew Will Tapley was in the picture, but the man seemed too stiff-shirted for Olivia. She emanated a carefree spirit. He loved the exuberance she displayed whether she was rushing off to a church commitment, working in the garden, or simply taking a few minutes to talk with him. The latter made his spirit soar.

No doubt her father favored Tapley. After all, he was becoming a minister. He couldn't compete with that but he also wasn't going to hide in the shadows. He'd crossed paths with Tapley on occasion, but the man seldom bothered to even tip his hat to him.

He wondered about Tapley's feelings toward Olivia. His own feelings for her grew stronger every day and the desire to draw her into his arms was becoming difficult to restrain. He swore inwardly at the thought of her in Tapley's arms.

"Good afternoon, Ben."

His last thought caused him to wince before acknowledging Olivia with a broad smile. "Watch your step. I've tried to pick up all the rusty nails but I could have missed some."

"She lifted her skirt and stepped carefully until she was only a few feet from him. "You've accomplished a great deal."

Ben looked up at the remaining partitions. "I hope to have the whole structure razed before I leave. I've got a good amount of boards saved to repair the barn. The rest of this will make decent fire burning." Ben stopped, suddenly embarrassed. "Sorry, I didn't mean to go on about my work."

"I like hearing you 'go on'."

Ben took in the warmth he saw in her eyes and smiled. He'd become more relaxed in her presence and he sensed she enjoyed their conversations. The air seemed to still when they were together, especially when they looked into each other's eyes without speaking. He wanted to put a name to what he was feeling and sensed she felt it too.

"Lovena asked me to bring you some molasses cookies."

When she held up the basket, he realized he'd lost himself in her eyes. Taking a few steps closer to where she stood, he unfolded the cloth napkin. "Mmm, they look delicious."

Olivia appeared suddenly shy. "I'm sure you'll love them." She thrust the basket toward him.

"Won't you have one with me? I was about to take a break. If you don't mind my appearance." He looked down at his dirty work trousers and tried to brush off grime.

"I don't mind at all."

Ben looked behind him at the stone wall that ran

along the back property. "Over there?"

He reached out for her hand. "Don't go tripping on those loose boards."

Taking his hand, Olivia allowed him to lead her to the wall. Before she could refuse him, he gripped her waist and lifted her up, setting her down on the top ledge.

She laughed. "I have climbed up and walked across this ledge since I was a little girl."

"Do you mind my help?" He winked at her before looking down at his rough hands. "I wouldn't blame you if you did." He jumped up and sat near her doing his best to leave a respectable amount of space between them. He was very aware of his soiled clothes next to her prim blue calico dress.

"You are a perfect gentleman."

Ben tipped his cap before eyeing the basket. "Are you going to offer me one of those cookies?"

Giving him a delightful grin, she placed the basket between them.

"Would you take one out? Don't want to get dirt on the rest of them."

Olivia lifted a large cookie and instead of handing it to him, put it up to his lips. "Shall I hold it for you as well?"

Ben gave a slanted grin and took a big bite, his lips touching her finger. "Hmm, sweet."

Their eyes met before she looked away, a smile playing on her lips.

"Are you going to keep the rest of the cookie away from me?"

Olivia took the cookie to his lips again.

"You must have one too."

"Instead of taking another one, she bit into the cookie she held in her hand.

"Olivia," Ben whispered hoarsely.

Their eyes locked.

There was no way he was imagining it. A strong attraction was growing between them and he wasn't one to walk away from even remote possibilities. He rested a hand on hers; she didn't move hers away. They remained that way, each seemingly lost in their own thoughts. Ben finally broke the silence. "I suppose I should get back to work before your father appears and rants about my lazy ways."

"He was busy at work in his study when I left the house."

Ben nodded. He wanted to remain right there with

her, but the temptation to draw her closer was growing too strong. Instead, he brushed a tiny crumb from the corner of her mouth before jumping from the ledge. He reached out his arms to help her down, but hesitated, waiting for her permission.

She raised her arms and rested her hands on his shoulders. Lifting her slowly, he set her feet on the grass. His hands tightened about her slim waist and he felt the soft flare of her hips beneath his palm. He loosened his hold, but didn't let go. Instead he lowered his head to her upturned face. Her lips parted, her eyes searching his. He was certain her thoughts matched his own.

Without dwelling on the consequences and thankful the trees blocked the view of the farmhouse, he touched his lips to hers, tenderly at first, then with more urgency. He breathed in her scent as she returned his kiss. The slight trembling of her lips beneath his caused him to stifle the desire to crush her more firmly to him. He drew his head back. Her eyes were closed and when she opened them, he wondered if she saw the hunger in his own. Reluctantly, he released her.

He watched as she worried her bottom lip. "I'm sorry," he whispered, though he doubted he sounded truly remorseful. "I don't know why I... Maybe it was those cookies."

"I'm not," she said softly before breaking into a smile. "Are you saying the cookies were the cause of the kiss?" she teased.

"Your lips were sweeter." He took a step away, his eyes never leaving hers. If he remained too close to her, he'd pull her back into his arms.

"I should get back. I... Here." She lifted the basket from the ledge and held it out to him. Their hands touched as he reached for it and neither let go until he relented and took it from her.

"Good day." She lifted the hem of her skirt and hurried away."

"Be careful," Ben called out when she nearly tripped on the scattered boards.

She turned back, wearing her beautiful smile that melted his insides. He remained standing there, watching her as she ran across the yard and onto the porch steps before disappearing into the house.

Closing his eyes, he took in a deep breath, letting it stream out slowly. The heat spreading through him had nothing to do with the outside temperature.

What am I doing? The reality of their stolen moment

sobered him. He'd kissed the pastor's daughter. What if her father had seen them? He would have been kicked off the property and what ridicule would Olivia have faced? His concern couldn't remove the pleasure he felt at kissing her, the sweetness of their shared cookie still on her lips.

William Tapley came to mind. He reached into the basket for another cookie. Taking a big bite, he pushed away thoughts bound to get him into deeper trouble.

He searched around for the tools he'd tossed aside and got back to work. After working for an hour, he stopped and wiped the sweat from his brow. He'd finished removing all the window glass from the front room and pulled out rusty nails holding the rotted wall boards. As he tugged at the loosened wood, dislodging a board, he caught sight of something nestled in the wall between two narrow pieces of bracing.

Reaching in, he pulled out a tattered book and turned it in his hands. It was covered in a cotton cloth faded and darkened with age, its edges ripped and shredded. Beneath the cloth, he could see the worn leather cover that must have protected it from the elements. Sheets of yellowed paper were stitched inside. He guessed it must have belonged to a farmhand or servant. Most likely the book had been hidden in the wall for years. Flipping through it, he saw that the writing appeared legible, though some words had faded and dampness had curled the corners of the pages. If it hadn't been bounded in leather, it would have been unreadable.

He closed the book but remained staring down at it. Should he give it to the minister? Burn it along with the rotted wood? If he destroyed the roughly made book that appeared to be a diary, it would keep its secrets. As he held it, the cotton fabric grew warm in his sweating hands. He wondered about its owner, most likely a woman, one who took the time to stitch the papers together and cover it in a flowered print now ragged and soiled. He couldn't toss it way. It might be more than an old journal left to waste away in the crevice of a wall, but a story of someone's life.

He tucked it into his back pocket. He had a job to finish. Later, he would decide what to do with the interesting find.

As the afternoon wore on, clouds gathered and the day turned darker. Rain would be coming soon. He razed the remaining wall and separated the good wood from the bad. He'd put in a good day, he thought, just as the first drops of rain fell. Once he'd gathered his tools and stored them in the barn, he mounted his horse for the ride home.

He hoped for one last glimpse of Olivia. Instead, he spied the carriage newly parked near the side porch. Will Tapley, shaking the raindrops from his hat, was climbing the porch steps and knocking on the Fuller's side door. Ben scowled and rode away.

OLIVIA WATCHED FROM her bedroom as William's carriage came to a halt below her window. With his exams coming soon, her father had offered to help him prepare. He'd naturally be invited to stay for dinner. After the meal, her father would make his usual excuses so William could direct his attention to her.

Just as the thought caused her shoulders to sag, she saw Ben ride off the property. She withdrew her hand from the curtain she'd pushed aside, walked over to her bed, and slumped down on its edge. What was she to do? She couldn't stop thinking about Ben and she had no desire to see William.

The sweet memory of Ben's lips on hers had filled her thoughts as she'd completed her afternoon chores and visited with church members. Mrs. Pearson brought some soap she'd made. Later, Mrs. Kimbell stopped by with a basket of candles and the Morton boy arrived with coal. While Olivia helped Lovena make pudding, the Widow Rogers arrived with a pie in hand as payment for her father's visit to her ailing son.

She'd escaped to her room only a half hour earlier, too little time to work through all the feelings stirring inside of her. At one moment joy bubbled up in her heart. As quickly, anxiety washed away the joy. What would her father say if he knew it was Ben who she wanted to be with, not William?

She closed her eyes, dwelling on the feel of Ben's arms around her and the ease in which he lifted her to the stone ledge. When he'd held her in his arms, waves of delighted warmth like sunbursts flowed through her. Even now, just thinking about him, her skin tingled. She folded her arms tightly about her and smiled. His kiss, just remembering caused her heart to soar. How could one kiss affect her so? No, it wasn't just the kiss but the way he looked at her, as if he were trying to read her thoughts through her eyes. She'd felt more in his gaze from the first day he'd introduced himself to her, his cap in hand.

Happiness. Yes, when she was with him she was happy. And when he was gone, needy for more of him.

Even when they could only wave a hello, it seemed each was looking for the other whether she was hanging laundry on the line, leaving for a church meeting, or when he was pulling at boards or piling wood in his wagon. Did she imagine she saw the same longing in his eyes as in hers?

She felt beautiful in his presence. His admiration seemed to wipe away past insecurities. Her mother, though she loved Olivia, couldn't hide her disappointment that her daughter wasn't blessed with her fair coloring and blond hair.

Thinking of her mother, she wished she was alive to talk to about what was happening to her. Ben, William, her strange dreams, her father's plans for her. On second thought, her mother wouldn't have understood. She would have been thrilled the Tapleys' son showed an interest in her daughter. They were a prominent family in town and her mother enjoyed the company of the wealthier parishioners, despite her professed humility.

Olivia had to admit since her mother's death, their home had grown more peaceful. Her mother's sharp voice and demands, usually meant for Lovena but at her worst toward her husband and daughter, often caused unnecessary drama and slammed doors. Still, she wished they could have had a closer relationship. Tonight she longed to have a mother to talk to, not only about the strange dreams but about Ben and new dreams that included him.

Speckles jumped on the bed suddenly, shaking her from her thoughts. She rubbed the cat's fur and forced her thoughts back to her impending evening. What if William tried to kiss her again? She had to talk to her father. Tell him she felt no more than friendship for William. *Father would understand, wouldn't he?* She needed to get through tonight and find the right time to talk to him tomorrow.

She stood and straightened her skirt but instead of walking to the door, she wrapped an arm around one of her tall bed posts. Resting her cheek against it, she thought of the woman in her dream and Lovena's reaction. Considering the maid's superstitious beliefs, she most likely wasn't the person to tell.

Maybe she should tell her father about the dreams. Would he believe their home might house a spirit? She doubted it. She imagined him telling her to have a glass of milk before bedtime to bring on a good night sleep.

What a strange day.

She took a moment to send up a prayer for God's guidance, took a deep breath and left the room. She had to stop delaying and get through this night.

"PLEASE BRING IN tea and those molasses cookies you made today," Reverend Fuller said to Lovena as he and William passed her on their way to the parlor. They'd been closed up in the study for the past hour.

"I planned to do just that," Lovena said, stepping aside as they entered the room, her hands pressed into her wide hips.

"Where's Olivia?" her father asked.

She's gone off to deliver a sympathy basket the church ladies put together for the widow, Mrs. Connors. Don't you worry, she knows Mr. Tapley's here." Her eyes caught William's only briefly before she walked away.

"Have a seat, William." The minister pointed to a chair next to his own and sat down. "I believe the last hour has been quite productive. Would you prefer a glass of wine?"

"Tea is fine." William gazed back at the now empty doorway. "Your maid was quite surly."

"She's been in a mood today. Unlike her, but her

bones act up on occasion. I take no offense. Most times she is agreeable."

"If our maid took such a tone, she'd be chastised or even let go, if my father had anything to do with it. You have great tolerance."

"We have discussed our different opinions on the treatment of household staff. Put the subject to rest. I have more important issues in mind."

"I assure you I didn't mean any disrespect."

The minister nodded. "I have some good news for you."

William leaned forward expectantly. "Yes?"

"I met with the church elders today. They've accepted my recommendation for you to serve as my assistant."

William's face broke into a gratifying smile.

"You'll receive only a pittance for your service as a deacon, but it will put you in good stead with the church. As they come to see your reverence for God's Word, you'll gain their admiration." He paused and looked hard into William's eyes. "After your ordination and if you have proved yourself, I'll recommend you as my replacement in the pulpit when I retire." He sat back wanting to gauge the young man's reaction. He saw relief and immense satisfaction in his expression.

Just as he'd expected.

"I am humbled by your faith in me."

Reverend Fuller allowed a few seconds to pass. He wanted William to digest the news and bathe a moment in his success. He would have been less hospitable to another candidate desiring so much of his time, preferring to work on his sermons rather than listen to William's sometimes arrogant stances. Despite his shortcomings, he was a righteous man, on a holy path and most important, the best husband he could find for his daughter. Olivia's future needed to be safeguarded. With glowing recommendations to the church elders, William would succeed in gaining his pulpit. More important, Olivia would become Mrs. Tapley and he could finally put his fears to rest. At least that was his prayer if God in his mercy allowed it.

He looked up when Lovena walked into the parlor and set down a tray that held a teapot, two cups, and a dish of cookies. She lifted the pot to pour but Reverend Fuller raised a hand.

"Leave it Lovena. We will help ourselves." He waited until the maid left the room. "Before Olivia returns, I'd like to discuss her future."

"I apologize for my awkwardness when I asked for your daughter's hand. I should have waited until I obtained a position."

"No apologies needed. You asked and I gave my blessing. It was not the time, however, to discuss my concerns about the marriage."

"I assure you, I possess noble principles. I will attempt to be the best of husbands."

"Your character is not at issue. I've observed your behaviors. There are other matters we need to settle." His voice took on a confidential tone. He'd put much thought in how to approach the subject. The offer of his pulpit had sufficiently gained the young man's attention, and hunger, if he calculated correctly.

"When did you plan to propose marriage to Olivia?"

"This evening on a carriage ride. Unfortunately, the rain has thwarted that idea. If you prefer I wait…"

"I'm sure you're anxious to receive her answer. Before you talk to my daughter, I must first be reassured of your complete commitment to the church."

William's shoulders visibly relaxed. "God's work comes first, though I shall be a devoted husband."

"I am pleased you have your priorities in order." He poured each of them a cup of tea, lifting his own to take a sip. He waited for William to do the same. "A sensitive matter must be discussed. One you shared with me a few months ago."

At that, William set down his cup and looked visibly pained. "I have feared my personal disclosure would cause you to refuse my petition. At that time, I didn't know my eyes would be on Olivia as my wife. If you remember I was discussing my desire, as a future minister, to be a good shepherd to my flock."

The reverend leaned closer to William, his voice softened in empathy. "Yes, of course. As your family's counselor, I was aware, at the first signs of your younger brother's condition. Your parents kept the situation private and took the necessary steps to have him institutionalized. If you remember I brought the subject up out of concern for your brother's welfare. The asylums do not always have the best reputations."

"He is being well cared for and will remain there permanently. Members of the church who are aware I have a brother, only a year younger than myself, believe he has an incurable illness of the body rather than of the mind. We wish to keep it that way. I am sure you understand."

"In our discussion you admitted your uncle, your

father's brother, had the same affliction."

William appeared uncomfortable but the minister had a purpose in reminding him of their conversation.

"My uncle's condition became evident at a young age as well. Fortunately for him, he died before adulthood, saving much hardship for him and his family."

"And due to this sensitive situation, you told me you have no desire to father children."

"With an uncle and brother similarly afflicted, I must assume the illness is hereditary. The medical community knows so little about these behaviors and some even mistakenly believe victims are cursed."

"Now that you are proposing marriage to my daughter, have you considered the implications of your decision?"

Silence followed the question.

"We must speak honestly," the minister urged.

"I prayed I'd be blessed with a wife who would support my calling. Your encouragement to court Olivia appeared to be a positive sign God was leading me, especially since you were aware of my family's personal situation." He hesitated. "Are you having second thoughts on your consent? Perhaps, you desire grandchildren?"

"I have no expectation for a grandchild. I doubt I will live long enough for such an event."

"Are you ill? I pray that's not the case."

"I have recently had discomforting signs that have caused me to question my mortality. I prefer not to worry my daughter. I trust you will keep my admission confidential."

"Most definitely. Please know I am here if you need assistance in any way."

The minister nodded dismissively. "To return to the matter at hand. As a minister, meeting all the needs of the church is a monumental task for one man. With a Godly wife beside you, the burden lessens, but there are few hours in a day your mind and heart are not on the needs of the church."

"I pray Olivia understands."

"Indeed, and because your work is so vital, your *personal* issue and decision has not affected my consent. Olivia has been a blessing to me. Yet, I admit fathering a child has caused me at times to give less attention to my church duties. It is for this reason I am adamant about leaving the church in the hands of one who is totally dedicated to the needs of the congregation."

"I want only to serve God and live according to His will."

"Olivia has grown up in the church and bred to serve others. As her father, I believe she could do no better than to be married to a man devoted to God. I pray Olivia will welcome your proposal tonight."

"I confess my concern. Olivia may feel differently about children. I have not broached the subject."

The minister looked toward the hallway before leaning closer. He spoke in a low voice meant for William's ears only. "I see no good purpose in sharing your family's affliction with Olivia *before* you marry or your thoughts on fatherhood."

William looked at him warily.

"No doubt you want to avoid a refusal."

"Yes, of course. If you think it's best to wait."

"I admit Olivia has talked of her desire to bear children. She is young and idealistic. In time, she'll understand and be more willing to accept your situation." Reverend Fuller reached for his tea cup, praying silently that God understood.

"I have feared her refusal for that very reason."

The minister's splayed hand urged a quieter tone. He

set his cup down with a clang on its saucer. "Then heed my warning. Avoid the subject until after you marry. If she insists on becoming a mother, adoption is always an option. Olivia has much love in her heart and many orphaned children need homes."

William heaved a sigh of relief. "You are quite right. I appreciate your counsel. I see no need to create a problem that may never become one."

"We are in agreement then." The minister rested back in his chair. His plan was far from perfect. "Perhaps a confidential discussion with a physician might be in order. Accidental pregnancies happen."

"I will take all precautions. I'm aware of ways to avoid a pregnancy. Never will I bring a child into the world with my brother's affliction. My family's suffering has been enough of a deterrent."

"I am confident you'll be the one to take over my pulpit after you and Olivia are married." He gave William a reassuring smile and noted the gratification on the young man's face. "A short engagement is best. I want to be around to see both of you settled."

He waved a hand at the comfortable room where they sat. "My grandfather built this house that has become the parsonage. It's a place of sanctuary for church members in need of prayer or consolation. Since I have no son to inherit, it will become yours once I have evidence, after your ordination, of your total commitment to the church."

"I am speechless at your generosity and honored you have placed so much faith and trust in me."

Reverend Fuller lifted his cup and took a sip of tea. He had chosen William wisely. His plan was the best he could think to protect Olivia. He must continue to pray for its fruition. The dreaded fear that ate at his insides might never materialize. In his daylight hours, he'd wondered if he was being irrational or if his fears were nurtured by guilt, but he could never be sure.

He heard his visitor clear his throat. Had William said something while he'd been lost in his thoughts? He looked down at his watch before taking a sip of tea. "Let's enjoy one of Lovena's molasses cookies and focus on future blessings."

LOVENA PRESSED HER back against the hallway wall that separated the parlor from the kitchen. While she was on her way to reheat their tea, she'd overheard too much of the conversation. She covered her mouth, a feeble attempt to swallow grief mixed with rage.

She had expected Tapley to ask for Olivia's hand, having recognized his ambition and the way he'd weaseled his way into the minister's good graces. Marrying Olivia would reinforce his chance to inherit the reverend's pulpit.

She didn't like or trust Tapley, not one bit. She saw how he turned down his nose to her and puffed up his narrow chest with his self-importance. In her mind, he wasn't a sincere man of God, just an ambitious one who knew how to get what he wanted. He hadn't fooled her.

What she hadn't been able to understand was why the reverend didn't see through Tapley's false modesty and posturing. Now she understood too well.

My poor Livie. He think he got it all figured out. He not just tryin' to protect her. He protectin' himself. Afraid she gonna learn the truth. He ain't thinkin' straight.

Lovena huffed at the thought as she returned to the kitchen. *Too much happenin' too fast. What you think of the minister's crazy plan, Narcissa? Is that why you come in here now makin' trouble?*

"Lovena?"

"I didn't see you come in."

"You appeared off somewhere," Olivia said as she

stepped into the kitchen from the porch and removed her shawl, shutting the door behind her.

"Just thinkin'. Your daddy and Mr. Tapley are in the parlor."

Olivia drew nearer and rested a hand on the maid's shoulder. "I'm concerned I upset you this morning when I told about my dreams."

"Don't you worry 'bout me. Go on. I suspect your Mr. Tapley is anxious to see you."

Olivia rolled her eyes at the maid before walking in the direction of the parlor.

Lovena exhaled a long, slow breath that steamed with greater anguish than the kettle boiling on the hearth.

CHAPTER FIVE

"THE WEATHER IS disappointing. I looked forward to taking another carriage ride with you this evening. Perhaps Sunday afternoon?" William asked as he and Olivia sat on the porch swing watching the rainfall.

"I'll be spending much of the afternoon at church. We're stitching Easter banners."

"Later Sunday evening?"

"William, I…" If only she could find the appropriate words to decline. "Our sewing may go into the evening hours. We have so little time to complete our projects. The other women are not as fortunate as I to have a housemaid. Lovena frees up so much of my time."

She wasn't lying. Easter preparations took valuable time away from the church women's household chores. But why couldn't she simply say no? Her stomach was in knots. She felt guilty. The longing in her heart wasn't for William. "I hope the rain stops soon. The daffodils are wilting under the downpour. They have given such a shower of color after this dismal winter."

William made no reply. She wondered if he was even

listening to her. He appeared uneasy. Just as the rain drummed harder against the roof of the covered porch, William lifted his arm and wrapped it around her shoulder, startling her. She stood abruptly, jarring the swing. *Lord, she was making a mess of things.* She pressed her palms against the porch rail, disregarding the splatter of raindrops on her face.

"What is it, Olivia?"

She looked toward the barn. Confusion added to the guilt. She should speak with her father first. She turned back toward William prepared to excuse herself and bid him good night. He must have followed her previous gaze and was staring in the direction of the barn.

"I saw that carpenter, Benjamin Pratt, ride away when I arrived. Your father told me he was working here. Have you spoken with him?"

Had he read her thoughts? "Yes, on occasion." She hoped her voice didn't betray her sudden tension.

"Please, Olivia. Come sit. You're getting wet." He reached for her arm to draw her toward the swing.

She hesitated but sat again, still unable to find the words that would discourage his attentions. She wondered if other women were more experienced in rejecting a suitor. She was too afraid of injuring feelings or handling the situation poorly.

William pulled a handkerchief from his pocket and wiped away raindrops from her cheeks. "I knew Pratt only from a school class he attended one year, though we seldom spoke more than a few words."

Struck by the direction of the conversation, she allowed him to continue his ministrations, admittedly curious about anything concerning Ben.

"I don't remember him to be an avid learner," he continued. "Understandable. After all, he'd been brought up by an uncle. Nice older gentleman, though uneducated."

"Uneducated? He is a carpenter of fine furniture."

"I didn't mean to suggest he was a simple laborer. I only meant the he's had no formal education to pass on to his nephew." He tucked the handkerchief back in his pocket, appearing slightly annoyed. "I admire his uncle for taking responsibility for a child coming from such an abysmal family life."

"Abysmal?"

William nodded grimly. "Dreadful situation. Pratt's father was the village drunkard. I remember my parents' disgust over his behavior. He couldn't care for his family. The church offered aid, but his father was too proud to accept any help. Rumors abounded that he beat his wife. In the end, the man drove his wagon into a ditch. Both he and his wife were killed. God only knows how such a background has affected Pratt. Unfortunately, evil tendencies can be passed on. Hopefully, his uncle's influence has helped to temper lasting damage. I recommend you be wary of too much conversation with the man."

"He converses well. I haven't sensed any deprivation in his character," she said with annoyance, while pushing back waves of compassion that nearly brought tears to her eyes. She'd had such a fortunate childhood while Ben knew nothing but suffering. She wanted to defend him from William's harsh judgments.

"Is he a diligent worker?" William asked, watching Olivia's expression more carefully than he had all evening. "Your father would not be happy if he's engaging in too much conversation when he should be working. Let's hope he hasn't taken to the bottle like his father."

"He works steadily. You can see he's torn down those old rooms and he's begun to repair the barn." Olivia couldn't miss William's furrowed brow. Once she'd been flattered by his attentions. Now she could barely look at him without distaste.

"Let us change the subject."

Olivia heard exasperation in his voice. She must bid him good evening. Unfortunately, William spoke before she had formed the words.

"My dear, I have something more important to discuss with you."

He leaned closer. Was he going to kiss her? No, please, not when Ben's kiss remained a warm memory. She pulled back in her seat, but she was already pressed against the arm of the wooden swing.

"So much of my time is spent in study and prayer, as you know. Papers need to be written, lecture notes studied…"

When he paused, Olivia forced herself to look at him and found he was looking up at the porch ceiling. He often appeared searching for the right words as if each sentence he spoke had to be prepared and interpreted correctly.

"I admit I fail miserably when it comes to sharing feelings," he said finally, lowering his eyes toward her.

"William…"

"Please, let me finish. I have sensed your unease. No doubt you noticed I was distracted. I apologize for not being more demonstrative in my affection." He reached for her hands, lifted them, and held them tightly in his.

Her eyes widened. She realized he'd been centered on his own behavior, blaming her apparent discomfort on his lack of attentiveness.

He smiled. "I am beside myself with anticipation tonight."

She wanted to wrench her hands from his. Something about the look on his face caused a rising dread in her chest.

He brought her hands closer to his lips. "Olivia, I would be most blest, especially blest, if you would do me the great honor of becoming my wife."

Her jaw dropped. He'd articulated each word with dramatic emphasis as if he'd practiced the proposal dozens of times. Now she understood his odd behavior, but she never expected the reason. Nor did she expect to feel nothing, nothing at all.

Except surprise.

And distress.

Her father would be delighted.

"Olivia?"

"I never expected… Father…" Why couldn't she just shout out, *No.* She was too stunned, numbed by the unexpected proposal.

William's lips spread into a wide grin. "I have spoken with your father and I am happy to say we have his blessing." He released her hands and cupped her face. "I believe it is God's will we be together, that you be my helpmate as I endeavor to do His will." He leaned closer to kiss her.

She pushed him away and jumped from her seat. The pounding in her chest matched the pounding rain overhead. "We truly don't know each other well enough." She pressed her body against the railing, everything in her wanting to flee.

William leaned forward on the swing. "I understand you didn't expect a proposal so soon, but we have a lifetime to get to know one another. Your father, perhaps he hasn't told you, but I am to be his assistant, to grow in my vocation. Imagine how you and I can work together in the church." Beaming, he reached out a hand. "My joy shall be complete when you say yes."

She backed away from him to escape his words and his eyes boring into hers. "I don't know what to say. I... Good night, William."

"But you haven't given me an answer."

She reached the door and pushed it open. Glancing

back, she saw the confusion on his face. "I'm sorry. I need time." She rushed into the house, shutting the door behind her. What else could she say to him? He'd spoken to her father and received his blessing. It's what her father wanted, what he'd hoped for, and believed was best for her. She pressed a trembling hand to her breast. Is that what stopped her from refusing William? How was she going to go against her father's wishes when she'd always trusted his guidance? He was going to be so disappointed in her, but she couldn't say yes. She just couldn't!

Lovena's head snapped toward the sound of the slammed door, nearly dropping the dish she'd just dried. "Livie, what's wrong?"

Olivia's eyes blurred with unshed tears.

Setting down the dish, Lovena went to her. "You better take a seat and breath. I'm guessin' you and your beau had a fight." She led her to a chair.

"Has he left?" Olivia's lips trembled as her eyes darted toward the closed door.

Lovena walked over to the window that faced the porch, the one she used to keep a cautious eye on her charge. "He's climbin' into his carriage and he lookin' none too happy."

Olivia walked to the table and sank into a chair. "William is not my beau, though it appears everyone else believes so. He has done a better job courting my father than courting me," Olivia burst out before covering her mouth and looking toward the parlor.

"Your father's gone up to bed. He left me to keep an eye out for you. You look like you need to talk."

"William believes it is God's will we marry. He's already talked to Father and received his blessing. What was I to say? Do I even have a voice in the matter?"

Lovena's large bosom lifted and sagged. She shook her head. "You been spending time with Mr. Tapley, goin' for walks and carriage rides. Didn't you plan to go with him to the spring dance the town been plannin' after Easter? In his mind, you and him were courtin' in a respectful way."

"Most of the time he was conversing with Father." Olivia's shoulders slumped. *Had she led him to believe she was expecting a proposal?* "I admit I was flattered by his attentions at first, but I hadn't considered our relationship went beyond friendship...until recently."

"A man's attentions to a pretty young woman ain't never a desire for only friendship."

"I hadn't meant to lead him to thinking I'd want to

marry him." She covered her face with her hands.

Lovena pushed out a chair and sat beside her. "I think you been enjoyin' Mr. Tapley's attentions until the Pratt boy started showin' up."

Olivia couldn't deny it. At first she was flattered by William's desire to spend time with her, but deeper feelings hadn't grown, despite the time they'd spent together. Even his kisses were forgettable. It was so different with Ben. Her heart leaped in her chest the minute she saw him arrive to begin his work. Her body tingled into the depth of her womb when they were together.

Lovena wiped away a tear that rolled down Olivia's cheek. "We can't control those feelin's inside, Livie, when the right boy stirs 'em up."

"What am I to do?" she pleaded. "Father will understand, won't he? He can't expect me to agree to marry a man I could never love."

AFTER OLIVIA WENT up to bed, Lovena remained sitting, her arms wrapped around her middle, rocking slowly back and forth and muttering to herself. "The reverend ain't gonna like hearing what Livie has to say. He wants her to marry the one he picked for her and nobody else." She released her arms and pressed her hands to her aproned knees. "Might save a lot a trouble for the girl if she accepts the proposal."

A familiar chill settled on her. Her words had ruffled the spirit. "Nothin' good gonna come of this Cissa. You best not interfere." She rubbed her goose-bumped arms, never doubting she was not alone. Rising from her seat, she removed her apron, hanging it on a kitchen hook. She carried her candle into her bedroom and closed the door, praying Narcissa's spirit wouldn't follow her.

Drained from the events of the day, she changed into her nightgown and turned her quilt down. She didn't get right into bed. Her thoughts were too filled with memories, and one in particular had sprung into her mind the moment she entered her room. She'd tried to dismiss it, but it echoed in her ears. No chance it was just a coincidence, she thought. Narcissa wasn't going to leave her alone.

It had to be the spirit's doing. She hadn't thought of the cross in years.

She walked to her dresser, stooped, and opened the bottom drawer. Reaching below folded scarves, she pulled out a tiny satchel made from an old handkerchief. Untying a strip of yarn that held it closed, she spread out the cloth on top of the dresser and lifted the gold cross concealed within. She rubbed her fingers against its jeweled surface before untangling its chain.

"I know you want me to give this to her, Cissa, but it ain't a good time. No, I fear for what gonna come. I got to wait for a proper time." She shook her head stubbornly and replaced the cross back in its handmade satchel, returning it to its hiding place.

"I ain't never defied a spirit before," she murmured, pushing the drawer shut with her foot before getting into bed. She closed her eyes and prayed for guidance while wondering what troubles would come tomorrow.

"OLIVIA, YOU ARE especially quiet," Reverend Fuller said the next evening as they sat in the parlor close to the fire. "You said little at dinner as well. Is something on your mind?"

She paused in her knitting and looked up at her father. He looked weary. He'd been gone most of the day officiating at a funeral and burial. Bringing up the discussion of William's proposal would add to his burdens, but she couldn't wait any longer.

She dropped her needlework in her lap and met his gaze. "William has asked me to marry him. Of course, you were aware of his plans. He told me you gave your blessing."

Her father set down his pipe. "Yes, I have been waiting to hear, though I expected more excitement in your voice or at least pleasure at his proposal."

"I hardly expected a proposal. I couldn't give him an answer. I was too shocked."

"Didn't you consider his visits over the past few months would lead to something more?" He looked at her quizzically before his expression changed to understanding. "Ah, I understand, a woman often likes to keep a gentleman waitin', but you will answer him soon, I pray."

"I consider him a friend, Father, not a future husband."

"*Friend?*"

She saw his face redden. She'd upset him.

"William doesn't need a friend. He needs a wife, a helpmate. I cannot think of a better match for you. He's intelligent, respected, and most important, of a Godly character. He will make a fine husband. A better one than you'll find among other men in this town."

"I don't love him."

He tossed a dismissive hand in the air. "Love grows

as you share in life's blessings and hardships. Women must marry out of necessity. In time you will find contentment. William will prove to be the right choice for you. What could be better for a child of a minister than to marry one? You know well the needs of a congregation. You have helped the needy of our church, visited the sick, prayed with those grieving, and rejoiced with those who have birthed a child. I can only imagine the good works the two of you will do together. And you cannot deny you have enjoyed his company."

If only she had not been so pleased by William's attentions in the beginning, before she'd become more familiar with his disposition. "I am not ready for marriage."

"Could it be that you feel some anxiety over becoming a wife? How I wish your mother was here to speak of things better said by a woman."

Olivia shook her head in despair. "It's not that." How could she make him understand? She felt nothing for William. With Ben she experienced joy and delicious intimate urges her friends giggled about, but she had only imagined. Urges she couldn't admit to her father. And more. Her heart warmed in his presence and a longing to see him, to be close to him had grown to a need so much more than simply desire. How could she explain what was happening within her? She didn't quite understand it herself except that she felt truly happy merely thinking about Ben.

She leaned toward her father, her hands clasped. "Please, allow me to make my own choice when the time feels right for marriage."

Reverend Fuller pressed back into his chair and exhaled an exasperated breath. "Olivia, you must listen to me. Haven't I always tried to guide you with wisdom and consideration for what was best for you?

"Yes," she said quietly. She couldn't deny that he had always been the best of fathers.

"I have prayed that God would send you a worthy partner. He has answered my prayers. You and William make an ideal couple and you are of a good age to marry. William's ordination is in a matter of weeks. He desires to wed before he takes on the duties of a church. As I prepare for retirement, I have high expectations for him. You must not keep him waiting. He may become impatient with you, even look to another. And you must consider the benefits of this marriage. I insist. Not only has he chosen a Godly vocation but he comes from a family of high standing and wealth. Who else has as much to offer you in our small community?"

How could she respond? She'd always respected her father's advice but his insistence was uncharacteristic.

He reached out a hand to her and she grasped his. "Olivia, I believe your behavior this evening demonstrates anxiety over the prospect of marriage. You will grow accustomed to the idea. Women do, you know." He smiled. His tone had softened and he looked at her as if he were speaking to a misguided child. "William will make a fine husband." He released her hand and lifted his Bible. "Before I retire from the pulpit, I fully expect to officiate at your wedding. We will say no more about it tonight."

Olivia opened her mouth to protest but shut it as quickly. How could she confess her heart had been captured by another man? Her fingers trembled as she picked up her knitting and tried to work a stitch. She and her father seldom had a disagreement that couldn't be settled through conversation but he had expected her to be pleased at the proposal. She'd surprised him.

Better to give him time to adjust to her position. Maybe tomorrow he'd be more open to listening to her heart. The thought relieved some of her anxiety. She needed only to think of how to refuse William in a kind way. She resumed her knitting. Only the crackling of the fire broke the silence in the room.

She gazed up at her father who had returned to reading his Bible. He'd aged over the past year. His hair was turning white and she noticed a slight pallor on his face. He'd been working too hard. She felt so much love for him and was truly sorry to disappoint him.

"Father, there is something else I'd like to talk to you about." He appreciated when she asked for counsel and she didn't want to end the night with the heavy silence that had grown between them. Pushing back the stitches on her needles, she set her knitting in the basket at her feet.

Her father looked up, closing his Bible.

"I've been having strange recurring dreams. I don't know what to make of them."

"You mustn't keep them to yourself. How many times have I said bringing things into the light dispels darkness?"

She nodded, unable to hold back a smile. "Many times from the pulpit."

"Secrets are a devil's playground. Tell me about these dreams so you can be rid of them."

She looked up at the candled chandelier above them,

recreating the dream in her mind. "There's a young woman, at least she appears young in my mind, but she remains in shadows. In earlier dreams, she's in a small, dark room, rocking in an old chair. At first, she seems peaceful, then terribly frightened." Olivia paused and looked toward the fireplace. "It's strange but I can almost feel her fear. And her sadness. It's as if I am with her and her pain is mine as well."

She gazed back at her father. "Yesterday morning I dreamt that she stood at my bedside. I felt her touch my cheek as I slept. I've wondered if it could be more than a dream. A spirit, perhaps? I know you don't believe in such things, but they seem more than just dreams. Her touch seemed so real, I've…" She stopped. Her father's countenance had changed.

He stared at her, open-mouthed, his eyes wide. She thought of Lovena's reaction to her dream. He seemed as disturbed. When he didn't say anything, she continued. "I've heard spirits of ancestors might remain in an old house, especially if they aren't at peace and unable to move on. I've never believed such stories, but there are so many unexplained mysteries. You have professed as much. Could it be possible? A great grandmother or great aunt?" Had her father grown paler? "I've upset you." Olivia slid over on the couch, nearer to her father's chair.

He appeared to shake himself from a stupor. "Your imagination is working overtime. I was born here. There are no spirits in this house."

Olivia shrank back at his surly tone.

"The more you ponder a dream, the more life you give it. Something must have startled you recently or it may be the time of year." He tossed the Bible on his side table, nearly knocking over a candle and stood. "Ah, that must be it. The forty days before Easter symbolize our Lord's suffering and our hearts are deeply affected." He walked to the fireplace, bending down to add a log.

"But the dreams return almost nightly. Don't you find that unusual?"

He reached for a poker and stabbed at the burning logs. "Not if you continue to allow it to fester in your thoughts. Has Lovena been feeding your imagination with her superstitions?"

"No. I didn't take the dreams too seriously until yesterday. When I awoke, I found myself looking around the room for her."

"Lovena?"

"No, the woman in my dreams."

Reverend Fuller made no reply. He remained staring into the fire until they both heard a rattling of china and looked toward the doorway.

"Why are you standing there, Lovena?" The reverend snapped.

"Bringing your evenin' tea," she said, as the teapot and cups quivered on the tray.

"Not tonight. I'm retiring early."

Lovena looked to Olivia. She nodded her refusal.

Her father waited until the maid left before addressing his daughter again.

"Push these dreams from your mind. The sacredness of this dark time creates a pall over our days and nights. Remember how the devil tempted Jesus in the wilderness. He has found a place in your dreams. Cast him off. Say extra prayers before sleep tonight." He returned the poker to its stand. "I will write some notes about that for next week's sermon." He gave his daughter a nod and left the room without another word.

Lovena returned after the minister had climbed the stairs to his room. "You look like you could use a cup a tea, Livie."

"I've made him angry." Olivia shook her head

slowly, mystified at her father's reaction. "And the way he barked at you. It's my refusal to accept William's proposal. I should have waited for a better night to tell him about my dream."

Lovena's eyes rolled toward the ceiling before she lowered them.

"His reaction was not unlike yours. He's always professed there are mysteries in this world only God understands. I don't know what to believe, but your reaction, and now his, leaves me puzzled. Father blames the dreams on the dark days before Easter." Olivia slumped back into the cushions of the couch and drew a frustrated breath.

Lovena set down the tea tray. "You know what he's like when he gets into talking about God and the devil. No doubt next week's sermon's gonna be filled with fire and brimstone."

"You're probably right. He looked pale. Easter week's planning puts a great deal of pressure on him. Telling him about my refusal to marry William and about my dreams may have been more than he could deal with tonight. Maybe tomorrow he'll be in a better place to listen to me."

"Have some tea and put today to rest. Don't know

about tomorrow, but it ain't doin' no good to ponder it
now.

Writin help me cry on paper and not just inside me.

CHAPTER SIX

BEN LOOKED BEHIND him for a second time. He'd been surveying an especially damaged part of the barn when he heard the scratching and rustling noise again. "Must be some field mice living in here," he said aloud.

He walked to the front of the barn and pushed open the doors. He'd closed them when he entered, hoping to keep in the coolness as he examined the rotting boards. The afternoon was warmer than usual for this time of year, and he'd be spent the last few hours outside clearing out debris from the rooms he'd torn down.

Gazing across the yard, he saw Olivia circling the house before kneeling on all fours and peering under the porch. He grinned as he admired her derriere raised in the air.

After a few minutes, she lifted herself up and brushed off her skirt before turning around. When she spotted him staring at her and grinning, she looked momentarily embarrassed before walking across the yard to him. As she drew closer, he saw she looked anxious.

"Olivia, what's the matter?"

"Speckles, I can't find her. She never leaves the house. She's old and spends most of the day curled up somewhere. I found the door open when I came back from the store."

Ben raised a hand to calm her. "Slow down. Who is Speckles?

She put a hand to her mouth. "I'm sorry. I'm babbling."

"No need to apologize. I want to help."

Ben watched her take a calming breath. "Speckles is my cat. I've had her most of my life. Lovena thinks one of the church boys filling the woodbin may have left the door open while she was in the attic gathering herbs. She's still searching in the house but Speckles is nowhere to be found."

As Ben listened, he remembered the scratching noises he'd heard earlier. "I wonder... I heard something scurrying around the barn." He smiled when he saw a sparkle return to her eyes. "Let's go look."

Once inside the barn, Ben pointed to a back corner. "The noise was coming from over there."

Olivia called out the cat's name as they both

searched.

"There!" Ben pointed toward the back wall. "I saw something move behind those old shovels. He grabbed Olivia's arm before she could rush over. "Let me look." He didn't want to scare her but it could be a rat and not a cat. He stepped quietly to the spot and grabbed the handle of a spade leaning against the wall and shook it. Speckles leaped out, a mouse in her mouth.

Olivia screamed as the cat skittered past her and under a hay wagon. Ben rushed to Olivia's side and wrapped his arms around her. When she looked at him, he couldn't hold his laughter in any longer. It didn't take long for her to realize the humor of the situation. She started laughing too. When their eyes met, Ben grew serious. Without a word, his lips came down on hers. He held nothing back, wanting all he felt for her to be evident in his kiss. He sensed only a moment of hesitation before she leaned into him and kissed him back. Her lips were so soft, so yielding. His tongue touched hers and his body reacted. Drawing her closer he deepened the kiss, his manhood pressing against her. He sensed her surprise, though she didn't withdraw from their embrace. He slowly released her lips and loosened his hold.

"My sweet Olivia," he murmured into her hair, breathing in the flowery scent. He didn't want to let her go. She belonged in his arms.

The cat's meowing broke the tender moment. They pulled apart reluctantly as Speckles fitted herself between their legs and meowed again.

Ben breathed out a sigh, thankful the cat had more sense than he did. Compromising the minister's daughter in the barn would not bode well for either of their reputations if they were discovered.

Olivia reached down and picked up Speckles who had released her catch at her feet. Ben kicked the dead mouse away.

"I better get back to the house," Olivia said almost shyly. "Lovena will start searching for me."

Ben walked her to the doors, opened them and without a word, watched her carry the wandering cat back home.

LYING IN BED that evening, Ben spent the last hour thinking about Olivia and wondering what to do about his apparent opponent, William Tapley. He needed some questions answered, but turning thoughts over and over in his mind wasn't helping.

He turned his attention to the diary book he'd discovered. After reading a few entries the night before, he had fallen asleep with it in his hand. He reached over to his night stand and picked it up. Adjusting the pillows behind him, he settled in to read a few more pages.

Today was a real nice sunny day, Aunt Iva. It still cool but the winter cold is long gone and daffodils are openin up. I scrub and rinse the laundry this mornin and I spent most of the afternoon plantin seeds in the garden and weedin a good part of it. But that not the best part of the day. Jimmy was workin here cleanin the barn and spreadin more hay. He tall and stringy and dark brown. He got a nice face and don't look much older en me. After supper I come back here and he give me a big toothy smile. I smiled back and he near stumbled when he went to climb up on his wagon. I held my lips tight together so I dont laugh. I like the way I feel when I see him like somethin in my inside is glowin. I feel pretty too. Maybe next time I get up the curage to say somethin to him. Just thinkin about it gives me warm shivers. Well, thats all I can write or the missus be complainin again bout my candle bein' lit too long.

Goodnight Aunt Iva,

Narcissa Dunn

BEN LOWERED THE worn book in his lap, guilt grating at his thoughts. He was reading a young woman's personal story. On the other hand, the diary had obviously been in the wall of those deserted rooms for years, long forgotten. According to earlier entries, Narcissa's mother had been a slave in Virginia. She gave Narcissa as a baby to her Aunt Iva, a freed slave, when the mother found out her master was going to sell the child. The aunt brought the girl with her to Connecticut and found work on the Fuller farm. She'd helped Narcissa make the book and taught her what she'd learned about writing from her previous owner. When the aunt died of pneumonia, Narcissa covered the leather-bound pages with material from one of her aunt's aprons as a token of appreciation and fondness.

Fascinating story so simply written, Ben thought. She'd been attracted to a boy named Jimmy. He thought of his own desire for Olivia and smiled. *I like the way I feel when I see him like somethin in my inside is glowin.* Yes, he could identify with her feelings. Narcissa Dunn just put it into words that made sense. He was tired but couldn't help but read one more entry before dousing his candle. He turned the page. The writing was sloppier, almost scribbled.

HE COME TO me last night and lay his heavy body on me. He whisper my name then he dug into me. It hurt Lord it hurt bad. I keep my eyes shut the whole time. His wet lips press into my neck and his hands rub me all over. When he done, I thought his wate gonna kill me for sure. He call me sweet honey, his breath heavin when he get up. I open my eyes and he lookin at me. In the light of the moon I could see his eyes. I want to see them. I dont know why. His eyes are kind in the day. They crinkle on the sides, smilin eyes. Maybe I need to know if they still smile. He cover me and leave. I smell wiskey and sweat. I laid in the wetness for a long time afraid to move. I don't want to know I'm still alive. I hold my breath until I can't hold it no more. When light come through the window, I close my eyes and hide under my blanket but I still smell him like he still there. I touch my soreness and see blood on my fingers. I start to scream but clamp my mouth shut. Better nobody no. Who they gonna believe? I need to get up and go to work, but I can't move. I hurt inside like I'm split in two.

BEN SLAMMED THE book closed, aghast at what he'd read, the image of the poor girl's pain etched in his mind. Though her writing was clumsy, each line was penned with raw emotion. He thought of the room where he'd found it and the torn, dirty mattress. Was that where the crime had been committed? He pictured a young colored girl terrified at the sight of her own blood, yet afraid to tell anyone. How alone she must have felt.

He'd entered into her world, one of suffering and pain. It would have been better if he'd never found the book, buried it, or burned it. But it was too late. He stared for a long time at the shabby flowered cover before tucking it under his mattress.

He doused his candle but lay awake, wondering who had taken advantage of her. Had she been abused by one of the farmhands? Was it the boy Jimmy she wrote about earlier? Whoever it was, she'd known the perpetrator. As a Negro farm worker, she would have had little credibility if she'd accused someone higher than her station, even let go for speaking up.

Should he give the diary to the minister? Or burn it as he'd thought previously, erasing the evidence of the woman's suffering? She'd hidden her writings for a reason.

He'd put in a long day and he needed to sleep. The remaining work at the Fullers' would take him no more than three weeks to finish, three weeks left relishing the closeness to Olivia. He'd make the most of his time.

Remembering the feel of her in his arms pulled him from the wretched story he'd just read. Seeing her every day was a pleasure and a liability. She liked him. He was sure of it. And she hadn't slapped him when he kissed her. Could she simply be a tease, a girl enjoying a bit of fun with a laborer? He didn't think so. There was something more between them.

But Tapley was in the picture and arriving at the parsonage too often for comfort.

Closing his eyes, he imagined more time alone with her. He'd admired her from afar for too long and now he was falling in love with her. He'd have to be careful or he'd be leaving the job with more than blisters.

The next morning he awoke feeling as if he'd fallen off his horse during the night. When he stood up to stretch, every bone seemed to groan under the effort. True, he'd been pounding, pulling, lifting, and tearing up planks daily without giving his body much of a rest, but the heaviness he felt had nothing to do with his labors.

The diary entries. *Damn, it's as if the woman's story climbed into my head and kicked at it all night.* Though he didn't remember dreaming, he'd had a restless night's sleep. He reached under his mattress and pulled out the book. It felt warm in his hands, most likely from his body weight resting on the mattress all night.

"What do I do with it?" He frowned, glaring at the book. He brushed through the lips of the pages with a finger. The last entry he'd read had created a weight on his heart. It was just an old diary, meant only for the eyes of its creator. If he gave it to the minister, what would he do with it? He sighed and stuffed it back under his mattress and got dressed. He'd deal with it later.

He left his room above the woodshop and walked down the steps that led outside. He'd been living there since he was fifteen when his uncle insisted it was time he moved out of the house. He'd said a young man needed his privacy and didn't need to hear 'an old man's snores'.

Once outside, he walked the few steps to the farmhouse and into the office his uncle used to see customers. The office had been the original parlor of the house. The kitchen and pantry were behind it, with two rooms to the side, one made into a small bedroom where their cook Hildy stayed when harsh weather made it difficult for her to walk the three miles to her home. The other was a sitting room that took the place of the former parlor. There were two bedrooms on the second floor and another smaller sitting room. The front porch wrapped around one side of the house and held his uncle's handmade rockers for a visitor's comfort as well as a nice advertisement for their quality workmanship.

He found his uncle sitting at his desk, leaning over some scattered sheets of paper, his nose nearly touching the one he was reading. Uncle Syl raised his eyes than dropped them again, fisting the paper he held. "How's he expect me to read the scratching on this page? The ink splats look like mouse droppings."

Ben took the paper from his uncle's outstretched hand. "If you cleaned those spectacles you're wearing you might be able to read better."

His uncle pulled off his glasses and rubbed the scratched lenses with a tail of his flannel shirt. "Time's coming for you take over the book work, Ben. My eyes aren't going to get any better."

Ben nodded in understanding. Uncle Syl was getting on in years and accustomed to putting in long days. His sore joints worsened during the winter months and soon he wouldn't be able to do much of the finer work. Though he encouraged Ben to learn every part of the trade, his uncle grew depressed and ornery when he could no longer do a task that at one time came easy to him.

Ben looked over the job description he held. "Mr. Johnson wants another bookcase to climb those crooked walls of his. Similar size to the last one, but I'll need to go out and do my own measurements. His are usually off by a few inches. I'll stop by this morning."

"You may as well take care of this one too. His uncle lifted a paper from the corner of his desk. It's going to keep us plenty busy once you finish with the Fuller's barn.

"Big job? Great. Whose it for?"

"Percival Tapley, the man who keeps his nose so high in the air, I'm surprised it don't catch flies. Wouldn't hurt for it to catch a mosquito or two."

Ben ignored his uncle's mockery. The name Tapley created too swift of a reaction in the pit of his stomach.

He reached for the job order. The last thing he wanted to do was to go to the Tapley house.

"The man wants us to build a fancy bedroom set, a surprise gift to his son and his future bride," his uncle smirked.

Ben's fingers tightened around the order his uncle had handed to him. "William Tapley is getting married?"

"It appears so. If you see him over at the Fuller's, don't say a word about the job. His father's ready to bust the buttons on the velvet vest he favors. Not only is his son going to be ordained in a few weeks but looks like he might be marrying the minister's daughter. Haven't heard any gossip about an engagement yet, but Percival is confident enough to order the set. If you ask me, marrying the minister's daughter places his son in a fine spot to take over Fuller's ministry when the old boy retires. Young William is not stupid. From what I've observed, he's ambitious and he's got the same nose as his father, pointed above everybody else's head."

Ben masked his anger and disbelief. He looked down at the job order, one corner crumpled in his clutched fist.

"Told Percival you'd bring over some wood samples.

You can get them ready before you leave. Not much else for you to do here this morning." His uncle stretched back in his chair.

Ben's dismal thoughts had blocked out his uncle's voice and turned his future hopes into dust. Refocusing, he looked up from the work order.

Uncle Syl eyed his nephew. "You slept through the birds this morning. They were noisy enough to wake the dead. You've been working hard. Try to get an extra hour or two of sleep tonight."

Ben nodded, setting the job order down on the desk. His uncle was in good spirits, especially with the news of a big job to work on through the summer and fall. He didn't want to dampen his mood and if he stayed any longer, he'd lose his composure. "Be back for supper." He walked out, forgetting to close the door behind him.

He arrived at the Fuller's after lunch. Unlike other days, he hadn't rushed to begin his work. Fortunately, the elder Tapley was away from home when he'd stopped at his house. Unsure whether to discuss the project with Mrs. Tapley, he said he'd return on another day. He wondered if he might be able to pass this one back to his uncle, claiming other work needed his attention.

Riding up to the barn, he dismounted and walked over to the pile of wood he'd gathered for the repairs. Though he'd covered the wood, the rain had been too heavy and had soaked through the canvas. He'd need to allow it to dry some. Fortunately, it was a bright sunny day. He began to spread the rain soaked boards, thinking of Olivia as he lifted each board.

He wondered if she was home or at the Meeting House. His mind couldn't make sense of her reaction to him and the news of a future marriage to Tapley. He was torn between wanting to see her and hoping he wouldn't.

He pushed himself to work faster, slamming each board down with greater intensity. He wished he'd never started this job, never gotten to know her. Better if she'd stayed in his imaginings. One thing was for certain, he needed to stay away from her. He'd known Tapley was spending a great deal of time at the parsonage being mentored by Reverend Fuller. He'd ignored rumors that he was seriously courting Olivia. *Fool.* The truth was Will Tapley was a welcomed visitor. Ben was the interloper.

He hadn't been able to control his need to get to know her. Though she appeared to have welcomed his advances, he'd taken advantage of each situation. She may have seen their meetings as an innocent flirtation gone too far while he'd grown serious. Even if he disliked Tapley, he had no right to impinge on a courtship the man obviously assumed would lead to marriage. He needed to get this job done and get away from here as soon as possible.

CHAPTER SEVEN

"GOOD MORNING, DR. Hines. You visitin' early today. I got some Johnny Cakes left from breakfast. You want to have a bite before you see the reverend?"

"No thank you, Lovena. I had my usual boiled egg and toast for breakfast. I told the pastor I'd stop by today whether he wanted me to or not. I've been keeping an eye on him. He's been looking pale on the pulpit."

She was glad he was checking on Reverend Fuller. He hadn't been looking good to her either. "If he ain't got his nose in the good book, he's out ministerin' wherever he's called. He says he'll rest when he can't serve no more."

"Sounds like Charles."

"He's in his study writin' his Easter sermon."

Lovena remained in the hall as the doctor made his way to the small study. He was dressed in his usual brown suit that had seen better days, but he carried himself with distinction. Serving the farming community often went beyond his human patients when a veterinarian wasn't available.

A rap on the back door pulled her from her thoughts. She returned to the kitchen and peered out to see Clara, a neighbor's maid, standing on the porch. She worked for one of the wealthier families in town, the Buckinghams. "Hello Clara, what you got for us today?"

"The missus wanted me to bring you some of the butter we've been churnin'."

"Mmm, hmm! I know just what I be doin' with that. The reverend been askin' for my pound cake and with strawberries comin' in another month, it'll be a treat. You tell her we thank her for her generosity."

"Somethin' smells good in there."

"I started real early this mornin' makin' chicken stew, bein' the day is so chilly. What's the news from the Buckinghams?"

"Those girls are busy sewing Easter dresses, fancier than usual. They plan to wear them to the dance comin' up too. Givin' their momma all kinds of headaches is what they're doin'."

"She has her hands full with those three girls. Ain't Lila gettin' married in June?"

"Yea, the missus got lucky marryin' her oldest off to

the blacksmith's son. He's a nice boy."

"Aaron, ain't it?"

The younger maid nodded. "Her second daughter, Jenny, is showin' some jealousy. She's only a year younger and figures it's her time too. Sometimes she eggs on her baby sister Beth, causin' no end of frustration for Lila who got so much on her mind. She's sewin' her weddin' dress and helpin' out with her sisters' dresses too. Little Beth's a sweet girl, but Jenny can twist her around her little finger. What's happenin' with Olivia? News around town is she'll be gettin' engaged soon to the Tapleys' son."

"Time will tell. I let them young people figure it out." Lovena wasn't about to tell the maid of her worries. Clara was one of the worst gossips among the servant folk.

"Well, I better be gettin' back."

"Tell Mrs. Buckingham we appreciate the butter."

"Sure will."

Lovena closed the door, stored the butter and returned to the hearth. After adding some seasonings to the stew, she checked the rising of her bread dough. When Olivia was done cleaning the bedrooms, Lovena would send her out to the chicken coop to bring back some fresh eggs so she could start the pound cake.

"I'll be off, Lovena," the doctor called, looking into the kitchen. "I told Charles he needs to take a daily nap. Please urge him to take my advice."

"I can try but he's one stubborn man."

"Has he been complaining of any chest pains lately?"

"No, but I seen him rubbin' his chest a couple'a times, now that you mention it." Lovena's expression turned to a concerned frown. "Why you ask?"

"His heart isn't as young as he would like to believe it is and his coloring concerns me. Just keep an eye on him. If you see anything that might cause alarm, send for me. I'd prefer not to say anything to his daughter, but her father needs to slow down. He's a few years older than me but he wants to believe he's a decade younger."

"I'll watch him close. Best not to say anything to Olivia unless it be needed." Lovena walked with the doctor to the front door, waved him off, and sighed as she shut the door. Too much going on lately, she thought, and only a week to Easter. She knew how busy both the minister and his daughter would be over the next few days, and she needed to keep her mind on the cooking for Easter Sunday. She wanted to be at her church on Easter morning so everything needed to be prepared beforehand.

The reverend been doin' too much and been walking around in a real dark mood. Oh, dear Jesus, what he thinkin' now that Livie told him about her dreams? He already upset Livie ain't jumpin' at the chance to marry Tapley. The poor girl don't want to marry him. She got eyes for that nice Pratt boy but she ain't never defied her daddy.

She looked up toward the ceiling, fear pressing in on her. *Lord, I know you listenin'. Narcissa, she had to carry a cross too heavy. Her spirit need to be restin', not bein' here causin' trouble. How come you ain't takin' her home? She always had spunk. Knowin' her, she refuses to go until things be made right. I'm scared'a what comin' about. I know you busy but I hope you keepin' an eye on her, a real close eye.*

She returned to her work shaking her head and praying her premonitions were figments of her imagination. She sensed a storm brewing, a storm that could tear down the walls the reverend built to protect Olivia.

"DON'T FORGET TO buy the yellow thread for sewin' the

ribbons on your bonnet." Lovena said to Olivia an hour later as the girl prepared to go to the store. "If the storekeeper don't have any, we can make do with white." Lovena pressed her hands against her hips as she watched Olivia peer out the window toward the barn. "You ain't gonna get your errands done that way."

"I was just noticing what a lovely day it is after the rain we've been having."

Uh huh. Lovena rolled her eyes. "You goin' right to choir practice from the store?"

"Yes, I'll be gone all day. We have only two rehearsals left before Easter services. A couple of the choir members offered to bring lunch pails.

Lovena saw a frown cross Olivia's face. She had little doubt it was because she'd miss seeing Benjamin Pratt. "You and your father don't seem to have a minute's rest this week."

"I plan to be at home all day tomorrow to help with the cooking. I know Father insists on Easter dinner at home though we've received more than a few invitations."

"I'm doin' just fine here. You do what you need to do." Lovena returned to wiping away flour that remained on the table but paused, giving in to her curiosity. "You have more of those dreams?"

"Not a dream really."

Lovena stared at her. "What you mean, *not really*?"

"I woke up this morning feeling as if she'd been there with me again. It feels so strange. Father believes the dreams will pass once Easter arrives. Maybe he's right. I've had a lot on my mind."

"You sure do."

"William is meeting with Father on Friday. When I see him after their session, I plan to refuse his proposal. Father expects me to "know my mind" by then and give him a favorable answer."

"Your daddy ain't bendin' is he?"

"He disregards my arguments. I hope to talk to him again tonight. Why does he believe William is the best choice I have for a husband? He has never ordered my life, only advised me. I would never have expected him to be so demanding of who I should marry. In the matter of William, he refuses to listen to my arguments. Why won't he take my desires into consideration?"

"I got no answers. He always been wantin' what he thinks is best for you." Lovena removed the dishtowel that covered her large mixing bowl and pressed down the risen dough with her knuckles. "You best get off to the store or you gonna be late for choir practice."

When Olivia closed the door behind her, Lovena heaved a weary sigh. She had no advice to offer Livie. Her father may be doing what's best. Who knows what the truth might bring?

"NICE TO SEE you this morning, Miss Olivia. You just missed all the excitement," the storekeeper said, wearing a welcoming smile.

"Oh? What did I miss, Mr. Grover?"

"James Seymour came barging in asking me to put up a notice for him. He needs to be confessing before Easter Sunday with all the swearing he was doing. May Bissel was in here shopping with her two little ones. She gathered them up and flew out of here so they wouldn't hear him cursing loud enough to raise spirits from hell's fires."

"Why was he upset?"

"Somebody's stray heifer broke into the fence he spent the week repairing. He tied up the creature and he's not going to return it or bring it to the pound until the owner fixes the fence and pays him for his wasted work. He's going everywhere putting up these signs to find the owner." Mr. Grover pointed to the large handwritten sign on his bulletin board. "I told him to get out before he chases away more customers. Told him I'd send him a bill for lost revenue. That shut him up. He's most likely off creating havoc somewhere else."

"I hope Mr. Seymour overcomes his rage before he finds the owner."

"It might be cheaper and safer for the owner not to fess up. Anyway, didn't mean to take you from your purpose today. What can I do for you?"

Olivia handed him the grocery list. "Lovena needs a few things delivered."

Mr. Grover looked over the list. "Got everything she needs, though I'm running low on sugar and super fine flour what with all the baking going on. I'll be sure to put some aside for her right away and get them out to her this afternoon. Is there anything else?"

"I'd like to look at your ribbons and threads."

"Popular items this week with all the ladies sewing Easter bonnets. Feast your eyes on the new fabrics too. I got in some nice summer prints and striped calico, even got some Philadelphia cotton."

"I'll do that. Thank you."

"You need any help, you just let me know."

Olivia walked toward the table displaying spools of

thread just as Lena Porter came bustling in. Olivia kept her eyes on the table not wanting to engage in a conversation, but it was too late. Lena was already walking her way.

"Good morning, Olivia. Getting your shopping done before rehearsal? I have been practicing the hymns all morning. Mr. Porter said it was like already being in church. I don't know if he meant it as a compliment though, with the look I saw on his face when he scooted out the door." Mrs. Porter chuckled. "Of course with you accompanying us on the organ, we sound a great deal better."

"Music always makes the difference. I'll be over as soon as I finish here." Olivia turned back to the display, but Mrs. Porter wasn't to be deterred. She squeezed her portly figure passed a corner and drew closer to her.

"How is that good looking beau of yours? I hear he'll be assisting the reverend at Sunday service. You must be pleased he's gained a position in your father's church."

"I beg your pardon, Lena, but the church belongs to all its members."

"Naturally, but with the two of you courting, it's a nice situation for Mr. Tapley. My friends all say what a handsome couple the two of you make and him just coming out of Yale Divinity School. You've done right well for yourself."

Olivia kept her eyes on the thread spools, wishing she could escape. Lena Porter seldom kept opinions or judgments to herself and it appeared others accepted that she and William were to marry. She couldn't stand in the center of the store and declare William was not her intended. Instead she forced a smile and walked to the fabrics. The woman followed right after her.

"I told my Emma she should be so fortunate as to marry a man of the cloth. I probably shouldn't tell you this, but she had her eye on Will Tapley, but once we saw him stopping by your father's house on a regular basis and seeing the two of you together sitting on the porch, we knew it wasn't meant to be. What a perfect match, a minister's daughter marrying a minister. Well, here I'm going on and don't even know if he's proposed yet. We're all waiting to hear the news."

Olivia's chest tightened. She wanted to blurt out there was no serious relationship and she had no desire to marry William but Mr. Grover already experienced enough excitement for one morning. The last thing she wanted to do was make a scene.

"Lena, I fear I'm going to be late for my church duties. I need to finish my errands and get over to the Meeting House."

"And here I am taking up your time. Well, I just want you to know how happy I am for you and Will Tapley."

Olivia pressed her lips together as the woman went on her way. She lifted the spool of thread she wanted and turned around, nearly dropping the spool. Ben was standing at the open door, his hand still on the knob, as Mrs. Porter brushed passed him.

Olivia froze. How much had he heard of the woman's chatter? Before she could lift a hand or call to him, he walked out, pulling the door closed behind him.

TIRED AND DEPRESSED, Olivia returned from the meeting hall late afternoon. Before she climbed the porch steps, she looked toward the barn hoping to see Ben, but if he'd been there, he was done for the day. Even if he was still working and she could talk to him, what could she say? He wouldn't have walked out without talking to her unless he'd overheard Lena Porter's exclamations. Not only did Lena's high pitched voice carry in the chorus at church but more so in a small general store.

She must tell William she appreciates his proposal but she can't accept. She prayed her father would forgive her for not accepting his choice. Only then could she talk to Ben. She might find out his feelings for her did not go beyond a flirtation, but his eyes said more. Regardless, she could not marry William.

When she entered the kitchen, she found the room empty but she could hear dishes rattling in the dining room. Before she could escape to her room, Lovena returned.

"I was beginnin' to wonder if you'd be home for dinner. Your daddy walked in an hour ago."

"I saw him in the church office briefly before meeting the choir. We're doing some new hymns so practice took longer than usual." She lifted the package she held. I bought thread and some ribbons. Did your delivery arrive from the store?"

"Sam Grover brought them over himself, leavin' his wife to mind the store. Even brought some coffee beans his wife ground especially for the pastor. Your daddy does love a fresh cup of coffee now and again. He told me all about James Seymour's fence and the heifer that near destroyed it."

"Was the owner found?"

"Turns out it belong to Mr. Snow, the shoemaker. Seymour got him to pay for repairs on the fence but Snow refused to do the repairin'. He agreed to make a new pair of shoes for Mrs. Seymour. I guess Mr. Snow came in the store grumbling about it."

"He is usually quite agreeable."

"He figures with the cost of the fence and makin' free shoes, he could buy another heifer."

"Probably true." Olivia walked toward the hall, hoping to avoid more conversation.

"How are you?"

Olivia turned around with a sigh. Lovena knew her too well. She probably looked as miserable as she felt. "I had a difficult day."

"You ready to talk about it?"

She walked over to the table, slumped down in a chair and began to tell her about the scene in the store. "Ben most likely heard every word of what Mrs. Porter said."

"But you don't know what he was thinkin'. If what he heard bothered him, he must have it as bad as you. Livie, you got yourself into a predicament."

"Was he here today?"

"He worked for a few hours this afternoon, mostly

inside the barn."

"I must talk to Father again tonight. He needs to know I am refusing William."

"I just don't know," Lovena murmured, wagging her head back and forth.

"I thought you liked Ben. He's a hard worker and kind. Father just needs to get to know him."

"Your father looks out for your best interests."

"You think I should marry William too?" She got up and pushed the chair under the table, scraping it against the wooden floor. "I can't talk about this anymore." She turned and rushed from the room.

"WHEN'S OLIVIA COMIN' down?" Lovena asked when the minister came into the dining room.

"She says she's not hungry. Why don't you take a dish up to her? She should have something to eat."

Lovena set a basket of bread on the table. "If you don't mind my saying so, you look like you carryin' a heavy burden."

The reverend gave a slow nod. "Lovena, I have placed a great deal of trust in you all these years."

She nodded.

"You've been here since before Olivia was born," he

said quietly.

"Yes, I have, and helped birth her too."

He lifted pained eyes to hers. "I have put much thought into Olivia's future. William is the right man for her. She must accept him."

Lovena didn't reply.

"I have been a good father, haven't I?"

"Yes. Olivia coulda done no better than you."

"You know I want what is best for her now."

"I believe that. Yes, I do."

He sagged back into his chair. "I need your help. My daughter is allowing her heart and not her head to decide her future."

Lovena crossed her arms tightly against her. "What you want me to do?"

"Convince her to accept William's proposal."

Bowing her head low, Lovena mumbled to herself as she straightened silverware next to each dish.

"Speak up. What are you muttering about?"

"It be hard for her to make that big decision now, and she don't have the feelin's for Mr. Tapley that goes along with a weddin'. You got your mind set on her marryin' him but…"

"I prefer not to discuss my reasons," he interrupted.

"You must trust I know what is best for my daughter."

"I worry, 'specially 'bout those dreams she been havin'."

His lips tightened. "They are only dreams, not reality or some spirit roaming the house as Olivia would like to believe. Ignore her talk of dreams. We can conjure up all kinds of explanations."

"It's just they seem…"

He cut her off again. "I don't want to hear your interpretation. I appreciate the loyalty you've given to our family. You agree I have treated you well?"

Lovena nodded, biting her lip.

"I expect your cooperation now. I have prayed long and hard for the Lord to guide me. I believe He has answered my prayers by sending William to me. He is a man not only devoted to God but one who desires to marry my daughter. I want you to help Olivia see God's hand in this union. I will continue to do the same."

He picked up his fork and lifted a chunk of beef from the serving dish. "Make up a dish for Olivia and tell her I expect her in the parlor within the hour."

"FATHER, PLEASE, I cannot bring myself to love William. I cannot marry him. I wish to have a good marriage, and I promise I will choose wisely when the time comes." Olivia sat stiffly on the edge of the sofa cushion while her father leaned back in his arm chair observing his daughter's discomfort.

"Have you been practicing your refusal to William as well?" He saw the startled look in his daughter's eyes and the pain, but he couldn't stop now. "I have spent many months with William and have come to know him well. I admit he tends toward egotism, not unusual for a man who has nearly completed his schooling at Yale. He is proud of his upcoming ordination, as he should be. Once he begins his work in the church, you will see a gradual change. A minister cannot preach Godly sermons, pray for the sick, or officiate at funerals without growing in humility. He'll be a good husband. Give him time."

"What can I say to have you understand?" Olivia pleaded, wringing her hands.

"I understand you are fearful. Marriage is a lifetime commitment, but it is a union blessed by God. You must choose well."

"But I have not *chosen* William. You have, Father."

He glared at her. "I will not abide your insolence. I've accepted William as my pupil and, prayerfully, my future successor. He has chosen you to court and to be his future wife. You have welcomed his overtures in the past. Has he not been a complete gentleman? Has he treated you with respect?"

Olivia's sighed. "Yes, he has been most respectful and proper."

"What more do you want? He's a man who desires to serve God. You believe you can do better?" He gripped the arms of his chair, his lips forming a straight, tight line.

"That is unfair! I'd hoped to have other feelings for him besides friendship."

He sucked in a weary breath. He seldom went against his daughter's desires, but this time he couldn't allow her to have her way. He must convince her. "Tender feelings grow. You will find it to be true once you are married."

"Father, I've been…talking to Benjamin Pratt."

"Who?" He leaned toward her, disbelieving what he suspected she was about to say. "The laborer working on the barn?"

"He's an apprentice to his uncle, a craftsman of fine furniture. Ben is intelligent and kind. I like him, a great deal."

He watched his daughter's visage change, her lips forming the hint of a hope-filled smile. *No,* he could not tolerate this. "Are you telling me you've begun a secret courtship with this man?"

"Not a courtship, conversations. I feel good when I'm with him. I believe he would like to court me." She looked suddenly embarrassed. "I… hope he would." She turned away, her clasped hands twisting in her lap. "I have never felt this way toward William."

"What is this nonsense?" His tone caused her eyes to grow wide. He hated himself for the disappointment he saw in them, but he loved her. He must protect her, even if she despised him for it. "Childish romantic notions, Olivia, that carry no common sense. I raised you …" He jerked back suddenly and closed his eyes. His face distorted into a grimace before he buckled over in his seat, pressing a hand to his chest, "Aaah," he moaned.

"Father, what is it?" Olivia gasped. She rushed from her seat and knelt at her father's side. "Lovena!"

"*Dear Lord,*" Lovena wailed when she came running and saw Olivia bending over her father. She hurried to him and braced his shoulder, pressing a thumb to his pulse. "Reverend, can you hear me?"

He moaned but remained buckled over.

"I'll get some cold cloths. Be right back." She rushed away, her heavy footfalls clambered across the floor toward the kitchen. "*Mercy, mercy.*"

When she returned, Olivia was still kneeling by him, tears rolling down her cheeks.

Lovena pressed a cloth to his forehead. "You need to find the doctor. I'll see to him."

Olivia didn't appear to hear her.

"Livie, go!"

She raised startled eyes to Lovena before pulling herself up and running from the room and out the door.

The minister kept his head bent nearly to his knees. Lovena was above him muttering prayers. His doctor consistently warned him to slow down. He should have no problem convincing him of an attack caused by too much stress; an attack his daughter must think could have been deadly. He was gambling on her devotion to him. He must do whatever it takes to make her bend to his wishes.

"HOW IS HE?" Olivia asked when Doctor Hines walked out of her father's bedroom. She'd been standing in the hall waiting anxiously to hear the doctor's prognosis.

"Let's go downstairs and talk," he answered,

indicating that he didn't want the minister to hear them discussing his condition.

After they descended the stairs, the doctor set his bag on a nearby hall table before turning to Olivia and giving her a compassionate smile. "I see the worry on your face, my dear. Take comfort. Your father is resting peacefully and he'll be back on the pulpit soon. I want him to stay in bed for a few days, however, and avoid any stress. His mind and body are tired. He doesn't allow himself enough leisure."

Olivia breathed a momentary sigh of relief before asking the question that weighed on her mind. "Was it his heart?"

"This incident appears to be more an attack of anxiety than a heart attack, but it is a warning for him to slow down. He needs to curtail his activities. If he doesn't, the next time may be more serious. I am sorry to have to be so blunt, but I've been worried about his overall health for some time."

"I fear we shall have a battle of wills."

The doctor shook his head grimly. "His stubbornness could be the death of him. Do you know of anything that might have triggered undue agitation? He appeared distraught. Once I determined he was out of danger, I was forced to give him a strong sedative."

Olivia didn't reply. How could she answer? Tell him her rebellion and her refusal to marry William caused the attack?

"I am sorry to add to your concern, Olivia. He is overworked and overburdened. Encourage him to slow down, but know you are not responsible if he refuses our advice." The doctor retrieved his medical bag and walked to the front door. "I'll look in on him again in the morning. Do your best to keep him calm and get some rest yourself."

Olivia waited until the doctor climbed into his carriage before closing the front door. She pressed her back against it and dropped her head into her hands.

Lovena walked over to her and rested a hand on her shoulder. "Livie, you heard the doctor. Go to your room and lie down. Your father be asleep for a good long time."

Olivia raised tired eyes to the maid. "Father was upset with me. I told him I wouldn't marry William. This was my fault."

"You stop that kind a talk. It was bound to happen what with the schedule he keeps."

"I told him about Ben. That I like him and he might

want to court me. Father was enraged."

Lovena wiped away a tear that slipped down Olivia's cheek. "You surprised him. He been thinkin' all along you and Mr. Tapley would marry."

"I gave him no reason to think otherwise until recently. If I refuse William, the news could... I can't even say it."

Lovena groaned. "You stop thinkin' the worse."

"When the doctor left me alone with him earlier, Father gripped my hand and begged me not to disappoint him. He wants only the best for me. He believes Ben is interfering with God's will and I need to stay away from his influence. Father spoke in barely a whisper as if it strained him to even say a few words. I tried to calm him. When Dr. Hines returned, he sent me from the room when he saw father's agitation." Olivia choked in a sob.

Grasping Olivia's chin, Olivia lifted her face to hers. "You need to let the night take care of itself. We gonna pray God has his way whatever that might be. Now you go and get a few hours sleep. It's after midnight. Nothing gonna change in the next few hours."

Olivia wiped her damp cheek with the back of her hand and nodded, her face a picture of hopelessness.

Once in her room, she curled up on her bed without undressing and pulled the quilt over her. The image of her father clasping his chest, his head heaving forward returned. She couldn't release the guilt that took her mind prisoner. She must have led William to believe she cared more for him. Her father assumed so. No doubt, her actions, her willingness to spend time with William, before she came to know Ben, led her father to give his blessing for their marriage. He expected her to be delighted at the proposal.

She'd shocked him.

Age had weakened him, and he carried the burdens of his congregation and spent exhaustive hours handling church business and ministering. She must stop her pleading for him to give in to her desires. Perhaps, selfish desires and foolish behavior. What if her continued refusal to marry William brought on another attack, worse than this one?

She couldn't live with herself. It would be her fault.

CHAPTER EIGHT

"WHAT A MISERABLE day," Ben muttered as he pulled off his boots and stretched out on his bed that night without undressing.

Bad enough he'd had to deal with the Tapley's furniture order, a bedroom set for Will Tapley's future marriage, but he'd walked in on a congratulatory conversation between Olivia and a town gossip. Had Tapley already asked for Olivia's hand? With the furniture order already sitting on his uncle's desk, it appeared so. Yet, how could he explain her attentions toward him? He hadn't imagined the attraction was mutual. Regardless, he needed to stay away from her, finish the barn and leave without looking back.

It didn't matter that he'd been attracted to her long before working for her father. Or, that their time together had given him the hope of a future with her. Tapley made a claim first and he'd ignored it.

He pushed himself from the bed and undressed. After pouring some water into his washbowl and adding lye soap, he scrubbed his face and hair and washed from head to toe the best he could with the remaining water. He went through the same ritual every night after working at the Fuller's. Cobwebs from the old rooms he'd razed clung to him and now that he was working in the barn, it wasn't much better.

Washed and settled into bed, he felt only slightly revived from his wretched day. He propped up his pillows and reached beneath his mattress for the mysterious diary. Entries he'd read previously stayed with him through the day and added to his melancholy mood. It was a depressing distraction, he mused, as he opened it. The next couple of pages were too difficult to read. The combination of moisture and dirt smeared the writing. He turned to the next readable page.

I WANT TO call you Rosalee becus your lips fancy like a rose growing up the side of the fence. Your hair dark but not black like mine and your skin be white. Imagine me bearin a white chile. You got nice color like pale honey. Your eyes dark like mine tho. I wonder if you gonna have smilin' eyes when you bigger. Now they look up at me like you surprised or somethin when you wake up. Most a the time you sleepin and I hold you close as can be. Forgive me for not wantin you. When my stomach started growin I was so scared. When I couldn't hide it I saw him watchin me. I see in his face he be afraid someone find what he did and he gotta pay the price. But you part of me and love is all I feel. Lovin my baby girl.

BEN PRESSED THE open diary to his chest, closed his eyes and exhaled an incredulous sigh. "She became pregnant." How difficult it must have been for her to carry a child conceived by force, he thought, and bearing a white child at that. "The father couldn't have been that man Jimmy she wrote about in an earlier entry," he murmured, shaking his head. "She obviously loved the child." He wondered if it could be a made-up story rather than a true account. He tested the thought but didn't believe it. There was too much emotion woven through the woman's words. He turned to the next page.

HE DON'T LOOK at me no more. Turns away when I walk by. He let me be. He let us be. Jimmy come to see me, talks with me in the night when he done with his chores. He was sweet on me before I become two. Now he has sad eyes. He know what happen but he don't say nothin.

He see you more white than black and has questions in his eyes and anger on his face when he look away. He smiles at you and holds your little white fingers in his brown hand and talks sweet to you. He holds my hand too and smiles but I only see his sad eyes.

BEN TURNED THE page slowly, drawn further into the woman's heartache. He wondered if she lived with the child in those cold rooms. And who was the father?

He kept reading.

The missus come to see you. She don't look at me. Only you. She scare me, Rosalee. When she leave I feel like snakes are crawlin under my skin. I hold you close to my breast and let you suck till there's no more to give, until you fall asleep peaceful, your softness melting into me like we be one.

Ben closed his eyes. He should get rid of the diary tomorrow, wipe out the thoughts hammering in his brain of a colored farm girl and a helpless baby, of secrets and sin. Instead, he turned the page, more curious to know the outcome of the poor woman's story. The next page was unreadable as well. Dampness had caused the pencil marks to fade but it wasn't just the effects of age and weather. Ben sensed the author was enraged and purposely marked the page with angry scribbles and blotches.

Were the blotches tears or was his imagination creating its own story? He tried to make out blurred half sentences and scratched out lines.

He sat up straighter in his bed and flipped through the next couple of pages that were much the same. It was as if the author was screaming into the pages with harsh strokes and couldn't find words to describe her agony. He flipped through the next couple of pages until the writing became more legible. His hands clutched the book tighter as he read. Was it rage for the sin or pain for this woman that caused his heart to pump harder in his chest?

I HOLD ROSE petals in my hands. They soft like your skin. I bring one flower in every day while they still alive. I try to remember the softness of my Rosalee but you gone. The missus want you. She can't have no baby of her own. She likes that you look white and she can claim you as her chile, like she bore you instead of me.

The mister he come and take you away. He says my wife, she wants Rosalee. She gonna act like it be her baby, like it didn't come from my body but from hers. It don't matter to her that you my flesh and blood. He promise me you gonna have nice things and be taught about Jesus. You cry wen he pull you from my arms. He hold you to his chest. Before he leave, he lay a gold cross and chain on my empty lap. He take you and leave me a cross. I hear you cry when he walk through the yard to the big white house. I don't look out the window. My body empty and feel cold like the cross in my lap.

BEN SLAMMED THE book shut and pushed it aside, a gnawing suspicion stabbing at him like knives. A chill ran through him. He was accustomed to sleeping naked but it wasn't the coldness in the room that chilled him but his dreaded thoughts.

Could it be? He took her to the big white house. He stared up at the wood beams in the ceiling. "God, this can't be, not the minister. I must be reading too much into this woman's story."

Or had he uncovered a scandalous truth hidden all these years? If the diary gave a true account and if his thoughts hadn't gone awry, Olivia was born to an uneducated, colored servant girl, her innocence taken from her by the one person who he would never have suspected, a man of God.

Olivia's father.

Olivia's coloring, deeper than her father's or mother's, gave credence to the woman's words. Olivia might be a mulatto, half Negro, half White, and stolen from her mother. Or, if relinquished, not out of a lack of love, but without a choice. What else could the woman have done?

Ben stared at the yellowed pages of the diary that lay open on the wooden floor. "To have your child taken from you," he murmured. He was an orphan himself but he remembered his parents' love. He knew he belonged and when they died, he grieved his loss. If his suspicions were correct, Olivia would never know her mother's sacrifice.

He couldn't deny his feelings for Olivia. Even this news, if it were true, didn't change the way he felt. His dreams were filled with her face, her laughter, and the softness of her lips on his. He was drawn to her as if it were as natural as breathing. Staring up at the ceiling, he pictured her face looking up to his. He pictured her taking a bite of the cookie he'd just tasted, her lips curving into a smile.

Was it possible the story was fiction? If it's a true

account, God help Olivia if the secret was revealed. His muscled arms tightened with rage at the sin that stained the child's birth and more, at the growing conviction that Olivia was the woman's child. Even those who professed strong Christian values saw the colored as a lesser race and undeserving of the same privileges as Whites. Though the North disdained slavery, negative views of Negroes ran rampant. The South was much worse but the attitude of superiority over the coloreds was prevalent everywhere. Many of his race refused to work, live, or share the same facilities. Disparaging remarks and jokes were common talk even among the most devout.

He thought of Lovena, the Fuller's maid. Olivia appeared fond of her, but as a servant or an equal? Had he carried feelings of superiority whether in his intellect or skin color? He never really gave it a great deal of thought. He hadn't befriended anyone who wasn't of his race, but the opportunity hadn't really presented itself.

Except for farm hands and the maids who worked in the wealthier homes, few Negroes lived in his community. He'd been affable and even helpful to workers he'd dealt with but kept to himself at most times anyway. The raw truth was there was a blatant and accepted separation of races and inter-marriage was either outlawed or frowned upon everywhere. Though they existed, most believed it was against nature for coloreds and whites to marry and their children were treated like oddities and with disdain.

The temptation to read more was there but he couldn't handle it, not tonight. He picked the book up from the floor and stuffed it under his mattress once again.

THE NEXT MORNING was bright and clear when he opened his eyes. Usually he bounded out of bed, especially when he realized he'd overslept, but sleep had escaped him most of the night. The words read the night before weighed him down. He couldn't let them go. He sat up and felt beneath the mattress until his hand found the cotton cloth of the cover. He prayed his suspicions were imagined, that more reading in the light of day would reveal mistaken beliefs about Olivia. He pulled out the diary and opened it to where he'd stopped reading the night before.

Jimmy is cryin today. I got no more tears. They dried up with my milk. I pack my things. The missus sendin me away. The mister gonna take me somewhere else to work. Jimmy want to come but the misses won't let him go. I ask mister to let me see you before I leave but he say no, "better this way," he say. But Jimmy, he sneak me in the house when it empty and everyone in church. Lovena won't tell no one. She promise me she gonna watch over you. She let me hold you and feed you. You like to hold the cross hanging round my neck. Before I say good bye, I give it to Lovena. I tell her to give it to you someday when the time be right.

Ben looked up from the page. "Lovena…she knows."

Could Olivia possibly know the truth? He dwelled on the thought for only a moment but discounted it.

He turned the page.

Today I got the biggest surprise. Jimmy come see me. He found out where I was sent. He ask everyone he meet at the market and where he get hay and such. Someone told him a pretty, colored girl got hired down the road. He was talkin' bout me. I think the word pretty come from Jimmy so as to make me smile. I almost fall over.

I was workin in the garden and Jimmy come up behind me. Seein him I feel the joy Jesus talk about. We find a place to talk and he tell me you not Rosalee Dunn anymore. You Olivia Fuller.

You still my Rosalee. He tell me you smilin all the time and you beautiful with big dark brown eyes. My eyes. He sees me in you. That make me feel all tingly inside. He talk to Lovena and he says he gonna take me to see you this Sunday when everybody gone again. I figure it might be the last time I see you. Im not doing so good. Been bleedin a lot. Ever since you been gone.

Ben closed Narcissa's diary and shoved it beneath the mattress. *Olivia is her child.* No doubt lingered. She may have died but in the smudged and soiled pages, her story remained. If only he'd never found it. If his curiosity hadn't caused him to take it home, if he'd destroyed it, he would have remained innocent of the truth. It would have been better that way.

He pushed himself off the bed, washed and dressed. He needed to get outside, breathe in fresh air and figure out what to do.

CHAPTER NINE

"FATHER, YOU'RE SUPPOSED to be in bed," Olivia scolded three days later when she found him sitting in an armchair reading.

"I've been in bed all day. I need to read through my sermon for Sunday."

"Doctor Hines insists you rest. No work."

"I've agreed to allow William to take over evening services but I need to be prepared to deliver the sermon on Easter. Did you speak with William after he visited with me?"

"Briefly, Mrs. Tapley arrived with him and sends her regards. She waited in the parlor and they left together." Olivia was glad she was able to avoid speaking to William alone.

"Have you given more thought to his proposal?"

"Father, I can see even the mention of it upset you. We'll talk at another time."

"Better my heart wear out trying to convince you of your foolishness. You have a man of God who wants to marry you and give you a life of serving the Lord as his partner. And what do you do? You flaunt yourself before a common laborer. A man you barely know. You behave as if William has not been courting you over the past few months. Like a …" He stopped and heaved a breath, one hand resting his chest.

"Please, you must stay calm. I did not flaunt myself. I wish I could explain to you my feelings. I don't understand them myself, except I don't love William."

She watched her father, looking for a sign of understanding. Instead, his face contorted in suppressed anger.

"I understand you're harboring romantic notions rather than being practical." He lowered his head, his hands pressed to the arms of his chair. The papers he'd been studying fell to the floor.

"*Father?*" Fear clutched her heart. She'd pledged not to bring up the subject again until her father was better. She had to leave it alone.

He stretched out an arm, trying to pick up the fallen manuscript. "Leave me. I need to finish my sermon."

"You must get back to bed." She leaned down and picked up the strewn sheets.

Her father's hand rested on her shoulder.

"Olivia, I beg you to listen to me."

She looked up in her crouched position. Her father's tone had softened to an impassioned plea.

"You must trust me. God brought William to our door. Promise me you will give your relationship with William time. Satan has put another obstacle in your path. First, those dreams you spoke of and now an intruder who is flattering you and turning you from God's will. I have prayed daily for your future to be secure, knowing I might not be here to see it."

"Don't talk like that. I won't hear of it."

"Promise me."

She looked into her father's eyes. Eyes that usually reflected kindness now appeared haunted. He must truly be afraid. Does he believe he is close to death? She shuddered at the thought. "I promise."

"And you'll stay away from Pratt? He's nearly done with the work. If I were well I'd demand he leave immediately. A few more days and he'll no longer be an intrusion. Once he's gone, your mind will return to what is right for you." He reached out his hand. "I have tried to be a good father, have I not?"

"You are a wonderful father," she said, avoiding his first question. Her heart yearned to see Ben again while fear for her father held her in its grip.

"Then trust me, Olivia." He reached out a hand. "Please, help me to my bed."

Defeated, Olivia took his arm as he lifted himself from the chair and walked slowly to his bed. She waited until he was settled comfortably under his quilt with two pillows stacked beneath his head.

"Be at peace, Father." She began to turn away but he grasped her arm.

"William will need your help over the next few days. I'm giving him a great deal of responsibility before his ordination. Review our Good Friday schedule with him and aid him in all the preparations for our Easter celebration."

She nodded, kissed him on the forehead and left the room, shutting the door quietly behind her. Pressing her back against the wall, she covered her mouth and sucked in a strangled sob. She'd made a promise, one against the desires of her heart. What else could she do?

Her desire for Ben had only grown stronger though she hadn't talked to him since he'd walked out of the country store. Was it even possible to fall in love in just a few weeks or was she truly being foolish, carried away by a rush of passion. She'd be spending the remainder of the week working with William discussing the church's schedule. They'd be working side by side just as they would do if they married.

She walked slowly to her room, trying to gain a grasp on when she'd stopped considering William in her future. Was it before Ben appeared?

Women married out of practicality and necessity and people change, mature. If she married William, would love and respect grow over time?

She'd never defied her father before. If her defiance led to another attack, she couldn't forgive herself. Her father gave her life. She couldn't allow selfish desires to take his away.

LITTLE TIME WAS left to think of her situation the next day. She rose early, looked in on her father, and found him sitting up in bed reading his sermon.

"Good morning. Are you feeling better today?"

"Not as good as I'd like. Getting old is wearing me down."

"It's nice to see a smile on your face."

"You're meeting with William today?"

"Yes, this afternoon." Her own smile faded.

Her father didn't notice. His eyes had returned to the papers he held.

"Perhaps you should allow him to take your place on Sunday."

"And not preach on Easter?" He flashed annoyed eyes at her. "It may be my last Easter celebration."

"Please don't talk like that."

"Take heart, Olivia. God willing, I'll be out of this bed and on the pulpit Sunday, praising the Lord."

Smiling at his optimism, she walked from the room. Before moving on to complete morning chores, she said a silent prayer for her father's recovery.

She arrived at the Meeting House at ten for the choir's final rehearsal. News had spread that the minister was on bed rest and William would assume some of his responsibilities. Choir members, having first asked about her father's condition, made polite remarks about William's new role in the church. When she'd turned her back to arrange music at the organ, however, she overheard a tactless parishioner murmur to another about William's convenient good fortune. She didn't miss an ensuing whisper, asking about an engagement. She willed herself to focus on the choir practice and not on the gossip.

After the rehearsal, she went home to check on her father. Lovena was adding slices of bread to a tray that already held a bowl of steaming soup.

"I was just takin' this up to your father. Got him sittin' by his bedroom window so he can feel the warm sunshine."

"I'll take it to him. He looks much better today, don't you think?"

"Yes, and in a good mood. I think he'll be up and about tomorrow."

"That's a relief," Olivia said, as she took the tray from Lovena.

"How are you doin'? I still see sadness in your eyes."

Olivia shrugged her shoulders but didn't answer her. What could she say? Too many thoughts were struggling for dominance in her mind. "It's a busy time."

"You need to eat. Let me pour a bowl for you."

"I'll eat later."

"*Livie.*"

"I'm not hungry." She ignored the maid's frustrated expression and carried the tray up to her father's room.

Seeing her father's smile of greeting as she walked through the door gave her greater encouragement that he was on the mend. When he grows stronger, she thought suddenly, she may be able to talk more rationally about her disenchantment with William. Maybe if she gave specific reasons that had nothing to do with Benjamin they could converse calmly. But what if she spurred another attack, she thought dismally, cutting off her hopeful imaginings. She returned her father's smile and stifled the hurt that tore at her heart.

"You look well. The rest has been good for you but please listen to the doctor. He wants you to shorten your schedule when you return to work. I will nag you to do just that."

"I'll try to appreciate your pestering. Your promise to me has lightened my spirits and with Lovena and the good doctor hovering over me all the time, how could I not improve?"

What could she say to that?

"I'm glad you're feeling better." She set the tray down on the table by his chair. "I must get back to the Meeting House."

"Of course. Give William my best."

She nodded before walking out, feeling worse than before she'd arrived.

When she approached the Meeting House less than a half hour later, she saw William outside the front entrance speaking with Ida Miller. The Millers' were new church members, having bought the Stokes' farm that went to near ruin when Isaac Stokes became sickly. He was forced to sell the farm for half its worth and moved to Wethersfield to live with his sister.

As Olivia came up the walk, she noticed Ida's flirtatious stance. She was an attractive girl close to her own age. Still out of their view, she heard Ida's laughter ring out and watched as she played with a blond curl beneath her attractive bonnet. Walking closer, she paused in her steps, wondering if she should interrupt their conversation. Her eyes narrowed in surprise when she overheard Ida's words.

"How wonderful to hear you preach, Mr. Tapley. Or should I call you *reverend*?"

"Not yet, but my ordination is not far away."

"When you preach, I shall pretend you are speaking just to me."

"You flatter me, Ida. I pray the congregation will pay as much attention."

Ida beamed, her hand reaching to touch William's coat sleeve.

Olivia couldn't hear William's reply. She didn't miss the look Ida gave him that bordered on hero worship and certainly attraction. Why not? William was attractive and confident. Hadn't she felt the same way about him during his first visits? Could she somehow recapture those feelings?

William must have seen her out of the corner of his eye because he immediately twisted his head toward her and took a step back. "Olivia, I've been waiting for you." He greeted her with an extra wide smile. "Miss Miller has asked if she might volunteer in some way in the church. Have you both met?"

"Yes, of course. Father and I make it a point to introduce ourselves to all new members."

She gave Ida a welcoming smile, sensing Ida wasn't particularly pleased at the interruption. "We always appreciate a member's desire to be of service. Our women's group has many upcoming projects starting after Easter and there never seems to be enough hands to accomplish everything. Our bulletin will list areas of need. The choir welcomes new members too and help is always needed for the children. Is there a special area where you would prefer to become involved?"

She realized she was prattling on without pause. The intimacy of William and Ida's conversation had left her feeling as if she were an intruder. William's always stately stance hadn't wavered but his tone appeared to invite Ida's praise. Of course, why wouldn't it? He was proud of his achievements and certainly enjoyed being admired.

"I haven't actually thought about how I would like to serve, but my family was very involved in our previous church," Ida chirped. "No doubt Mother and Father will also take a role. Working on improvements to the farm has taken up most of their time."

"I understand."

"I shall be sure to check the bulletin. I must go now." Ida fluffed strands of curls off her shoulder. "Thank you, Miss Fuller."

"Please call me Olivia."

"It was a pleasure to see you, Mr. Tapley." With a demure smile and a swirl of her skirt, she turned away and walked across the green to the street.

William's gaze darted in her direction before turning his attention back to Olivia. He took her arm and led her through the door of the Meeting House and into her father's office.

The office held a mahogany desk that appeared decades old and the pastor's chair, its leather backing and seat worn and faded from wear. The surface of the desk was neat with a short pile of books set to one side and papers neatly stacked on the other. Two straight back chairs with straw-weaved seats faced the desk for visitors. Wooden shelves filled with books covered two walls. The other two, painted white, were bare except for a couple of candle sconces.

"Miss Miller appears quite taken with you," Olivia said, as they entered.

"She must not be aware my heart belongs to you," William said, taking her father's seat and waving a hand toward one of the other chairs.

Olivia sat, reluctantly, pressing her lips together and wishing she hadn't voiced her observation. She wanted to keep this meeting on the business of the church and avoid any talk of their relationship. Furthermore, seeing William in her father's chair was unsettling.

"How is Reverend Fuller today? My mother and I left quite worried yesterday despite hearing he is recovering well."

"He appears improved."

William clasped his hands and rested them on the desk. "Good to hear. While he recuperates, I'm prepared to take on as much responsibility as the church is willing to give me. In fact, I'm meeting with the elders this afternoon to offer any service they'll entrust upon me."

"Did Father suggest you meet with them?"

"No, I... I didn't mean it to sound as if I were going over his head." William appeared offended. "No doubt the elders are concerned for your father's health as well as the ministry of the church. Age is a beast that is difficult to tackle. I want them to know I'm available for any duties that might need immediate attention."

Olivia's eyes narrowed but she said no more about it. They needed to work together congenially for the next three days. Though William acted pompous and self-righteous at times, he would be a hard worker in his calling.

And she needed to remember her promise.

How could she defy her father at this time? He had weakened before her eyes. She knew of no one who prayed as fervently and served with more self-sacrifice. At times it seemed as if he were driven to prove to God he was worthy. She'd seen him often enough on his knees in prayer and repentance, though she doubted he had more than trivial sins to repent.

He wanted the best for her. She must try to give her relationship with William more time. With every thought of submission to her father's wishes, desire for

Ben bloomed in her heart. What was she to do?

"Olivia?"

She looked up into William's inquisitive eyes. She realized while she was fingering papers on her father's desk, her thoughts had strayed.

She straightened her shoulders and pushed a paper toward William. "My father lists everyone's duties throughout Holy Week as well as his own. Once you study it, I'll be happy to answer any questions you have."

He took the paper from her and sat back in the chair. His appraisal of the schedule gave her a moment to gather her wits, clear her mind of intruding thoughts and focus on what needed to be done.

CHAPTER TEN

LOVENA HAD HER first good night's sleep since Reverend Fuller's attack, awakening only once to check on him. As she rose to face the day, her shoulders hunched forward and her eyes grew large. The bottom drawer to her chest gaped open. She hadn't left it like that. The room was too tiny to allow anything out of place without stumbling into it. A vague recall of a jarring sound as she slept rose in her memory. Her eyes had fluttered open. Hearing nothing more she'd fallen back into an exhausted sleep.

She stepped closer to the chest, seeds of fear sprouting within her until her dread was realized. Narcissa's gold cross, its chain pulled taut, lay on top of the handkerchief it had been wrapped in. Muffling a scream, Lovena scanned the room. Nothing else was out of place. Had she walked in her sleep and taken the cross out of its hiding place?

No, her instinct told her otherwise. She closed the drawer slowly and stepped away from it. Though she couldn't see Narcissa's spirit, she felt her presence and knew what she wanted. Numbly, she dressed and forced herself from the room to begin her chores.

She worked nonstop all morning, preparing meals for the day. After beating down bread dough a second time, she slammed a cupboard door, then another one. She couldn't find a utensil she needed. Nothing had gone right since the discovery. The memory of the open drawer and the cross lying there still caused her hands to tremble and left her with a sick feeling in her stomach. She was surprised she was able to act normally when Olivia came home at noon. Thankfully, Livie spent a brief time with her father and left soon after to return to the Meeting House. Lovena breathed a sigh of relief. Now that the house was quiet, the laundry done, and dinner cooking, she couldn't hold her anxiety in any longer.

She slumped against the kitchen counter, knowing her imagination hadn't been playing tricks on her. Ever since the old rooms were razed and Livie revealed her dreams, she'd sensed Narcissa's spirit. She'd been roaming about the house, standing over Olivia's bed and dwelling in her dreams. Now she'd become more daring.

"You angry I ain't given the cross to Olivia? Ooh,

girl, you be scarin' me and you becomin' a nuisance." Her eyes darted about the kitchen. "I'm gettin' old and tired. Why you scarin' me so? If I give your baby the cross, it gonna cause problems, big problems. The reverend, he been sickly. What seein' the cross 'round his daughter's neck gonna do to him, or me? It's a bad time, Cissa."

A sudden clap of thunder seemed to shake the sides of the house. Lovena shuddered and clasped her hands to her heart before shaking her head at the wildness of her thoughts. No way could Narcissa cause the sky to rumble.

"Lordy, I forgot the sheets! They gonna get soaked. Picking up her laundry basket, she hurried out to the clothes line and began pulling off clothes pins and gathering the sheets and pillowcases. Before she could finish, the skies opened up and the rain came down in a torrent, pelting her as she tore at the last of the laundry and thrust it into her straw basket. She rushed toward the porch steps but tripped on the sheets hanging over the side of the basket. The container tumbled from her arms as she slipped and fell onto the wet grass, crying out in pain when her wrist twisted in an awkward angle.

She tried to push herself up with her knees but the

wet grass caused her to slip more. She tried to crawl but winced when she put pressure on one ankle. Her wrist ached and after a few tries, she fell flat, exhausted. She finally gave in to her weakness, her cheek resting in the muddy grass. She wondered if she was going to die right there in the cold rain. She was, after all, at a good age to die.

"Narcissa? You see me lyin' here, girl? You be mad at me but you never been mean spirited. I was just clumsy, that's all." She continued mumbling to herself. Though her mind told her it was an accident, she couldn't erase the vision of the cross lying in the open drawer. "If I don't get some help, Cissa, your baby ain't never gonna get that cross." The only response was the sound of clanging tin as raindrops pounded on cans in the backyard.

"Lord, I'm in a real fix," she said, shivering as the rain fell, creating a muddy pool around her heavy soaked body.

BEN ARRIVED AT the parsonage later in the afternoon. He preferred to stay away but he couldn't use the weather as an excuse any longer. The heavy rains had ceased, leaving only a fine drizzle. He hoped he could put in a couple of solid work hours inside the barn and leave without being noticed. It would be a good day to see if there were any major leaks, especially above the hay lofts.

As he passed the side porch, he saw the overturned basket of laundry first before realizing a body lay next to it.

"Oh, my God." He saw immediately it was the Fuller's maid. He pulled his horse to a stop and jumped off.

"Lovena?"

She didn't answer. She lay totally still soaked to the skin, her eyes closed. He grabbed her shoulders and shook her gently. When she moaned, he breathed a sigh of relief.

"*No,* Narcissa, please," Lovena murmured. "It be a bad time."

Narcissa? The maid's words were nearly inaudible, but he'd heard it. His thoughts went immediately to the diary.

"Lovena, do you hear me?" He patted her arm, not wanting to frighten her. "It's Benjamin Pratt." Her body shivered beneath his touch.

"Cissa, you best leave."

She continued to mumble but her words were becoming inarticulate. She was hallucinating, or dreaming. He looked up at the house. He hated to leave her but he needed to find help. He rushed up the porch steps and banged on the door. No one answered. Returning to her side, he grasped her arms, shaking her more firmly. Her eyes fluttered and widened.

"Can you hear me? It's Ben."

She twisted her head toward the sound of his voice.

"Ben? I thought..." She looked up at him. "I... I got clumsy. The sheets...they gonna need to be washed again."

Ben couldn't help but grin. "Let's not worry about them right now."

She pressed her palms to the ground and tried to lift herself but moaned in pain. "Can't offer you no cookies today."

He exhaled a relieved breath. Her humor told him she'd heal.

"My wrist. It aches and my ankle, it got twisted."

"How does your back feel?"

"I got a strong back. It's the rest of me that let me down." She tried again to twist toward him.

"I'm going to help you sit up. You tell me if I'm

hurting you."

Grasping her upper arms, he lifted her carefully until she was in a slumped, sitting position. He pulled off his coat and wrapped it around her shoulders. "Is anyone home? No one answered the door."

"The reverend's in bed. He been ailin'. Livie, she's at the meetin' house."

"Let see if we can get you inside."

"You ain't gonna be able to lift me."

"Let me worry about that. I'm going to try to get you on your feet. When I do, see if you can put pressure on at least one foot and lean against me."

"I got too much weight on me."

"I'm not leaving you on the wet ground." He wrapped her arm around his shoulder and pushed himself up with his knees until she was able to press one foot into the ground. When she put weight on the other, she let out a wail.

"Try not to put pressure on that foot. Lean on me." He pulled her toward the porch steps. "Grab onto the railing."

Together, they took the step slowly. Her ankle was at most sprained but not broken, he thought.

"Just a few more feet, Lovena."

"You a good man," she said as he pushed open the door and helped her into the kitchen to the nearest chair. He eased her down and she collapsed into it.

"You're still shivering. Is there a blanket nearby?"

"Back there in my bedroom."

Ben followed her eyes to a closed door at the other end of the kitchen. "I'll be right back." Entering the tiny bedroom, he grabbed the quilt folded at the foot of her bed. Returning to her side, he wrapped it around her shoulders. "I should find Reverend Fuller."

"No, leave him be. Best get Olivia at the meetin' house. She'll know what to do."

Ben grimaced when he saw her chin quiver. She must still be cold. She needed to get out of those wet clothes and be put to bed. This was not the time to balk at seeing Olivia. "I'll go find her." He started toward the back door but paused." Can I get you anything before I leave?" He looked toward the kitchen fireplace at the cast iron bucket hooked above the fire. "Is there hot water? I can make you some tea."

"No, but add more water to that. Who knows how long I been out there. Don't need the fire burnin' a hole in a good pot."

Ben did as she asked, understanding the woman's

duties came first in her mind. Later he'd go out to the well and refill the water buckets.

He didn't like leaving her alone but there seemed to be no choice. "I'll be right back with Olivia."

"Benjamin."

"Yes? Do you need something else?"

"Thank you. I thought I gonna be dyin' out there."

Ben walked toward the kitchen door, weighing the significance of what he wanted to ask her. "You were mumbling, Lovena."

"What I say?"

He heard an edge of panic in her words. Better not to say too much, he thought. "You said something about it being a bad time."

She lowered her eyes, shaking her head side to side before looking back at him. "Did I say anythin' else?"

"Not much more." He didn't want to upset her. She looked pitiable with mud caked on her face and a head scarf that was now half falling off. "You're going to be fine. I'll be back as soon as I can."

Ben hurried out the door, mounted his horse and rode swiftly to the Town Green. When he reached the Meeting House, he swung out of his saddle and wrapped the reins hastily to the post.

After rapping on the closed door, he pulled it open, wasting no time waiting for a response. The darkened hallway opened up to the large meeting area with its rows of wooden pews. He saw Olivia and Tapley in conversation at the podium. Tapley was giving Olivia his rapt attention and once again Ben felt like an intruder. He supposed they belonged together, just like this, going about the business of the church.

He cleared his throat.

Olivia turned. "Ben?"

William took an immediate step forward. "Pratt. You're dripping mud on the floor. Have you been drinking? This is no place…"

Ben cut him off. "Olivia, Lovena needs you at home."

Her hand flew to her mouth. "My father?"

"No, it's Lovena. She needs help."

"What?" William snapped before Ben could explain. "How impertinent for a maid to interrupt church business."

"Lovena wouldn't call for me unless it was important," Olivia shot back. She closed the distance between her and Ben and looked back at William. "I must leave."

"We need to finish before I meet with the elders," William countered. "Is there no one else who can see to her request?"

Ben heard the irritation in Tapley's voice. He wasn't surprised. Self-importance was a Tapley male trait. His needs would come before a maid's.

"Something must have happened. I need get home now." She looked at Ben. "Is Lovena all right?"

"I found her lying outside in the mud. She must have fallen while doing laundry. I helped her into the kitchen. She's chilled and shaken, drenched by the heavy rains. She has some injuries."

"Oh, no! She must get out of those wet clothes and we need to get the doctor." She shot a look back to William as if seeking his help, but his expression didn't leave room for aid or empathy. With a shake of her head, she hurried to the door with Ben following behind her.

"Olivia, wait," William called out, striding toward them. "You're not going to undress the woman. Allow me to get Lottie, our maid. She'll care for Lovena's personal needs. Pratt can find the doctor." He lifted a brow to Ben.

"I need to be with her," Olivia said between gritted

teeth.

"I gladly offer our maid's services. I'll deliver her to your house within the hour."

"She's not needed. I can help Lovena."

William reached out for her arm. "Olivia, consider the appropriateness. Your maid will feel more comfortable with Lottie's help. Your father would agree."

Ignoring William's protests, she rushed out the door, gesturing to Ben with a nod.

"You can ride with me," Ben said as they both clambered down the steps.

Olivia allowed him to lift her onto his saddle. He swung his body up behind her. In minutes they were at the parsonage. After helping Olivia dismount, he followed her in. Lovena remained slumped in the chair, the quilt drawn tightly around her.

Olivia rushed to her side and knelt down, ignoring the muddied floor. "I am so sorry I wasn't here."

"You was doin' your work. I was doin' mine. Ain't nothin' to apologize for."

"What happened?"

"I was tryin' to get the sheets in before the rain came. Only half pulled them off before it started. I slipped and down I went. Couldn't get up. Those sheets are soaked and full a mud."

"I'm not concerned for the sheets. Where do you hurt?"

Ben watched as Olivia rubbed her thumb across the maid's cheek to remove dried mud.

"Nothin's broken. My ankle's sore and my wrist needs to be wrapped up or I'm gonna be useless in the kitchen."

"Let's get you to your room and out of those wet clothes. The doctor needs to look in on you."

"I'm a sorry mess. Just need to get wrapped up is all."

"We'll let the doctor decide that."

"What's happened here?" The minister stood in the doorway in his robe, his eyes fixed on the scene.

Olivia looked up in surprise at her father's appearance. "Lovena fell outside in the rain. Ben found her. He came for me. We need to get the doctor to look at her injuries."

"Anything broken?" The minister's face held concern, while his eyes narrowed at Ben's presence.

"No, just sore. I be good as new tomorrow."

"I'll go find Doctor Hines," Ben offered.

"It's not necessary," Reverend Fuller said abruptly. "I'm expecting a visit from him. Olivia and I will see to Lovena. You can get back to work."

"Father," Olivia murmured, looking at him imploringly.

"Thank you for your help, Pratt," Reverend Fuller said in an amended tone.

Ben nodded and glanced briefly at Olivia and Lovena before turning to leave.

"Thank you," Olivia said, giving him a grateful smile.

Her father said no more until Ben closed the door behind him. "Let's get her into her room."

"You shouldn't be helpin' me. Why you down here in the kitchen?"

"The house was unreasonably quiet. I'm accustomed to you charging in and making sure I'm behaving myself." He reached for Lovena's arm.

She shook her arm away from his helping hand. "If Olivia gives me her shoulder, I can make it. You get yourself back to bed."

"I feel better than I look. Better than you do at the moment."

Lovena gave him a surrendering grimace. He and

Olivia eased her up and helped her to the bedroom, settling her in a chair by her bed.

"Olivia, I'll leave you to help her but first I want to speak with you." He eyed the door, letting his daughter know he wanted to have a private conversation.

"I'll be right back, Lovena," Olivia promised and followed her father.

"I can manage," the maid called out.

Olivia gave her a scornful look and closed the door behind her.

"Father, please go back to bed."

"I'm tired of everyone telling me to get back in bed."

"Dr. Hines will give you the devil if he finds you roaming around."

The minister grumbled. "When Lovena is settled, come to my room and tell me about your meeting with William. I want to know if he's well prepared for the services tonight and tomorrow."

"We were nearly finished when Ben arrived."

"Do I detect some anger?"

"I'm annoyed at William. He was more concerned with continuing our meeting than Lovena's condition."

"He may not have realized the immediacy."

"It's more. He said it was not my place to attend to

her. He offered to bring his maid, insisting it was more appropriate. Haven't you noticed how condescending he's been to Lovena in the past? I don't think it's just her station, but her color."

Her father sighed. "Lovena is family to us, but that's not the case in many households." Before he could say more, someone rapped on the kitchen door.

"I hope it's the doctor," Olivia said, leaving her father's side. Instead, it was Tapley's Negro maid.

"Mr. Tapley dropped me off. He says Lovena needs some tending. He going back to the meetin' house, Miss Olivia. He told me to tell you he be pleased if you meet him there once everything's settled here."

"Olivia, invite her in." The minister walked to the door. "Lottie, it's kind of you to come and help," he said, ignoring his daughter's frown.

"Mr. Tapley says Lovena might need help over the next few days. He told me to set two more plates for Easter dinner for you and Miss Fuller. Lovena most likely won't be up to preparin' dinner."

"That is kind of him. My daughter and I will discuss Easter plans later. Lovena's room is back there." He pointed toward her door. "You can go see her now. Olivia will join you shortly."

"Father, please."

He put up a staying hand. "Allow the maid to attend to Lovena."

Olivia waited until Lottie was out of sight. "Lovena's been here for me since I was born. I want to be the one to help her," she pleaded. "I told William we had no need of his maid."

"Please look at his offer as a kindness. Have you considered Lovena may feel more comfortable having his maid help her? She's the first to remind us of her position. We must take her feelings into consideration too."

"You're trying to smooth over William's bigotry. You taught me long ago God does not look at the color of a person's skin but at the heart."

"William has strong opinions, opinions prevalent in our world. He's young. Allow God's grace to work in him. Go, do what you can for Lovena."

Olivia hesitated. She wanted to say more but held her tongue. Instead, she turned away and walked back to Lovena's room.

REVEREND FULLER RETURNED to his room, feeling depressed. He hadn't missed the concern on Pratt's face.

The man showed genuine empathy. He'd watched the brief interchange of glances between Pratt and Olivia as they knelt beside Lovena. His thoughts went to William, so much like his father, proud, narrow minded, and with little tolerance.

If he didn't carry such a burden, would he choose William for Olivia? He was pushing her into a marriage she didn't want. He thought of his own barren marriage and wanted more for his daughter. But he had serious matters to consider. Their world left little room for mistakes of breeding. He'd sinned and Olivia was the product of his sin.

He must protect her

Rather than return to bed, he sat in an arm chair in his darkened bedroom remembering the nightmares that woke him too many nights, sweating, and shaking from fear. Nightmares of Olivia walking toward him, a baby in her arms, a colored child. He couldn't erase the look of horror on her face. He knew the mind played tricks when asleep but the image left him questioning to the point of near madness in his darkest hours.

In the light of day, he'd dispel his fear as irrational. Olivia was darker skinned than he or his wife but she was white to the world. If she married a white man, it stood to reason her children would be no darker than their mother. But still the nightmares persisted. Were they the devil's making or his guilt that caused his fear? Or a warning? Could Olivia birth a child with her mother's color or Negro features? Had science proved otherwise? He knew children picked up traits from previous generations. He himself inherited his grandfather's curly hair while both his parents' hair was straight. He'd often been told he looked more like his grandfather than his own father. What if she bore a darker child with coarse hair? He didn't know the answer but his nightmares were enough to convince him to take his fears seriously. She must never find out the truth.

Despite his repentance, his guilt and shame refused to abate. He was a fraud as a minister and the worst of sinners. The fear his daughter would discover his sin and her origins had grown stronger as his health weakened. As long as he was alive, he believed he could protect her but he was getting old and weary.

The nightmares had increased as Olivia drew closer to marriageable age, causing his dreaded obsessions to gnaw at his insides. He'd become convinced she would discover the truth through her off springs. Every time he read or heard about the vicious crimes against people of color, he cringed, knowing his own daughter could be a victim of the worst prejudices if the truth were revealed. He'd pleaded to God for answers.

Then William Tapley arrived at his door asking for his counsel and instruction. When William divulged his pledge never to father a child, the light of hope infused the minister's darkness. God was showing mercy, answering his fervent prayers in a way he could never have imagined. Olivia and William would make an ideal couple and more important, William was studying for the ministry. He was the perfect partner for his daughter who had been brought up to serve the church.

The young man needn't ever know Olivia's heritage. She was white, like her father. God had called William to serve and led him to the minister's door. Together, William and Olivia could find contentment apart from raising their own child.

The minister covered his face with his hands. Was he deluding himself? His declarations to protect her were genuine but he was saving himself and his reputation too. What would his congregation think of him if they knew the truth? Worse, what would Olivia think of him? He loved his daughter with his whole heart. He couldn't bear her rejection. How could she live with the knowledge she was birthed by a Negro servant who he'd taken advantage of in drunken lust?

He drew his hands down and closed his eyes, remembering, despite so many attempts to wipe out that night from his mind.

His wife had once again refused him. When she realized she could never bear a child, she had no use for the sexual intimacy marriage allows. That night she'd rejected him again. He'd poured himself a glass of whiskey and took the bottle out on the porch. It was a warm night and though he seldom over imbibed, believing Christians should be moderate in all things, that night, he ignored his scruples. His wife was in bed and he was alone in the dark, nursing his misery.

He saw the lit candle in Narcissa Dunn's window and thought about her. He'd noticed her during the day, plucking weeds, her backside lifted as she worked. Having been with the family since she was a child, she'd become a fetching woman, flirtatious in her posturing. He'd tried not to notice. He was a minister of God, after all, but the image of her hips swaying when she walked stayed in his mind.

He continued drinking and watching the candle

flicker in her window. He watched her shadow as she undressed. Shouldn't she have doused the candle, he'd thought. He convinced himself that she knew he was watching, enjoyed tantalizing him, and would welcome his advances. He couldn't take his eyes off her or stop his lustful thoughts. The liquor weakened mindfulness and his imagination took control, created a false reality and erased his common sense.

When she doused the candle, he remained on his porch, staring at the darkened window until the bottle was empty. His sexual urges took over. He tossed the bottle over the railing and stumbled down the porch steps.

He remembered when he reached the barn, being closer to her wasn't enough. He wanted to satisfy her desires and his own. No one else was living in the other rooms and he needed to see her. He'd become obsessed with thoughts of watching her as she slept. Or was she waiting for him? In his drunken state, he'd convinced himself that she wanted him.

He opened the door to her room and peered inside, saw she was curled up in bed. His body reacted. He wanted to touch her. Commonsense fled. If he could just see what she looked like in her bed clothes, he'd leave. He drew her covers down and saw she wore only a thin cotton gown, lifted to her thighs as she slept. The moon lit the room enough for him to see her long brown legs before she twisted on her mattress. One of her hands reached down to pull at the covers in her sleep. He remembered seeing the curve of her breast as she tugged at the blanket gripped in his hand. The aching in his groin overcame any feeble thought of decency that remained.

Her eyes opened. He'd wanted to speak sweet words to her, but his mind went numb. His hands roamed over her body, touching her breasts, her thighs, her core. He'd believed in that dark moment that she liked his touch. She wasn't fighting him. Her body became still.

Later, he couldn't remember how he'd gotten on top of her. But he remembered her tightness, his need, and his own body heaving, reaching his climax. He remembered lifting himself off her and covering her up. She never uttered a word.

When he walked outside, he must have fallen. He woke later on the ground. It wasn't light yet, but he knew dawn wasn't far away. Clouded memories of the night before returned. Why was he outside the barn lying in the dirt? At first he thought he'd been dreaming but his body told him otherwise. He looked up toward the window above him, Narcissa's window. He rose to his knees and wretched violently until he felt hollow inside and black with sin. He stumbled the remaining distance to the house, removed his shoes and crept to his room like a thief.

His wife slept in the spare bedroom. He was careful not to make a sound as he passed her door. Once in his room, he'd fallen on his bed. He remembered wishing for death but instead, he slept. It wasn't until his wife rapped on his closed door, scolding him for sleeping late, that he forced himself to face the day. He'd awakened with a horrid headache. Sober and wrought with shame, he'd wept as he'd never wept before, crying silently out to God to forgive him.

He feared the day and what would come of it. Once he'd forced himself to wash, dress, and leave the safety of his bedroom, he prepared himself to face the horror and censure of those around him, but nothing happened. The household was busy as usual and no one remarked on his silence. He'd gone immediately to his library and when church members began to call, he acted the part of their devout minister. Later in the day, he'd ventured outside and saw Narcissa working in the garden. She had looked up at him for only an instant before her frightened eyes lowered.

Days passed and his crime appeared buried as deep as the crops Narcissa planted. She must have realized if she told anyone, they wouldn't believe her, not a colored's word against the minister. His guilt grew more intense. He had taken advantage of a woman whose race unfortunately delegated her to silence when abused. No one would listen, except one of her station and race, and what could they do except sympathize? With his respected position in the community, he would have denied any allegation, the deplorable man he was. Instead, his crime marred his soul as rust corrodes metal.

When he discovered she was pregnant, he'd tried to convince himself someone else was the father. Once the baby was born, he could no longer deny the child, born white, was his. It was his wife who took matters into her own hands when she realized, with immediate but concealed horror, the truth.

Lovena was Narcissa's midwife and the only one present when Olivia was born. He'd observed the maid's protectiveness toward Narcissa during the pregnancy and could never forget the look the maid gave him after having delivered the baby in those cold rooms next to the barn. His fear of discovery so overwhelmed him, he hadn't even offered a comfortable bed for Narcissa to birth the child. All her needs were left up to Lovena.

The winter that year was especially frigid and his wife suffered with constant colds. Unable to attend to her church duties, she remained in her room near a warm fire during the remaining winter months. As she was heavy set, no one dared to disagree with the pastor's wife when she told them she had been pregnant and kept it a secret, expressing her fear she might miscarry as she had done so many times before.

His wife would keep his secret if he delivered the baby to her and sent Narcissa away.

CHAPTER ELEVEN

WILLIAM ARRIVED TO pick up Lottie early that evening. Olivia heard the carriage turn into the drive while she was filling a pitcher of water in the kitchen. Not wanting to see him, she went immediately to Lovena's room and sent Lottie out. By the maid's hurried response, she guessed William didn't like being kept waiting. When Olivia opened the kitchen door for Lottie, she saw William about to step down from the carriage.

"We appreciate your help, Lottie," she said half closing the door as the maid walked through it onto the porch. Please tell Mr. Tapley I am unable to visit tonight." Thankfully, William wasn't looking her way. After closing the door, she breathed a relieved sigh when the carriage wheels grated along the stone drive to the road. She retrieved the water pitcher and returned to Lovena's room.

"You not s`pose to be takin' care'a me. I got myself into this muddle," Lovena said as Olivia poured her a glass of water.

"I like helping you. You need to stay off your feet. Father and I can manage until you're feeling better."

Before Olivia walked out, she saw a bottom drawer left partially open. "You don't need to be tripping on this." When she leaned down to close it, a sparkle drew her attention. She looked closer. "Lovena, how lovely." She lifted the gold, jeweled cross by its delicate chain and admired its beauty. "I've never seen you wear this. It's... Lovena, what's the matter?" The maid's shoulders had lifted from her pillow and she looked terrified.

"I shut that drawer this mornin'. I know I did."

"It's nothing to be upset about. Lottie may have opened it looking for your nightgown."

Lovena's eyes remained wide as she glared about the room before slumping back on her pillows looking almost defeated.

"Does the cross carry a personal memory, one you prefer not to talk about? I'm sorry if my curiosity…"

"That cross ain't mine. I *closed* the drawer," Lovena mumbled, staring at Olivia's hand that held the cross. "She want it open."

"Who? Lottie?"

Lovena sucked in her bottom lip as if afraid to say

more. Olivia wondered if her fall had disturbed her more than originally thought.

"It be yours," she said finally.

"What?" Olivia looked back at the cross, bewildered. A terrible thought crossed her mind. Had the maid stolen it? No, not Lovena. It wasn't in her to do such a thing.

"It was your momma's. She wanted me to give it to you one day. I was waitin'."

"My mother's cross? Why wouldn't she have given to me? Did she ask you to give it to me on a special occasion? My wedding day? Don't be upset that I found it. I'm surprised she didn't leave it with Father. Perhaps she didn't trust he'd follow her wishes and give it to me sooner. He must know about it."

"He knows."

"You sound almost morose. Please don't be disappointed that I discovered it. Today is Good Friday when our Lord died on the cross. What a perfect day to find my mother's gift." She wrapped the chain around her neck and hooked the clasp. "It feels good to have nice thoughts of my mother today."

"She want you to have it. It be out of my hands."

What an odd answer, Olivia thought. "Do you mind

if I wear it now?"

"It best you keep it under your dress. Your father don't need any surprises."

"You think he would be displeased?"

"He's preparin' for his sermon on Sunday. You don't want old memories interruptin' his thoughts. Who knows what might cause him trouble? Keep it hidden, for now."

Olivia could think of other things that would upset him much more, but she was aware of Lovena's superstitious nature. "If you think it's best." Fingering the cross for a few seconds, she tucked it under the collar of her dress and pressed her palm over it. "It feels warm. Thank you for taking care of it for me."

She walked to the door. "Rest now and don't worry about chores." After shutting the door behind her, she paused and touched the covered cross again. Though she and her mother always had a strained relationship, she felt a surge of love as well as sadness that she couldn't share the moment with her. Then she thought of Lovena's odd behavior. The poor woman was lying on the ground in the pouring rain for hours. Maybe her overreaction comes from exhaustion and stress. *What a strange day.* Usually her father expected Good Friday to be spent quietly and in prayer. Because of her busyness, she'd given little thought to the meaning of the day.

"Lord, forgive me for being so wrapped up in the day's events that I haven't taken time to dwell on your sacrifice." She was interrupted by a knock on the front door. Had William returned? "Please don't let it be him," she murmured, still harboring too much anger.

She was pleased and relieved when she opened the door to find the doctor smiling at her. "Doctor Hines, welcome."

"I apologize I wasn't here sooner, my dear. The rains created a dark and dismal day and brought more house calls than expected. How is your father?"

"He appears better, but I'm afraid you have two patients to look in on this evening. The doctor raised a brow as Olivia closed the door behind him. "It's Lovena. Let me take your coat and I'll tell you all about it."

BEN STAYED WORKING on the Fuller's barn until near dark. Olivia most likely didn't know that he'd remained. He kept his horse in the barn while he worked. Liberty snorted occasionally as if sensing Ben's troubled mood. Not unusual.

Uncle Syl had given Liberty to Ben shortly after his parents were killed. His uncle brought the horse home after the animal was found unattended and starving. Its owner had died alone on his farm and his stock left unattended for weeks. After being told stories of the cracked Liberty Bell in Pennsylvania, its history, and attempts to repair the damage, Ben decided to name the horse *Liberty* and was determined to bring him back to health. They bonded immediately, their bruised spirits healing together. They became inseparable. Ben considered Liberty his best friend and he figured the feeling was mutual.

While Ben worked he looked out toward the house occasionally. He saw Tapley arrive and leave his maid behind and later return to fetch her.

The man obviously didn't take Olivia's wishes into consideration. When Ben packed up his tools and closed up the barn, he was glad to see the doctor had arrived. He hoped Lovena was doing better. The poor woman was more concerned about being a bother than taking care of herself.

If only he'd arrived sooner. She must have been out there lying in the mud for hours. Despite the reason for collecting Olivia at the Meeting House and rushing her to the parsonage, he couldn't help remembering how good it felt to have Olivia snuggled close to him on his horse, even for a short time. She didn't belong with Tapley, but what could Ben do about it if she chose to marry him?

He recalled the image of Olivia and William standing together discussing church business. His chest clenched at the sight before he was forced to gain their attention. She was too kind, too giving, and Tapley was, in Ben's mind, cold and calculating, regardless of the fact he was going into the Lord's service.

He needed to stop dwelling on their relationship. Something other worldly was going on that boggled his mind. Why was he the one to find a diary of long hidden secrets he shouldn't know about? And today, Lovena uttered Narcissa's name when he tried to rouse her. Too much of a coincidence.

A thought struck him.

What if Lovena knew about the diary and had forgotten about it. Maybe she remembered while he was tearing down the walls. He racked his brain, trying to conjure up the maid's exact words. *No, not a good time,* she'd said. She was telling Narcissa to leave. Yes, she was definitely hallucinating if she was talking to a dead woman. Maybe she feared he'd found the book. What other reason would cause her to say the woman's name just as he arrived to help her.

Narcissa wrote about Lovena in her entries. Maybe he needed to tell the maid he'd found it. No, better to wait until she's healed. He might be able to ease her mind. Let her know the secrets were safe with him.

LATE THAT NIGHT after helping his uncle with some paperwork, chopping wood, and doing some clean up in the shop, Ben settled into bed. He reached beneath his mattress, pulled out the diary. and leafed through the pages until he found where he'd left off.

Jimmy and Lovena sneek me in. I can't believe my eyes. You already five months old and sitting up in a high chair. I cry happy tears when I see you so healthy. I sit down in the kitchen and Lovena puts you in my arms and you don't cry. You just look up at me. Lovena tells me about the stories the missus been sayin about her gypsy relations bein the cause of your skin color. Your skin not pasty like hers cuz you are of my skin and bones.

Missus can pretend all she want but her lies dont cover the truth. I hold you and tell you about me and

Aunt Iva and stories my aunt told me about my parents, your gramma Ruthie, and your grandaddy Jeremiah Dunn. They all gone by now. I think I be with them soon. I tell you as much as I can about them and pour love into my words. Lovena take you when I gotta leave and you reach your arms out to me and I cry. They happy tears cuz you gonna *live a good life. Lord, I be happy I got to see you again. You felt soft in my arms. It was hard sayin good by.*

Jimmy waitin to take me back before the Fullers come back from church. I want to come to my old room once more before I go. So here I sit for a little while, rememberin seein you for the first time. Oh the joy I felt. It caused me to shiver all over. I wanted to be where you was born and write to you one last time. Writin help me cry on paper and not just inside me. I wish I could steal you away but I know I can't take care of you. Jimmys worried cuz I got skinny and don't look so good. Not everything heals up the way it should after a baby be born.

You be Olivia now but you always be my Rosalee. I tell Jesus to take good care of you. I don't have anything to give you but a cross and all the love deep inside me. They can't feed you or keep you warm.

You gonna learn to read and write better than me.
You gonna have pretty dresses and be treated speshal,
like a white chile. The mister, he did a sinful thing but
God blessed me. I feel happiness thinkin' about the
moment Lovena put you in my arms and the hours I be
with you. They worth all the pain. Forgivin is hard but
it be God's way and what he wants from me. I leave my
heart with you, my sweet Rosalee.

Ben slapped the book down on the night stand and
covered his eyes. *Rosalee. Rosalee Dunn, not Olivia.*
Thoughts flew through his mind like bats in the rafters.
Her father. *My God.* She mustn't know. Why would
she? No one would guess she wasn't white.

He pictured her smooth, golden skin, like silk to his
touch. Darker than her father's. *Still, no one would*
guess. He's a minister, by God!

This morning he'd promised himself he was going to
stay away from Olivia, but he was left no choice when
Lovena ask him to fetch her. Seeing Olivia left him with
an even deeper desire for her. He'd tried to believe she
was meant to be with William but he'd seen her attitude
toward his callousness. The man was wrapped up in his
own self-worth and Ben wondered how he could love
anyone but himself. Was it because her father approved

of him?

Swearing, he reached for the diary to curb vengeful thoughts that were rearing up toward Tapley. He was spying into someone's secret life where he didn't belong, but he couldn't stop. He turned the page but there was no more to read. Her last words were for her daughter. She must have closed the book and hid it in the wall before she left. She was ill. Had she died shortly after?

He shoved the book under his mattress, laid back and rested an arm over his eyes. Should he talk to Lovena? She'd kept the secret all these years. Why not reassure her that he would do the same?

SATURDAY MORNING CHORES gave Olivia little time to think about the day before. The doctor wanted Lovena to rest her ankle for a couple of days. Despite the maid's insistence to get out of bed, Olivia stayed firm. Thankfully, Lovena had completed most of the Easter dinner preparations earlier in the week.

Olivia and her father made the decision together to stay home on Easter Sunday despite the many invitations, including William's. Church members usually stopped by the parsonage later Easter afternoon, bringing desserts, breads or small Easter gifts. It would still be a busy day.

When she heard horse's hooves clomping up the stone path, her heart leaped. *Ben?* Though she'd thanked him for his help the day before, she wanted to once again express her gratitude.

She wanted to see him.

William would be officiating at church service tonight. She had no plans to attend, preferring to stay home with her father. He'd stayed in his room since yesterday afternoon, leaving her concerned. She'd expected he'd be working at his desk in his study by now. Illness seldom kept him in bed for long.

Had telling him about her anger at William aggravated his condition? She didn't want to upset him but his adamant belief that she should welcome William's proposal baffled her. Why didn't he trust her to decide her own future?

When the horse and rider came into view, her heart sank. It was William. She'd avoided seeing him when he came for Lottie, but she had no choice now. When his maid came to the door earlier, Lovena was happy to see her. Admittedly, her father was right. Lovena grew more upset when Olivia tried to serve her. Still, William hadn't listened to her the day before or followed her wishes.

She removed her apron and opened the door unable to even force a smile. She'd wanted to spend the day in quiet contemplation. Well, that was not entirely true. She'd hoped to see Ben.

"Hello, William." She didn't invite him in.

"Good morning. It's such a beautiful day I thought we might walk together to the Meeting House. I'll leave my horse here and retrieve it when we return."

"The doctor is coming this morning to see Father and Lovena. I want to be here." Olivia saw disappointment cross his features.

"I understand. I hope Lottie has been a help to you. This weekend could not have been a worse time for your maid to be unavailable. With your father convalescing, you must be beside yourself."

She wanted to reiterate what she'd told him yesterday, that she could have handled the situation without his maid's help. But there was no reason to appear ungrateful. Lottie's presence was appreciated. Lovena blamed herself for her accident and she didn't want to burden Olivia. If only she could make Lovena see that caring for her was not a chore but a way to thank her for her constant care.

"Lottie has been a great help but you must need her home. I can manage without her." Her tone was clipped. She couldn't seem to hide her anger and she needed to put it aside.

"Lottie manages to complete her own duties despite the few hours she spends here. May I come in?"

Olivia stepped aside but did not invite him into the parlor.

"I was not in the best mood yesterday, Olivia. I apologize for my brashness. I was quite anxious. Your father has placed much trust in me. I wanted to be sure I performed all my responsibilities to the best of my ability. Pratt's interruption caused me to behave badly. I'd hoped sending our maid to help would be seen as a kind gesture, perhaps an apology for my behavior."

Olivia blinked at William's humble façade. He held his hat in his hands, his head slightly bowed as he made his apologies. Perhaps he truly realized he'd behaved badly, offering his maid as an act of contrition and not what she had suspected.

"I accept your apology, William."

"Thank you. How is Lovena today?"

"Resting comfortably but she's anxious to get back to

her chores. The doctor wants her to avoid putting weight on her foot for a few days and her wrist needs healing.

"If Lottie has eased some of your worry than I can rest easy I did not overstep."

Olivia nodded. His apologies were becoming tedious. She could not marry this man!

"I hope you understand the stress I was under. Fortunately my meeting with the elders turned out to be quite productive. They explained the accounting of the pew costs, budgetary restraints and other practical items. Further, many church members stayed after last night's service and approved of my sermon. I felt quite gratified."

William's mood changed from humility to exhilaration. Regardless, Olivia felt his meeting with the elders was presumptuous since he was simply to be an assistant to her father. She almost told him so but remained silent. He would find her opinion flawed in some way. Besides, her anger hadn't totally dissolved. She needed to take more time to pray this afternoon.

"Will you be coming to the Meeting House after lunch?"

Olivia had nearly forgotten the reason he'd come.

She did not want to leave the house and she doubted she could be any more help to him. He was becoming quite comfortable in his new position.

"I'm not going today. The choir is all set for tomorrow and I have too much to do here."

"Olivia, your duties to the church come first."

"My duties today are here at home. No doubt you will do fine as my father's substitute this evening."

William looked off toward the parlor as if he were trying to compose himself. "I was hoping we could talk. This may not be the best time, but you haven't given me an answer to my proposal. I hoped we would announce our engagement on Easter."

Was he blind to her reaction to him? He saw little fault in his behavior and most likely felt she should be honored he wanted to marry her, especially with her father's blessing. Maybe if she shared her feelings or lack of them, he'd withdraw his proposal. Her father would surely accept it if William changed his mind. That might be the answer. He couldn't possibly be interested in a marriage where feelings weren't mutual.

"William, I need…"

"I am doing it again," William said, interrupting her. "You have so much on your mind and I'm being thoughtless. Next week is soon enough to discuss our future together. This Holy weekend should be on the Lord's work and my thoughts focused on the service tonight. Please tell your father everything is going well. And, Olivia, take care. You look tired."

William was already heading to the door before she could say more. Better to wait until after Easter to talk to him, she thought. She needed to consider her words and leave William with a measure of pride to withdraw his suit.

He paused before stepping on to the porch. "If your father is not up to doing his Easter sermon, he only needs to say the word. Assure him I'll do my best to meet the needs of the church."

She nodded, refusing to comment on his offer to take over the pulpit tomorrow. He was obviously more than willing. How was it she had not seen more of his arrogance in the past months when her father was mentoring him? She felt a pang of guilt. No doubt she'd been too flattered by his initial attention.

"I look forward to our talk next week." He smiled. "And to our future as well." He donned his hat and left.

Olivia stared after him, his quick departure leaving no time for her to reply to his final words.

No sooner had he disappeared from view when Ben rode up the drive. She stepped outside, hoping he would stop to talk with her. How differently his arrival made her feel. When he slowed and she waved, he brought Liberty to a stop.

"Hello, Olivia." He gave her a hesitant smile. "Good to see you. I thought I'd put in a few hours today. I hope to be done with the barn early next week."

"Father shall be pleased."

"It's a repair and with old wood, but it should last a few more years, God willing."

"Ben." She stepped down from the porch. As she walked closer, he dismounted. "Thank you again for helping Lovena and for coming for me."

"I was glad to help." He looked uncomfortable at being the center of her gratitude. "How is she feeling today?"

"Much better. She seldom takes time to rest and now she has no choice."

"Good. I saw Tapley ride off toward the green."

"Yes, he apologized for his behavior yesterday when you came for me."

Ben clipped his thumbs in his pant pockets and looked skyward before turning his gaze back to her.

"The gossips believe you and he will marry."

Olivia's chin dropped. It was the last thing she expected him to say. "I haven't given him an answer."

"I see. So, he has asked." He looked out across the yard before returning his gaze to her. "You love him?"

Olivia's mouth dropped open. She was surprised at the intimacy of his question and pleased he cared. She couldn't lie, not to him. "No... I don't. My father believes it is God's will that we marry."

"And what does your heart say?"

His eyes were boring into hers now. "Father expects me to say yes. He believes I will grow to love him."

"That's not what I asked. What do you believe?"

"Oh, Ben." Her voice trembled. "How do I answer you?" She hoped her eyes would tell the story.

He drew closer and brushed her cheek with his palm. "Follow your heart, Olivia."

She sensed he wanted to say more but he turned and grasped the horse's reins.

"I need to get to work. Please give Lovena my regards."

Still stunned by his question, she remained where she was, watching him lead his horse toward the barn. He didn't look back.

Returning to the house, she closed the door behind her and brushed a hand to the cheek Ben had smoothed with his palm. Her heart spoke louder than words could express. She was deeply in love with Benjamin Pratt.

BEN COULDN'T REMAIN talking to Olivia. His desire to reach out and wrap his arms around her was too overwhelming. He wanted to protect her, to take her away from the secrets and lies she'd lived with all her life.

Opening the barn doors, he looked around at the work that needed to be finished but his thoughts remained on seeing Olivia. His uncle's often expressed words of wisdom came to mind. "We seldom see the true nature of others' lives, their sadness or sorrow." Ben had looked upon the Fullers as the ideal family, his own tainted with scandal.

Now he knew too much about Olivia, more than she knew about herself, and it didn't matter to him. He'd wanted to wipe away the sadness he saw in her eyes. And why was her father bent on her marrying Tapley?

None of it made sense.

Unless… Did Fuller believe a man of God might be more forgiving if he found out the truth? What other reason could there be?

He grabbed a piece of wood that lay at his feet, measuring its size before hammering it into place. He needed to finish this job and leave. Every time he saw Olivia, he'd be tormented, not only with the need to hold her, but with the truth he couldn't reveal.

She doesn't love Tapley, but her father has a strong hold on her. He's getting older and she is devoted to him. Ben felt disgust for the man. He was a preacher of God's Word and he defiled the Word with his actions. He may have been a good father but he gained a daughter through an outrageous sin. And now he wants to control her future.

Damn! He poured himself into his work, anger pushing him to work faster. He was surprised when he heard the barn door open. Turning, he saw Reverend Fuller.

"How are you doing, Pratt?"

Ben swallowed the rage that sprang up in his throat. "Another day or two and I should be done."

"You've done a good job. Will you be spending Easter with your uncle?"

"Yes, we have little family otherwise."

He waited for Fuller to say more, but the man simple

stared as if he were contemplating or measuring his words.

"You will finish by Tuesday, Wednesday the latest?"

"Yes, everything should be done by then."

Fuller said no more. He turned and walked away. Ben watched him hesitate before disappearing down the path.

The man was anxious to be rid of him. Ben wondered if Olivia said something to him about their conversations or if her father could have seen them talking together.

Tossing the hammer to the floor, Ben cursed. It wasn't right. The man preached morality but he crossed the line. He shattered a life! Now he was controlling Olivia's future. Minister of God or not, he couldn't fathom Tapley abiding the truth about Olivia.

None of it made sense.

He packed up his tools and left the barn. As he rode away, he wondered if Lovena approved of Olivia's marriage to Tapley. He must talk to her soon. Would she give him justifiable reasons Ben would be forced to accept?

CHAPTER TWELVE

A SLIGHT BREEZE brushed Olivia' cheek as she slept.

My sweet Rosalee. You so pretty. I'm leaving soon. Jesus been patient with me, but he calling me home. He been after me to forgive your daddy. It been hard but if I wanna live with the Lord, I need to do as Jesus did on the cross. When your daddy give me that gold cross and take you away, I want to spit on it. I beg Jesus to forgive me. The Lord, he carried a heavier cross but I refused to think on it. I keep my rage at your daddy closer to me than Jesus' sacrifice. It was bad what your daddy did but he gave me you, even if I got to hold you for only a little while. Jesus let me watch you grow into a beautiful woman and a good one too. And your daddy, he been a good father. I got to give him that.

Olivia stirred, turning her head restlessly, but her eyes remained closed.

My Rosalee, questions stirrin' inside you. You don't know what they is yet but they there. It be a mystery but you know me in your heart and my dyin don't change that. Nobody can break the bond between a momma and her baby.

I know you be in love. Me too…once. You don't want to let go a love. Hope and lovin deep is what keep us close. I love you most in the whole world. That's why I stay and watch over you. Jesus know that be true and he let me. Your daddy thinkin' he protectin' you, but he got to trust God's way not his own. I got to believe the Lord gonna work it out.

Olivia sighed softly in her sleep.

My pretty girl. Bitterness be gone from your momma's heart but the truth got to show its face sooner or later. You got to follow your heart.

A soft feathery breeze swept over Olivia's bed as light streamed through the shadowy darkness. She turned on her back, her arms restless beneath the covers. When her eyes opened, they adjusted to the semi-darkness. She looked toward the window and saw glimmers of light slice through the edges of her window shade.

Bits and pieces of her dream returned.

You've got to follow your heart. Her breath caught. She'd dreamt of the woman again and she'd spoken the same words Ben had said to her. Maybe it wasn't a dream. Had Narcissa come to visit her once more?

Olivia felt calm as if she'd been nurtured in her sleep. But she'd held on to Ben's words, *follow your heart.* She'd repeated them in her thoughts often. They must have found their way into her dreams.

Olivia fingered the cross she wore, trying to remember more. But it was just a dream, only a dream.

She hadn't dreamt of the mystery woman in over a week. She sifted through another flicker of memory. *I feel as if she came to say goodbye.* The thought nearly brought Olivia to tears. Why did she feel such sadness? She recalled her father's words when she first told him about the repeated dreams. He'd blamed it on the devil's work. Was Narcissa leaving now that Easter had arrived?

But the woman wasn't evil. Olivia had sense warmth from her, even love.

Sun filled the room now with its light. She needed to get up, dress, and look in on her father. Most likely he was already dressed and studying his Easter sermon.

She pulled away the covers. "Speckles? She clicked her tongue. *Odd.* The cat was always asleep at the foot of her bed. She remembered her jumping up on the bed when she retired and cuddling with her for a few minutes then settling down in her usual spot. The bedroom door was still closed. She swung her legs off the bed and looked around.

Meow. The mewing came from under the bed. Kneeling, Olivia coaxed her cat out and lifted her in her arms. The cat shivered and clawed her shoulders. "What is it, Speckles?"

She settled the cat at the foot of the bed, rubbing her ears to calm her. *How strange.* "Speckles, did you see her? Is this woman more than a dream?"

Putting the mystery aside, Olivia dressed quickly and carried her cape and Easter bonnet down the stairs. When she entered the kitchen, her father, dressed in his best suit, was just getting up from the breakfast table. Lovena stood at the sink, leaning on a cane, and washing dishes.

"Let me help, Lovena. You should be resting your ankle."

"The doctor said I can start puttin' more weight on it. Sit and eat some eggs and toast.

Olivia looked at the table set festively with a vase of fresh spring flowers in the center. "There is no stopping you. This afternoon, I'll serve dinner."

"You let me go at my own pace, Livie. Sit now, the eggs gettin' cold.

"Father?"

He was walking from the kitchen toward his study. "We have some time," he called back. "I thought of something to add to my sermon. Be ready in fifteen minutes. There's a chill in the air."

Olivia sat and added a spoonful of scrambled eggs to her dish. "Did Father seem well at breakfast?" she asked Lovena as the maid set a cup of tea before her.

"He was quieter than usual but you know how he is about his sermons, especially on Easter."

Olivia smiled. She looked forward to Easter morning service. The atmosphere was joyous, the music brought everyone to their feet, and her father's words stirred the church to greater praise. The past week had been especially difficult, but she'd come to a stronger place through all the unexpected problems. Father was feeling well and when the time was right, she'd sit down with him again and be clearer about her issues concerning William. She realized that telling her father she didn't love William wasn't enough reason for her sensible father who wanted the best for her. She would be clearer about her dissatisfaction with William's behaviors.

Most important, she was determined to follow her

heart.

She hoped, as they celebrated Christ's resurrection, the day would bring renewed faith and hope for the future she'd dreamed about with the man she loved.

BEN THOUGHT HIS uncle might attend church this morning but when he entered the house, he found him sitting at the kitchen table nursing a cup of coffee and still in his bed clothes.

"My bones are acting up this morning. I don't think I'd do well sitting in a long service. I'll do my own praying right here."

Ben nodded and poured a cup of coffee.

"Don't want to stop you from going."

"I plan to ride down to the Snip and toss in a line. I'll do my talking to Jesus there." He figured it was the best place for him to pray today. If he went to the Meeting House, his eyes would be on Olivia, not on the purpose of the visit. He reached for a piece of toast.

"The sun will be sparkling on the water today. I think the Lord might like to be out fishing too," Uncle Syl said, handing Ben the jelly jar.

Ben smeared some on his toast and set it aside. He sat for another half hour talking with his uncle before gathering his fishing gear. He hitched the rod and gear to straps on his saddle and mounted Liberty.

As he rode toward the lake, he thought of the afternoon he'd found Lovena on the ground. She'd been a sorry sight. It must be difficult for her to complete even the lightest chores. Being confronted by the minister yesterday had put him in a foul mood. He should have asked before he left if he could help out in some way.

Reverend Fuller and his daughter would be at the Meeting House all morning. He doubted Lovena would be able to attend church. After fishing, maybe he'd stop by and see how she was faring.

When he reached the lake, he headed toward his favorite fishing spot. He dismounted and tied Liberty to a nearby tree and untied his gear. Once he was settled on a slope with his fishing line tossed in the water, he said his usual prayers. He preferred to pray for others rather than himself, but this morning he couldn't help but pray for a future with Olivia. The water was calm and the morning quiet and peaceful. He couldn't say the same for his thoughts.

What if Olivia's father pressed her into accepting William's proposal? The thought made him curse aloud.

No one was about. He was alone with nature and his God and too many things were happening. Working at the Fuller's was meant to be a straightforward job. Instead, he'd uncovered scandalous secrets and fallen in love with a woman practically promised to another. He had obviously caused conflict for Olivia and drawn the ire of her father.

"God, I need help. Are you listening?" he called out as he lifted the rod and flung its line further into the lake. Except for the quacking of a couple of ducks that floated by, he heard no answer. Maybe he didn't like sitting in church for hours at a time. but he wasn't an atheist. He believed in God and he could sure use his help right now.

After an hour, he'd caught nothing and in truth he really wasn't trying. Most times, he'd throw the fish he caught back in anyway. He remained at the lake, willing himself to relax, but after a couple of hours he packed up his gear. If he thought he could have a peaceful morning, he was kidding himself. He was confused and angry, perplexed about what to do with the diary, angry Olivia's father wanted Tapley as her husband, and even angrier at himself that he couldn't let her go.

Leaving the lake, he rode toward the parsonage. He'd

stop by for just a few minutes to see if Lovena needed a helping hand. Telling her about the book could wait another day.

Not on Easter.

Even when a good time arrived, how would he approach the subject? *I found Narcissa Dunn's diary and its entries could destroy the Fuller family.*

REVEREND FULLER SHOOK the hands of church members as they entered the Meeting House. Regulars commented about his absence and expressed gratitude at his return. Their kind words increased his guilt. He'd faked an attack but the truth was he really didn't feel well. He'd been especially tired over the past few weeks. Using his health to control Olivia was another grave sin. It seemed there was no end to his deception, but what else could he do to protect her?

Olivia's dreams brought back memories he'd tried unsuccessfully to bury. The Easter season was a time for circumspection. Were his plans for Olivia unacceptable to God? William's lack of empathy toward Lovena didn't help his cause either.

Remorse weighed him down as he approached the pulpit. He'd spent an hour with the Lord before daybreak pleading for mercy and forgiveness. He wanted to stand before his congregation cleansed and without sin. After all, he was preaching redemption. He'd encouraged the church to confess their failings and be cleansed for Easter morning. But he didn't feel redeemed.

Walking to the pulpit, he nodded to William who was standing by to assist and then to Olivia to begin the first hymn.

Christ the Lord is ris'n today, Alleluia!
Sons of men and angels say, Alleluia!
Raise your joys and triumphs high, Alleluia!
Sing, ye heav'ns and earth, reply, Alleluia!

As THE CHURCH members raised their voices in praise, his heaviness began to lift. He gazed toward his daughter as she played the organ and led the singing. He felt pride and humility for her gift to him. He watched William in his starched cravat and black coat as his voice rose in exultation to the Lord.

Yes, everything would work out and Olivia would be secure and protected as William's wife. Deception displeased God, but He understands human frailty. He works through our sins to bring good, the minister mused as the hymn concluded and the congregation sat down. He lifted his face to the Lord and offered opening prayers, reciting Romans 8:28, the theme for his Easter sermon.

"And we know that in all things God works for the good of those who love him, who have been called according to his purpose."

Before he continued, he smiled at the congregation and down at his daughter who was seated before him in the front pew. Shards of sun sliced through the Meeting House windows, causing an object on her bodice to glisten. His shoulder bent forward as he gazed more closely.

God, no. His hands clasped his chest. *It can't be.* His mouth remained open but no words emerged. He could only stare at the cross that hung from his daughter's neck, his grandmother's cross, the one he'd dropped into the folds of Narcissa's skirt before walking away with her child. His body swayed, his eyes no longer seeing his congregation, only the cross, before he crumbled to the floor.

Church members shrieked and in the distance he heard the stomping of feet, but they seemed far away.

Someone had grasped his shoulders and eased his fall. It was the last thing he remembered before he passed out.

When he woke, Doctor Hines was leaning over him, a stethoscope pressed to his chest. He looked up to see his daughter, her eyes wide with fear.

"It was too soon for him to be up on the pulpit. I warned him. Much too soon." Dr. Hines muttered, after he pulled away his instrument.

"My sermon, I…" The image of the cross returned. He sucked in a breath and closed his eyes.

"William followed your notes and ended the service early."

He'd heard what Olivia said but he didn't respond. He was confused. Had he imagined it? He tried to look at his daughter but the doctor was kneeling over him again.

"We need to get him home. His heartbeat is weak but it's stable. His exertion this morning was more than he could handle." The doctor turned his eyes back to his patient. "I'm going to keep a close watch on you, Charles. You're a tough old bird but you're not made of steel. Your heart needs more rest. I want you to stay in bed until I tell you that you can get out, and not just in a few days. When you improve, I expect you to cut your workload in half if you hope to live to see grandchildren." When the doctor looked away, the reverend blanched at his mention of grandchildren.

"I need a couple of church members to help me put him into my carriage," the doctor said, standing up.

Olivia took the doctor's place by her father's side. Reverend Fuller looked up. He didn't look into her face but at the cross dangling from her neck as she leaned over him. He hadn't imagined it. He knew that cross and God help him, he feared its presence. He turned away and closed his eyes.

OLIVIA WAITED OUTSIDE her father's bedroom until Doctor Hines completed another examination.

"How is he?" she asked when he finally opened the door.

"Fair. I'll return in a couple of hours and have another look at him."

"I am so grateful you were there." She choked up unable to go on. He rested a hand on her shoulder. "I think he's going to make it through this if he behaves himself during recuperation."

She drew a relieved breath. "Thank you, doctor. I'll see you out."

"No, I'll see myself out. Olivia, he's asked to be left alone. Why not get some rest?"

Olivia nodded and waited until Doctor Hines disappeared down the stairs before opening her father's bedroom door. He would certainly want to see her. She approached her father's bed and touched his forehead. His eyes were closed. He hadn't said a word to her since his attack and she needed to hear his voice.

"Father, I'm here."

His eyes remained shut though she was sure she saw them flicker. Rather than opening them, he turned his head away from her.

"I love you." She kissed his bearded cheek, waited, and when he didn't acknowledge her, she stepped back and with an anxious sigh, left the room.

She walked slowly down the stairs. Why didn't he respond to her? Even in the carriage, he was aware but didn't look at her. Though she wanted to believe it was her imagination, she sensed he was purposely avoiding her.

When she entered the kitchen, Lovena was stirring a pot over the fire. Olivia sat at the table, bent over, her head resting on her crossed arms. She didn't hear the maid walk over to her, but felt a hand on her slumped shoulders.

"Your daddy's in good hands, Livie. He likely wasn't ready to be up there preachin' so soon. You know how stubborn he can be."

"He seemed fine," Olivia said without lifting her head, tears dampening her sleeves. "Just as he was ready to begin his sermon, he looked at me. I was sitting in the first row in my usual place. I smiled at him. All of a sudden his expression changed almost to *horror*. I can't even describe it. Maybe a pain seized him. I don't know."

"The doctor says he holdin' his own."

"I felt as if I caused it."

"Don't be ridiculous, girl. You ain't caused nothin'." Lovena pulled a chair out and settled next to Olivia, wrapping an arm around her shoulders.

"I'll never forget the look on his face before he fell back. Thankfully, William caught his fall. The church was in a frenzy."

"He must have gotten a chest pain right at that moment. Don't you go blamin' yourself."

"Thank God Dr. Hines was there. I was so frightened. I thought he was dying. I was never so afraid." Olivia lifted her head and wiped her eyes.

"You got to put him in God's hands. The good doctor wouldn't have left if he thought he was in immediate danger." Lovena settled back in her chair. We just gotta keep him from…" Lovena sucked in a gasp. The cane she held clattered to the floor.

"What?" Olivia reached down for the cane and gave it to the maid.

"The cross. Dear Lord, he saw it. Oh, *mercy!"*

Olivia pressed a hand to her chest where the cross lay. "What are you talking about?"

"Didn't I say not to wear it? That it gonna bring bad luck? You should have listened to me. The cross done it. It was the cross."

"*What* is going on in here?" William stood at the kitchen doorway, anger reddening his pale complexion. "I heard you from the parlor." He snapped, glaring at Lovena. "Why would you tell Olivia not to wear a cross? I've been wary of your influence on her. You people, with all your superstitions and lack of spiritual guidance!" His eyes flashed to Olivia. "Is this the rubbish she teaches you?"

He reached out and wrapped his fingers around the cross hanging from her neck. "She tells you not to wear this, that it is bad luck?" He glared again at the maid, spitting out his words. "You *heathen*. I told the reverend that Olivia was too close to you. I told him that the ignorance of your race needed to be guarded against. But he refused to listen." He jerked his head back toward Olivia. "I swear when we are married, she will have no place in our Godly household."

"William! Stop!" Olivia screamed, aghast at his rage. She tried to pull his hand from his hold on the cross.

William unfurled his fingers, releasing the cross from his grip. He appeared to be making an attempt to calm his wrath, though his face remained red. "Olivia, forgive me for raising my voice, but this is righteous anger. The cross is the symbol of Christ's sacrifice. How fitting you should wear it on Easter. For her to tell you the sight of it could have caused your father's attack is blasphemous. Don't you see what she's doing? My dear, I dread to think what other superstitious falsehoods she's told you. You must be shielded from this kind of sacrilege."

"I don't need to be shielded. Lovena is not a heathen nor is she any less a human being than any of us!" Disgust at his prejudice sickened her. Her own questions begged answers, but she could no longer abide his ignorance or his disrespect.

"Why are you here?"

He looked stunned by her reaction. "I was waiting in the parlor. Dr. Hines told me you were with your father. I wanted to be here for you. I didn't know you were in the kitchen until I heard her shriek." His eyes darted to Lovena and back to Olivia. "Do you understand what she was saying to you? It was sacrilegious garbage."

"I want you to leave. *Now.*"

"*I* should leave? For heaven's sake, I am trying to protect you."

"I don't need your protection. Please leave."

"I'll go, but mark my words I cannot abide this after our marriage. If it wasn't for…"

"Wasn't for what?"

William pressed his lips together, leaving her question hanging in the air between them. He turned to leave but paused as if collecting himself. "I plan to offer my services to the church in your father's absence, but I must leave for New Haven this week to take my final exams. I pray the church will be in capable hands."

"Reverend Slater has been called in the past to officiate when my father is unable to do so. No doubt the elders have already contacted him. You needn't worry about the church's capabilities," Olivia said indignantly.

William stared at her, appearing dumbfounded, before walking from the room.

Olivia waited until she heard the front door slam shut before turning back to Lovena. "I apologize for William's callous remarks."

The maid waved a hand as if to brush off her apology. "He goin' to be a fire and brimstone preacher someday."

Olivia knew Lovena had grown a tough skin against racists' remarks. She'd talk to her again about William's unwarranted tirade but now she needed answers. "Tell me about this cross and why you believe it caused my father's heart attack."

REVEREND FULLER MOANED as his arm stretched out over the bed as if it were trying to wave something away. "Why have you come? Leave me be, *please*."

Olivia stood motionless inside the threshold of her father's room, watching as he thrashed around and mumbled. It appeared as if he were having a nightmare. Tucking the cross under her collar, she walked to her father's bedside and looked down at him. He appeared to be sleeping, sweat beading on his forehead. She reached for a cloth that lay on his night stand and wiped away the perspiration. "Father?" she said softly, but he didn't respond though he became still.

Once his breath grew even, she left the room and went to her own. Unclipping the chain around her neck, she deposited the cross in a box on her bureau and lay on her bed. The cross stood for something and she had to find out what it meant. Lovena refused to answer her questions and Olivia had left the kitchen in a huff. It seemed only her father could answer them. Whatever it was, it was powerful enough to bring her father to his knees and put fear into Lovena's eyes.

BEN ARRIVED AT the Fuller's late the next morning and worked steadily until mid-day. After placing the last of his tools in the wagon, he stood with bent elbows and hands cinched at his waist looking at the last of his repairs, a barn door, patched with the salvageable boards.

The job was done. He had no other reasons to linger. Yet, he found it difficult to leave. He'd hoped he would see Olivia but he didn't expect it. He wanted to knock on the door when he first arrived to see how she was doing but decided against it when he saw the doctor's carriage in the yard.

The grief he'd seen on Olivia's face Easter Sunday still cut into his heart. He'd reached the parsonage that morning when he'd observed her father being helped into the house with the doctor close behind. Olivia held the door, tears streaming down her face. Her father appeared deathly ill. He found out later what had occurred from their cook as she served Easter dinner. The news of the minister's collapse in church had spread across town in just a few hours.

He climbed up on his wagon and started down the drive. When he heard the door of the parsonage creak open and shut, his heart took a sudden leap. Olivia stood on the porch. He brought the wagon to a halt.

"Hello, Ben." She stepped down and walked toward him.

He tipped his cap. He was so glad to see her. Nothing else mattered. She was there, speaking to him, and she had told him she didn't love William. Her admission gave him hope. For now, with her father so ill, there was little he could do to push his suit.

He drew the horse to a stop and jumped from the wagon. "How are you?" He sobered when he saw that her face looked pale and drawn. "I heard about your father. I'm sorry. How is he doing?"

"It's hard to say. He's been sleeping each time I've looked in on him." She rested a hand on the side of the wagon. "The doctor is with him now. I hope to visit with Father once Dr. Hines leaves but I'm afraid I'll upset him."

"Why would you think you'd upset him?"

Ben watched Olivia's shoulders sag. He wanted to reach out to her but held back.

"Are you superstitious?"

Ben raised a brow. He'd given little thought to superstition until recently. "Why do you ask?"

Olivia looked across the lawn toward the stone ledge where they'd sat once sharing one of Lovena's cookies. "Do you have time to sit with me for awhile?"

Ben smiled. He couldn't think of anything he'd want more. He walked along side Olivia through the yard. When they reached the wall, she paused and looked at him. He understood her unspoken request. He lifted her to the ledge and joined her.

She looked down and fingered a button on the sweater she wore. "I plan to tell William I cannot marry him."

A knot that had been squeezing Ben's heart,

loosened. "Should I be disappointed?"

"I hope not, but I believe my father will be."

"You haven't told him."

"No, he's too ill."

"He wants what's best for you."

"Do you think marrying William is best for me?"

Ben reached for her hand and held it to his chest before looking into her eyes. He wanted to kiss her rather than answer her question. Tossing aside his qualms, he pulled her to him, bringing his lips down to hers. She welcomed his kiss.

When he released her, he brushed the back of his knuckles gently across her cheek to the curve of her neck. "Did I answer your question?" She gave him a trembling smile, tears welling in her eyes. Wrapping her in his arms again, he trailed gentle kisses along her forehead before lowering his forehead to hers. He loved everything about her and he didn't give a damn about anything else.

"I love you," he whispered when he drew back. The happiness he saw on her face gave him the courage to go on. "Would you refuse if I asked you to marry me?"

A tear slipped from the corner of her eye. He wiped it away. He knew her answer. He held her to him, resting his chin on her hair and breathing in its scent. This was right. He knew it deep in his soul. They had to find a way to be together.

She pulled away slowly and held his face in her hands." I love you, Benjamin Pratt. I think I fell in love with you the first time you spoke to me."

"I fell in love with you long ago." He grinned at the surprised look on her face. "At a distance." He reached for her hand. "You asked me before if I believe in superstition. Tell me why."

"Something happened yesterday that makes little sense to me."

"And?"

"I don't want to burden you with my problems. I need to talk to my father but I feel as if he is avoiding even looking at me."

"Most likely it's his condition. You won't burden me. I want to know everything about you. Now what's this about superstition?"

She took a breath and pulled at the chain around her neck until the cross that had rested beneath her collar was visible. She told him about finding it and Lovena's warning.

"I respected her request but yesterday I forgot to tuck

it under my collar when I dressed for church. Father saw it just as he was about to begin his sermon. The last thing I remember is a look of dread on his face before he collapsed."

As she talked, Ben hoped he hid his astonishment. Narcissa's story flashed through his mind. He couldn't possibly tell her what he knew. "Heart attacks can come on quite sudden."

"Yes, but when Lovena saw I wore the cross openly, she became really upset. She blamed my father's attack on the cross. I felt as if I did something terribly wrong."

Ben looked away, rubbing his forehead. He had a clear picture of what happened. Her father must have recognized the cross he'd left with Narcissa after taking her child.

"You think I'm being foolish."

"No, I don't, but you must listen to me. You're not to blame for your father's collapse. Erase the thought from your mind."

Olivia's lower lip trembled. "Thank you. I know Lovena has a superstitious nature. Could it be only a coincidence? I pray Father will help me understand what happened. He's not clear in his mind right now and sleeping most of the time. I need to wait until he's stronger before I can ask him."

Ben wrapped an arm around her shoulders. "I don't know if I believe in superstition, but I believe God has a plan for us. My uncle may not be a regular churchgoer but he taught me to pray. After my parents died, I couldn't make sense of it and refused to believe God existed. When my uncle took me in, raised me, taught me his trade, I realized I was just where I was supposed to be. You and I are meant to be together."

"I don't want to be anywhere else." Olivia rested her head on his shoulder.

They held each other's hands, leaning into each other, until they heard church bells ring in the distance.

"I've lost track of time. I want to talk to the doctor before he leaves."

Ben jumped down from the wall and grasping her waist, he lifted her, hesitating, before setting her feet on the ground. He was tempted to draw her back into his arms but he didn't, understanding her need to go to her father.

"I've completed the barn repairs, but I'll stop in to see you tomorrow afternoon. And when your father is feeling better, I'll talk to him."

Olivia reached a hand to his shoulder and pressed a

kiss on his lips. Smiling, she turned and hurried away. Ben watched her as she skirted around the copse of trees that hid the house from view.

He returned to the wagon and leaned against it, hardly believing his good fortune. Should he tell his uncle that he asked Olivia to marry him? No, better to wait until he can talk more to Olivia and discuss their future. For the moment, he pushed away the truths the entries brought to light. So much had happened in such a short time, he could barely grasp all the implications and couldn't fathom what the next days would bring.

He felt little empathy for Reverend Fuller's condition. He wondered how he was going to react when Olivia tells him that she refuses to marry Tapley and when Ben approaches him to ask for her hand. He needed to bide his time. Nothing could be done until the minister's health improved. Meanwhile, he had a great deal to think about.

CHAPTER THIRTEEN

"OLIVIA, I WAS looking for you," Dr. Hines said, as he stepped outside onto the porch.

"I'm sorry, I was… How is my father?"

"Let's sit a minute." The doctor didn't wait for a response but set his bag down and sat on the top step of the porch.

She followed the doctor's lead and sat next to him. Seeing his worried expression, she feared the worst.

"My dear, I doubt your father will return to the pulpit any time soon, if at all. His heart, I believe, has been severely damaged. He's quite weak and he seems…lost."

"I don't understand."

"He's confused. It could be his body trying to adjust to a new reality. His age, a weakened heart and stress can create havoc in the mind."

"Are you saying his mental facilities have been affected?" She thought of how her father had been avoiding even looking at her.

"It's most likely temporary. He appears disorientated

and fearful."

"My father, afraid? Does he fear he might die?" She clutched her throat to push down growing panic.

"I can't say. At one moment he knows who I am and seems to be listening to me and in another he becomes agitated, mumbling about the wrath of God and sin. It makes little sense what he says. I wanted you to be prepared. I recommend you keep him comfortable and calm. I'll return this evening and examine him again. There's little we can do. His recuperation is in God's hands."

Olivia didn't know what to say. Her father had always been clear minded.

The doctor stood and picked up his black bag before offering her a hand as she rose from her seat.

"I'll go look in on him now."

"You may be a comfort to him. Don't stay too long. Tomorrow he may be more himself. We need to give him time."

"Thank you," Olivia said in a near whisper. She remained on the porch until the doctor climbed up on his carriage seat and rode away. Before entering the house, she looked toward the barn. Ben was standing at the door watching her.

She raised a hand in farewell. Hope with a shadow of guilt remained as she walked in the house. She wished Lovena was there to talk to but Olivia had insisted earlier that she go to her room and rest. To her surprise, Lovena went willingly. She, too, was getting older, like her father. One day they would both be gone. The thought cut deep into Olivia's heart.

Taking a fortifying breath she walked through the hall and up the stairs. When she reached her father's door, she knocked softly before she opened it and peered in. Her father's head was turned away toward the window. She stepped quietly to his bedside.

His face turned slowly toward her and to Olivia's surprise his eyes were red brimmed and his cheeks damp from tears. She'd never seen her father cry.

"Father?" She sat on the edge of his bed.

"My Olivia," he whispered, reaching up and smoothing back strands of her hair that had escaped her cap.

"Why are you crying? You must believe you will recover." She wiped his cheek gently with her fingers.

"My child, believe I love you. I never meant to hurt you." His voice cracked as another tear rolled down his cheek.

The sorrow that echoed from his voice and visage brought tears to her eyes. She grasped his hand in hers. "You have been the best of fathers."

"I beg you. Forgive me."

"You have done nothing that needs forgiveness."

"No, you don't understand. I have wronged you. I have sinned and God is holding me accountable."

The doctor was right. Her father was confused. She needed to calm him. "You are not well. Your mind is playing tricks on you. God, no doubt, holds you in great favor. You have served him well. It's time for you to take care of yourself. Perhaps your illness is a sign that it's time to retire and enjoy the years you have left."

"*No*, you must listen."

Though his voice was weak, she heard the demand in his tone.

He turned his head away and began to mumble to himself. She realized he was quoting the Bible. She was accustomed to him uttering verses by memory almost daily. His Bible was his guidance and his closest friend, he would say. She turned her ear closer and recognized the verse from the Gospel of Luke.

For nothing is secret that shall not be made manifest; neither anything hid that shall not be made known...

She didn't know what to think. "Father, what is wrong?"

He turned back to her and clenched her fingers in his. "My daughter, I committed a grave sin, an unforgiveable one, despite my repentance. Unless I confess, she won't go away."

Olivia rubbed his damp forehead. "Who won't go away?" He was hallucinating but denying his present reality might cause him more upset. She felt helpless at what to do.

"Your mother. I can't rest knowing she has no peace. It's my fault, all my fault."

"You were good to her." Olivia forced a smile. "I urge you, rest now. You'll feel better tomorrow."

His eyes went to her neckline. "What happen to the cross? Is my guilt so strong that I imagined you wearing it? Did I imagine her presence?" He lifted his hand and rubbed his eyes as if he could erase what he'd seen. "Where is the cross?"

"I don't understand. Why does it disturb you?"

"It was real then, not the imaginings of a guilty mind. I gave it to your mother, a pitiful offering. I saw the anguish, the despair on her face, the accusation. How I have prayed for God to forgive me, to cleanse me of my sin. Over and over, I've prayed, but she remains. I must confess."

"You are confused and you're scaring me."

"Listen to me. Your mother's life was ruined because of my sin. I am responsible for her death."

Olivia heaved a relieved sigh. "Mother had been ill for a long time. She died peacefully. Don't you remember? You're carrying unearned guilt. She died of illness that you had no control over. There was nothing you could have done."

His eyes bore into hers. His chin trembled, his mouth opening and closing before the words came pouring out. "Olivia, your mother died months after you were born. Etta raised you as her own child, but she did not birth you."

Olivia's mouth dropped open before she let out a gasp. "I won't hear this!"

"You must. I am telling you the truth."

"Are you saying you're not my father?" She feared his answer as she watched the tears slide down his face. She didn't wipe them away nor did he.

"You are my natural child. I…committed a grave sin. Your mother, your true mother…her circumstances…she couldn't take care of you." He sucked in a shaky breath. "No, that's not true. No more deception."

She sat frozen, disbelieving. She saw weariness on his face. More than weariness, defeat, but she couldn't utter a word of comfort. Her mind pulled her from the belief that he was delusional, to another, one too incredible to absorb.

"We didn't allow her to take care of you. Etta was unable to carry a child to full term. She wanted you. We knew we could give you more. It seemed right and I convinced myself…" He stopped as he heaved in a sob. "I beg your forgiveness." His lips trembled while more tears rolled down, disappearing into his beard.

He no longer sounded confused. His words poured out as if he'd held them in for far too long. *Dear God, am I being pulled into his madness?* She pressed a hand to her lips until she could no longer hold in the question she feared to ask. "Who was my birth mother?"

He turned his head away from her and stared at the wall beyond the bed. "She was here this morning. I must give her rest or I will have none."

He was hallucinating, wasn't he? A sudden thought caused her to shrink back. "My dreams, were they of her?"

"I don't know."

"Who was my mother? Tell me!"

A sob escaped his lips before he turned back and looked into her eyes. "She was a domestic, working here at the parsonage. Her name was…Narcissa, Narcissa Dunn." He winced at the mention of her name. "Lovena can tell you about her."

"She knows all this?" She squeezed her eyes shut and shook her head, wanting to erase her father's words and block out his expression that couldn't deny them. She pressed a hand to her chest and felt the cross beneath her dress. "Lovena gave me the cross."

"My grandmother's, a paltry substitute for taking a child from a mother's arms." He seemed to be talking to himself. "I forgot about it. Never thought I'd see it again."

"Lovena told me it was my mother's." Her voice sounded dull to her own ears as if she wasn't connected to the words. "I assumed it was the mother I've known all my life. She didn't lead me to think otherwise. She told me not to let you see it. I couldn't understand why she'd want me to hide it from you."

"God wanted me to see it. I was to preach of the Lord's redemption. Praise him for his forgiveness, but I carried the weight of guilt in my heart. I feared hurting you, Olivia. I thought your marriage to William would protect you from the truth."

"Protect me," she whispered. Her voice edged with anger. There was that word again. "Protect me from what?"

"I don't know. I was afraid, afraid you'd find out. I wanted to shield you from the sorrow the truth could bring. I tried to consider all possibilities but my efforts were all wasted. Now you must carry a burden you don't deserve. I fear I won't be here to help you carry it."

Olivia stood, her hands clenched to her sides. "I need to leave." She backed away from the bed. His voice had grown weaker and she'd lost the ability to hear anymore.

He reached out. "Don't go, not yet."

She stared at his open hand, extended to her. She shook her head and ran from the room.

Lying on her bed, she stared up at the ceiling. Thoughts she'd pushed away years before, surfaced; times in her life when her mother's look made her feel as if she was unacceptable, like she didn't belong. She had none of her mother's features, her blond hair, her thin lips or her light-skin. She'd mollified those feelings, deciding everyone must have a place in their heart where they felt different, a place set aside for God and that would be filled when life was over. Now she realized they had carried a deeper meaning, one she could never have imagined.

"Livie?" Lovena knocked quietly before pushing open the door that had been left slightly ajar. "You best get up. The doctor gonna be comin' back soon." She walked into the darkened room and lit the candle by Olivia's bed, before going to the washstand and dampening a washcloth. "You need to eat something too. Ain't gonna do any good if you get sick." She turned and stopped her chattering when she saw Olivia's face. "What's wrong, honey? You worryin' about your daddy?"

Olivia sat up and glared at the woman she'd known her entire life. "What do you know of my mother? What do you know of Narcissa Dunn?"

Lovena's hands dropped to her side, the washcloth falling from her fingers. She bent down with a weary sigh and picked it up.

Olivia watched the maid's eyes fill with tears as she took a step closer to the bed. Her father hadn't been hallucinating. Lovena's face revealed the truth in his confession.

"Father told me. It was her cross, wasn't it? My real mother, *Narcissa*. The dreams I had of a woman standing by my bed, touching my cheek, humming a song. She was coming to me in my dreams. I knew her once, didn't I? That's why I felt no fear, only comfort from her. *Rosalee*, she'd whispered. She was talking to me, wasn't she? Is that what she named me? Tell me!"

Lovena nodded.

"I need to know everything. Come and sit." She skirted over to the other side of her bed, making room. When Lovena remained standing, Olivia patted the quilt. "Your ankle is still weak. *Sit*." With obvious reluctance, the maid sat on the edge of the bed. Olivia watched as Lovena wiped the dampness from her eyes. They took on a faraway look as if her thoughts were slipping back into the past.

"Narcissa was a sweet girl," she said finally, her voice low and wistful. "She could be sassy too." She looked back at Olivia. "Sometimes I see her in you. You have her eyes and times when you look at me I think of her, 'specially when you pout. You have her pretty shape too." Lovena bowed her head, rubbing her brow.

"Tell me more." Olivia's hands clenched her quilt in an attempt to calm the waves of confusion she feared could drown her. "How long did she work here?"

"She be just a chile when she come here with her Aunt Iva. Iva, she worked for your granddaddy and when she die, Cissa stayed on. She became a beautiful young woman."

Olivia's body jerked suddenly as a memory pierced through the fog she'd been trying to escape from. *No*.

Lovena must have sensed her anguish. She laid a hand on Olivia's arm but Olivia brushed it away.

Could it be? She'd been told that her grandfather hired only Negro women because white girls never stayed. They'd be trained and in no time, leave to get married. She folded her knees to her chest and wrapped her arms tightly around them. "My mother was Negro." She didn't ask it, she claimed it. "That's why I'm darker skinned than..." She stopped and stared at the maid though she already knew there would be no denial.

Lovena pressed her lips together. Her lowered lids told the truth.

"I'm colored...like you." She'd said it with dead calmness. Her insides seemed hollow, emptied of who she'd thought she was.

"Your daddy, he wanted to give you a life better than you woulda had with your mama. Narcissa understood."

"Did she give me to him?"

Lovena didn't answer.

"Did she?" Olivia bent forward, anger replacing the deadness she'd felt.

"Mrs. Fuller want you. You looked white and it was her husband's baby too. Them keepin' you was the best for you in the end. Your momma got sick. She died a few months after you were born. Oh, Livie." Lovena reached out again to grasp her hand.

Olivia stiffened from her touch.

She retreated, resting her hands in her lap. "Narcissa, she love you. I want you to know. She got to hold you and talk to you and tell you stories. She knew you would be well taken care of."

Olivia stared at the maid, all remnants of disbelief dissolved. She dropped her head into her folded arms.

"Livie."

"Please, leave. Now. I beg you."

Lovena lifted herself from the bed and walked slowly to the door, hesitating, before shutting it quietly behind her.

Sobs racked Olivia's body as an unthinkable reality

consumed her. Each time she thought she had control over her tears, a new realization hit as if she were in a ravaging ocean, one giant wave after another slamming into her and drawing her back into her new reality.

An hour went by before her tears were finally spent. She wiped the dampness from her raw cheeks and pushed herself up from her fetal position. Propping herself up against her pillows, she smoothed one hand over the other as if she were trying to see something she hadn't seen before. She pressed one finger into her skin, rubbing it back and forth, transfixed for a moment, awed, as if she had never been aware of its texture.

Memories surfaced from her childhood and suddenly made sense. She was perhaps five when a church woman asked her mother if Olivia had been adopted. Her mother had scoffed at the remark and prattled on about a bit of gypsy mixed into her good English background.

Another time, when she was eight or nine, her mother added vinegar to her bath and scrubbed her face with a vinegar-soaked cloth. When her father heard about it, he grew furious. She overheard their muffled voices arguing. It never happened again.

As she grew older and others commented on her

attractiveness, her mother took greater pride in her daughter's coloring and dark eyes. Yet, she'd still insisted on choosing the colors for her dresses when she realized some shades appeared to lighten her complexion while others darkened it.

Another recollection caused her to suck in a breath. Her mother had posed her on a garden swing holding a bouquet of spring flowers and painted her. She'd wanted to see the painting but her mother wouldn't allow it until she was finished. When it was finally unveiled, Olivia had recoiled in disbelief.

Though her mother had captured her face and pose, she'd painted her with a lighter skin tone, even adding highlights to her nearly black hair. Her mother bristled at Olivia's reaction and insisted she'd captured the glow of her skin in the sunshine. The painting caused another argument when her father realized what his wife had done and refused to hang it. Olivia never saw it again.

To her, it was the first time she had truly acknowledged that her mother didn't see her as she was but rather as she wished her daughter to be, a fair-skinned child instead of a toss back to a gypsy relative who didn't belong in the family tree. Now she understood. Her coloring didn't come from a gypsy but from a colored woman.

She was bi-racial, a mulatto.

She repeated the word *mulatto*, tasted it, tried to absorb it, but it was like a foreign substance that didn't fit all she believed about who she was. Her thoughts turned to her father's adulterous act. Did he have a secret affair with her real mother or worse, had he taken advantage of the worker? No, her father was not capable of such an act. He was gentle, caring and wise. Those were the words that she would have described him only hours before.

Lovena had told her about masters who took advantage of female slaves. Slaves were considered property bought and sold like livestock. Many families hired Negroes for farm work or household help and treated them poorly, but her father wasn't one of them. He railed against slavery in the South and lectured against inhumane treatment of those who serve. Yet, was he any better than the worst of them?

She squeezed her eyes shut and pressed her face against her knees. What was she to do now? She thought of the woman in her dreams. "Are you here with me?" Olivia whispered, looking about the room before sighing. "You come only in dreams. I need to see you, touch you, hear you." She recalled the woman's words in the last dream. *Follow your heart.* "Are you aware of Father's desire for me to marry William? Do you know of Ben?"

Just thinking of Ben caused the tears to begin again. *He's lost to me now. He's in love with the woman I was yesterday. I don't even know who I am today.* She bent her head to her knees and let more tears fall.

My Rosalee

Olivia's head shot up. The room was dark except for the flickering candle.

God gives only the grace for today. Don't bury faith and hope, Rosalee. Follow your heart.

"If only I could see you," Olivia pleaded, getting on her knees and looking around the dark room. She felt the soft wisp of gentle fingers on her cheek. She lifted a hand but stopped, allowing the sensation to linger. She reached out but there was nothing to hold onto.

"Follow your heart." Olivia repeated the same words from her dream, from Ben's lips, but only pain filled her heart, not faith and hope. Was love lost to her too? Emptiness was what she felt, the emptiness of realizing she didn't belong as the daughter of a white mother. Yet, something eased inside her. She gazed around the room again, before slumping back and closing her eyes. She revisited the words she'd heard. But from where? In her spirit? Her mother? She remained still for a long time before pushing herself from the bed.

Determined.

She needed to find out about Narcissa Dunn, her own birth, and who she was meant to be.

CHAPTER FOURTEEN

WHEN BEN ARRIVED at the parsonage the next afternoon, Lovena answered the door but couldn't bring herself to give the young man a welcoming smile.

"Hello, I've come to see Olivia. She's expecting me this afternoon."

"She ain't seein' nobody today. She's restin'."

"I see. I… suppose she's gotten little sleep caring for her father."

Lovena nodded. She wasn't about to tell him why Olivia refused to leave her bedroom.

"Please tell her I stopped by." He started to turn away but turned back. "How is Reverend Fuller today?"

"He's doin' as well as can be expected."

"And how are you?" He was looking down at the cane her hand rested on.

"Don't think I need this anymore." She lifted the cane. "The doctor want me to use it when my ankle starts feelin' tired. One ache leaves and another comes. It jus' happens with gettin' old."

The smile he gave her didn't erase the

disappointment his face revealed when she'd told him Olivia wasn't available.

"I'll stop again tomorrow. Good day." He hesitated as if he had more to say, but appeared to think better of it. Tipping his cap, he walked off the porch.

After closing the door, she returned to pulling at her pastry dough, kneading it harder than necessary. Olivia remained angry at her because she refused to answer more of her questions. She sensed Livie couldn't take in much more so she had to put up with the girl's anger for the time being.

"What gonna happen now that she knows the truth?" she muttered. You been leavin' me alone, Cissa, now she got the cross. I guess it be all you wanted from me. You been causin' all this trouble cuz of the reverend's choice for Livie's husband. Ain't that right? Can't say I blame you. I don't like that Tapley boy much either. I couldn't't'a done anything about it."

She paused in her kneading. "Ain't you somethin'." Lovena's sarcasm turned to a more tender understanding. "I know you never got to choose a man or experience lovin'. Is that what you want for your girl?" She formed a ball with the dough and tossed it in a bowl before brushing the flour that covered her work table into a pail. "Whatever you doin', you been creatin' a mess and the only mess I know how to clean up right now is this flour. If you're still hangin' around, what you gonna do about your girl's heartache?"

BEN RODE AWAY from the parsonage wondering if Olivia was having second thoughts about their relationship. He didn't want to believe it. They'd professed their love to each other. No, her father's illness must be the cause. He'd come again tomorrow.

He pulled at his horse's reins and turned up the street toward the blacksmith's. When he dismounted in front of the shop, he was surprised to see William Tapley walking out the door.

Tapley tipped his hat. "Pratt. Nice to have a sunny day. Does your horse need shoeing?"

"No, my uncle has the blacksmith sharpening some tools." As he tied his horse to a post, he eyed the black suit Tapley was wearing. "What's your business?"

"On my way to New Haven. I have final exams this week. No doubt all will go well and I'll be ordained by summer." He lifted his nose in self-satisfaction.

"Congratulations."

"Would have been out of town a half hour ago but

one of the horses favored a hoof. Sure enough the smithy found a stone wedged in its shoe."

Ben nodded. He had no desire to carry on a friendly conversation with Tapley.

"How is it going at the parsonage?" Tapley asked as Ben started up the steps. "Are you done with your work there?"

Ben paused with one foot on the bottom step. He rested an arm on the wooden railing, sensing Tapley had an objective for asking. "Yes, finished yesterday."

"Good. You must have heard the reverend passed out in church. Terrible. The faithful were nearly inconsolable. I calmed them as best I could."

"I'm sure you did." Tapley didn't seem to notice Ben's subtle hint at sarcasm. "Will you be officiating during his convalescence?"

"This coming Sunday, I think. From what the doctor says, the minister is going to be laid up for some time. I assured the elders I'm available to serve in any way I'm needed. Once my exams are finished, the date for my ordination will be set. Of course, we pray for the reverend's swift recovery."

"Of course."

"After all, Olivia and I want her father to officiate at

our wedding."

Ben's eyes narrowed at the emphasis Tapley placed on his statement.

"We have her father's blessing, naturally. I must focus on my exams this week, and Olivia is beside herself with grief over her father's illness. Not a good time to announce our engagement. When her father regains his strength, I feel confident we can begin to plan our future together."

"Really," Ben said flatly. It appeared Olivia had not yet rejected William's proposal.

"I don't believe I'm revealing any secrets, Pratt, by telling you Reverend Fuller plans to retire soon. I'm pleased to say he has expressed his desire that I take over his ministry, God willing. I am humbled by his faith in me. He expects Olivia and I will reside at the parsonage. When that time comes, I shall enjoy the sweat of your labor on the barn. No doubt you've done a commendable job."

Ben didn't miss the backhanded compliment. He wondered if Tapley's condescending tone was deliberate or just his usual haughty demeanor.

Tapley continued. "I've noticed the house needs repairs as well. With Reverend Fuller's advanced age and failing health, he hasn't been able to keep up with the maintenance. The church members help but they can only do so much. I may bring more work your way." He smiled, as if he were offering a generous gift. "Well, I must be off. Have a good day."

Ben watched Tapley's pride-filled stride as he headed toward his carriage. He wondered if he knew of Ben's attraction to Olivia. It seemed the man wanted to put him in his place. Tapley's overconfidence and assumptions grated at Ben. They were just assumptions, weren't they? Or would her father's illness sway Olivia? Could that be why she didn't see him? No, he refused to accept that she'd changed her mind.

He was glad Tapley was out of the picture for a few days. He smiled at that thought. Today, he had work to do but tomorrow he and Olivia needed to have a talk.

"IT'S GOOD TO see you up and dressed," Lovena said as Olivia entered the kitchen the next morning.

Olivia nodded but said nothing. Having seen the doctor's carriage arrive from her bedroom window, she forced herself to face the day. She wanted to speak with Dr. Hines. Despite her anger and confusion, she needed to know if her father was improving.

"Bein' mad at me ain't gonna help you through this, Livie. Why don't we sit down and talk about it?"

"I really don't know what to say, Lovena. I don't know who I am anymore."

"You know who you are. Everythin' inside you hasn't changed," the maid said matter-of-factly as she carried a plate of cheeses to the table.

"Really?" Olivia settled into a chair and picked up a slice of cheese, her first piece of solid food since the morning before. "Isn't our past a part of who we are? The mother I knew was quite proud of her ancestry. It is no longer mine. I don't know anything about my true mother's heritage, except she was Negro. You, more than I, are aware of how that one fact alone alters my entire past, present and future."

Lovena carried a jar of strawberry preserves and a basket of biscuits to the breakfast table. "Eat, Livie. Starvin' yourself ain't gonna help none."

"I want answers. What kind of a man is my father? Why did the woman who raised me pretend I was her own blood?"

Lovena took a seat and let her vent.

"Were there ever gypsy ancestors?" Olivia snorted. "No need to answer that question. But how else could she rationalize a daughter whose skin and hair were so different from her own? All lies!"

"Livie…"

"You too. I was the only one kept in the dark."

"Listen to me. You know our blood be all the same color." She held up the scarred finger she'd cut years before. "And our hearts the same to the Lord."

Olivia remembered her childhood conversations with Lovena but her rage stifled any acknowledgement. "Tell me more about Narcissa Dunn. Is she buried nearby? I could visit her grave. Do you know where it is?"

"Lordy, you givin' yourself more grief than you already carryin'."

"Please, don't keep anything from me."

Lovena clasped her hands and stared with her lips pressed together, as if she were weighing the impact of her unspoken words. Finally, she sat back and began. "Your daddy paid for her burial and her stone. He had it engraved. Jimmy and me, we put flowers on it many times. He's moved away now, the boy your momma cared about."

Olivia rested her elbows on the table. "Tell me about Jimmy."

"He was sweet on your mama. Nice boy. He did

some farm work here for a time."

Lovena's words made it clearer to Olivia that love was not a part of her parents' joining. She was about to ask her more but footsteps sounded on the hall stairs.

"I need to talk to Dr. Hines." Olivia rose and left the room.

"How is my father?" she asked immediately when the doctor reached the bottom step.

He didn't answer immediately. His eyes were scrutinizing Olivia's face. "What's wrong, my dear? You look pale, exhausted, in fact. Have you had sleepless nights worrying about him? I must ease your mind."

"I am tired, yes. How is he?"

"His heartbeat is slower than I would like, but it's become steadier and that's a good sign. Thankfully, his mind appears clearer, though he says little. He seems quite depressed. He's a man accustomed to being in control and busy. Now he has no choice but to remain in bed and take care of his needs rather than the church. No doubt it's the reason for his depression. He's as comfortable as possible. I'll be keeping a close eye on him."

"You'll be returning later?"

"I'll stop by again this evening. I must get over to the Johnson's house. Their young son Michael is doing poorly. He has a spring cold I fear may be turning into pneumonia."

"I am so sorry to hear that." Olivia pushed her own gloom aside. The family belonged to their church. Little Mike was born sickly and remained frail. She knew he might not be able to overcome a serious affliction. "I'll pray for him and his family."

"I know you will."

After the doctor left, Olivia walked into the parlor and sank into a cushioned chair. She thought of what her father would do with the doctor's news concerning Michael Johnson. He'd toss aside his work and rush over to the Johnson's house to pray with them. He'd put a call out to the church to gather in prayer. Now, the congregation was without a minister to lead them until Reverend Slater arrived.

William wasn't returning from Yale Divinity until Saturday. Would he even consider visiting the sick over other duties of the church? She rubbed her forehead and sighed. She wasn't being fair. He wasn't ordained yet and as her father had insisted, William needed to grow into the role of pastor.

Pushing herself up from her seat, she went back to the kitchen. She found Lovena buttering a biscuit before setting it down at Olivia's customary seat.

"You sit right down here and eat more. I don't need two people sick in this house."

Olivia obliged rather than argue. She took a few bites of the biscuit and a slice of cheese, her thoughts still on the sick child. After a few sips of the tea, she stood abruptly. "I'm going to the Meeting House."

Lovena gave her a questioning look.

"The Johnson's young son is sick. We need to begin a prayer chain and church members may be able to take over some of the family's farm chores."

Lovena gave her a broad smile. "Bless you for takin' on your father's duties. That's who you are, Livie. I'm proud a you. But first eat some more. You need strength to do those good deeds."

Olivia broke off a piece of the biscuit and picked up another slice of cheese. She munched on them while she considered what else she needed to do. "When I return, I'm going to talk to Father. Dr. Hines said he saw some improvement in his condition. He may be ready to answer more of my questions."

"You do what you got to do." Lovena raised a hand as if in surrender.

Walking from the room, Olivia focused on prayers for little Michael rather than her own troubles.

BEN RAPPED ON the Fuller's kitchen door early that afternoon.

"Hello, Benjamin," Lovena said, greeting him with a smile.

"Hello, ma'am. I hope you're feeling well this morning."

"Not complainin'. Does no good anyways."

"Have I come at a bad time?"

"Ain't no good time in this house lately. Come in." Lovena stepped aside.

Ben walked in and look around, hoping to see some sign that Olivia was nearby. "Has the pastor's condition shown improvement today?"

"He's about the same. Time will tell."

He looked over the maid's shoulder. "Is Olivia with him?"

"I'm sorry, Benjamin, you missed her today. She's off visitin' one of the church families. They have a sick little one."

"I see." He couldn't mask his disappointment.

"A church lady brought some fresh ground coffee this week. I'll pour you a cup. I'll have one too. It be a good time for me to get the weight off my ankle."

He came close to bidding her good day but thought better of it. It might be the right time to mention the diary.

"Go have a seat at the table. I'll get the coffee." After pouring two cups, she joined him. "I appreciate what you did for me the other day. I wouldn't't'a wanted Livie or her father to find me in the mud, lookin' like a wet burlap sack'a potatoes that fell off a wagon."

Ben gave a half laugh. He liked that she could find humor in what had been a grave situation for her. "I was glad I could help. Looks like you're getting around better."

"Been usin' the cane only in the evenin' now, but I won't be needin' it much longer."

"Maybe you should take more short rests during the day."

Lovena bellowed with laughter. "I can see me now, sittin' with my feet up in the air when there's work to do."

"If it's what's needed."

"You're a good man, Benjamin. There's a lot a folks around here think us maids don't need no rest. Thankfully, the Fullers aren't one a them. I appreciate your concern but the ankle's healin' up fine."

"And your wrist?" He stared at the bandage.

"Nothin's broken. It's just takin' its time to heal."

"Good to hear." Wrapping his hands around the warm coffee cup, he stared down into the liquid. *Should he tell her now?* Telling her about the diary was harder than he thought it would be. He'd be stirring up more trouble for her than she needs right now.

"You look like you got somethin' heavy on your mind."

He raised his eyes toward hers before nodding slowly. Setting the cup down, he fingered its handle.

"Come on now, what's eatin' at you? No doubt it got to do with Olivia."

"I don't know how to begin and you have a lot going on."

She tapped her brow. "I still got a bit'a room in here. Go on. Always best to start at the beginnin'. Ain't nothin' surprise me anymore. 'specially after the past couple'a days."

He paused and took a sip of coffee before setting it

aside. "The other day when I found you on the ground, you were mumbling."

"You mentioned that before. I was half outta my wits. What was I babblin' about? I don't remember anything except bein' soaked to my bones in mud."

Her hearty laughter relieved some of his tension. She was trying to put him at ease.

"You called out a name. *Narcissa.*"

Her expression changed instantly. She gave him a wary look but made no reply.

He bit at his top lip before pushing himself to continue. "I found a handmade book, a journal, written by a woman named Narcissa Dunn. It was hidden behind a wall board in the front room I was tearing down. When you said her name the other day, I thought you might have known about it."

"Lord," Lovena's lips formed a large O. Her eyes widened and she pressed a hand to her breast. She said nothing for a moment as if she were digesting not only the news but the raw reality behind it. Finally, she rested her elbows on the table and stared long and hard at Ben before speaking, her voice grave. "When one stone falls off the heap, they all come tumblin' down, don't they?"

Ben wasn't sure what she was referring to, but when she said no more, he went on. "Some of the writing is smudged and unreadable from dampness and age, but it's a diary and enough is legible."

She leaned toward him with narrowed eyes. "You read it?"

Her voice wasn't exactly accusing but her disturbed expression remained. Guilt pierced him like a poisoned arrow.

"I should have burned it."

She didn't agree or reply. Instead, she leaned back and stared beyond him. "I forgot how that girl liked to write. Her aunt was one smart lady. Iva learned from a woman she worked for years back and taught Cissa. I seen her writin' in that book when I was livin' in those old rooms, but it wasn't my business to ask her what she was writin'."

Ben could tell she was lost in memories, sad ones. He waited until she fixed anguished eyes on his.

"What she write? It best you tell me."

Too late for regrets or recriminations, he thought. He looked around the larger kitchen area and off toward the hallway.

"Ain't nobody here who can listen. The minister's up

in bed and Livie won't be back for some time."

"She wrote about a child, an infant."

Lovena closed her eyes, her head swaying side to side.

Ben didn't know what to say or do. He'd opened a Pandora's Box he couldn't close. He waited until she signaled him to go on.

"Tell me all you know."

Dread seized him. He was going to expose a secret that should have remained buried. "It's not my intention to upset you. I should never have read it."

Lovena sat back in her seat, more composed. She didn't say anything. Instead, she seemed to be searching his face for something more. "Maybe so; maybe not."

"She wrote…." He stopped and cleared his throat. "She'd been taken advantage of and became pregnant. She had the baby and it was taken from her."

He gauged her reaction. Her lips were pressed tightly together as if she were afraid of what he was about to say.

"Go on."

"I don't know if it's for me to repeat." He grimaced. "Damn, my curiosity. It was her private story. I wouldn't be telling you but it seemed you were a friend."

"'cause I said her name?"

"No, she wrote about you. She wrote that you helped her so she could see the baby."

Lovena's face was a dark portrait of sorrow. "What else?"

Ben wished he had a better way to phrase the truth. "I know Olivia is her child." No denial came. "You've always known, haven't you?" The news was not a shock to her. "I promise I won't breathe a word. I'll give the diary to you or destroy it if you prefer."

"Narcissa, is this more of your doin'?" Lovena muttered, not to him but to the room itself. She reached out and laid her hand on his. "Benjamin, ever since those rooms been torn down, she been causin' all kinds a trouble."

"Are you saying she's not dead?" The thought had never occurred to him. She'd written she was ill but maybe she survived.

"She been dead a long time," Lovena said with a grim nod.

His brow stitched in confusion.

"The dead don't always live in peace."

"I don't understand." He didn't believe in ghosts

roaming around. This entire situation was becoming more bizarre.

"You in love with my Livie? Don't you give me that look. I'm not blind. I see more than you think."

He couldn't fool this woman. It seemed as if she could look right through him. "Yes. I know Will Tapley has asked her to marry him. He expects her to say yes. I also know Reverend Fuller has given him his blessing."

"And what you think about that? You don't have to answer me. I can see by the look on your face you think the same way I do. How do you feel now you know the truth about her?"

Ben saw Lovena's jaw stiffen. She looked like a protective mother prepared to do battle. "I love Olivia." He looked down at the maid's dark hand covering his. "When I read her mother's words and realized the truth of her birth, I was shocked, disbelieving. Angry. I thought of Olivia never knowing this woman who loved her. I felt sad for both of them. Yes, I love Olivia, the way she looks, the way she talks and laughs, but it's more." Ben reached for his coffee cup and sipped, feeling embarrassed at exposing his feelings. "I feel a new kind of loneliness when I'm not with her," he said finally, putting the cup down. "She's become a necessary part of me."

He looked up and saw a quiver of a smile on Lovena's lips. Her hand tightened on his. "I haven't answered your question. No, the truth of her birth has no effect on my feelings but her father wants her to marry Tapley. He must have a great deal of trust in him."

"He tryin' to protect his daughter."

Ben heard something more in her voice. Compassion? "You care about him, even after what he did?"

"He done a terrible, terrible thing. It took me a long time to find mercy in my heart. He has to answer to God for his sins but he been a good father to Livie. I'm not makin' no excuses for him. He got to live with what he did. But he done his best by his chile, regardless. I stayed because I wanted to look after her for Cissa's sake." She stopped, sighed, and reached for her cup, slipping the coffee slowly.

Ben felt she wanted to say more. The woman had a big heart. As far as he was concerned, the man deserved punishment rather than praise for being a decent father.

"I see the look on your face, Ben. You're weighin' the heaviness of sin and you figure it don't deserve any lightenin' with forgiveness. All's I can say is I've come to know he's a good man that let the sin'a lust take hold a him. I don't think he's ever forgiven himself. For years now, I seen him spend hours bent down on his knees praying, pleadin' with God. I know it cuz I seen the look on his face when I've had to interrupt him cuz someone's come to call. He'd have this pleadin' shadow on him like he been beggin' and ain't gotten no relief. He been in a prison sufferin' inside himself. Now he's worryin' about Livie's future, 'specially since she's of marryin' age and he's getting closer to the end. I think if the world was different, he might'a told her the truth, but you know how it is for us Negroes. He never wanted her to find out and have to suffer for his sin in a different way.

Ben couldn't deny the truth of Lovena's words. The North might have outlawed slavery but there were still households that enslaved and many who believed Negroes could never be accepted as equal to men of his own skin, despite abolitionists' fervor.

"He believes Tapley is the answer to his prayers?" Ben didn't mask his disgust.

"The minister, he's not thinkin' right. He's afraid."

Ben shook his head, thinking of Tapley's arrogance.

Perhaps the minister hasn't seen that side of the man, though it was difficult to miss. "Does he think Tapley's vocation will cause him to accept the truth if it's revealed? Or does he plan to tell him?"

"He hopin' the truth will stay hidden if she marries Mr. Tapley."

He combed a hand through his hair in frustration. He wasn't going to force her to reveal anything she'd be sorry for later. He'd already placed enough of a burden on her.

The sound of carriage wheels on the stone path ended the discussion.

Lovena lifted herself from her chair and went to the door with Ben close behind.

"Look like we havin' visitors from church, most likely wantin' to check on their minister."

"You need to attend to them. I'd appreciate if you'd tell Olivia I stopped by."

She placed a hand on his arm as he reached for the doorknob. "We gonna talk again, Ben. We need to keep our secrets for now, and you best pray about what best to do with that old book."

He nodded and walked out, feeling no better than when he arrived.

Chapter Fifteen

OLIVIA REMOVED HER shawl, folding it over her arm as she walked home from the Johnson's modest farm house. The day was growing warmer and her long-sleeved dress, even without the shawl, felt uncomfortable. She'd been so busy lately with church duties and other issues in the household that summer dresses she'd begun to sew in early March remained unfinished. Last year's dresses would have to do. Summer clothing was the least of her worries.

After her visits this afternoon, the thick cloud of rage that consumed her over her father's betrayal had been pierced by the reality of his service to others. She'd been stopped on the street and on the Town Green by concerned citizens. Church members were gathered at the Meeting House to pray for him. When they saw her, they couldn't say enough about her father's caring and selfless deeds.

They acted as if he were on his death bed. The thought made her cringe. He'd been a worthy pastor and had accomplished much in their small town. No one appeared to know his dark secret. She wondered what they would think of him if they knew. And how would they treat her?

She thought of her visit with the Johnson family. Mr. Johnson brought her to the boy's bedside where his wife was keeping vigil. Hearing the child's choking cough confirmed the cold had gone into his chest. She'd touched his feverish forehead to say a quiet prayer. When the child looked up at her with his pale blue eyes, tears threatened, but she'd forced a smile. How she wanted children of her own. She could only imagine the pain the family was going through seeing their innocent child suffering.

The Johnsons thanked her for coming and sent their good wishes to her father. Their parting words remained with her. "You are kind and giving like your father. God bless you both."

Visiting the sick and infirm, praying for those near death and giving them hope of heaven was her father's calling. He never treated these visits as a chore but rather a blessing to him. He was humbled by other's faith in his prayers. How could he commit adultery and give so unselfishly to others' welfare? Live with lies and yet save souls?

Could she forgive him? Despite his good deeds, his deceit left her numb.

As she drew closer to home, she thought about the prejudice toward the colored community. She'd read stories about the treatment of mixed raced children, mulattos, as they were called. Mulatto, her label now. Many were barred from white society and looked at as unnaturally born. She'd read that some who passed for white refused any contact with their colored families. With all the stories about the cruel treatment of slaves in the South and the abuse of free Negroes in the North, what were their choices? Colored laborers brought in during the harvests were often treated poorly and with disregard. She'd read and heard enough about social concerns and separation of races. Should she continue the lie?

Suddenly a dog crossed her path and ran into a nearby field. Ironically, the dog had a spotted coat, brown and white. She couldn't help but think many of the colored were treated like dogs. Her father had voiced his anger often when he'd heard a story of violence against a minority.

And what was her real mother like? Did she fight to keep her or give her up willingly? Lovena said Narcissa loved her, held her, and told her family stories. If only she could tap into those memories lost somewhere in her infant mind.

And there was Benjamin. He'd fallen in love with the woman she was yesterday. What would his reaction be if he learned her mother was Negro? They'd never discussed social issues. For all she knew, he could have prejudicial views. All her beliefs of fairness and equality came from standing outside the colored world. Now when she looked in a mirror, fear frowned back at her and mocked her ignorance.

She'd thought she held no prejudice. Instead, she wanted to erase the truth of her birth, return to her ignorance, her white world where she looked upon the stigma Negroes lived with daily and simply empathized. She didn't want to carry the burden African Americans carried in their hearts for decades.

She thought of her father's insistence she marry William. Why? Did he believe his vocation would keep him from turning from her if he learned the truth, or that their children would be protected under the umbrella of the church? Olivia wasn't naïve. As easily as some church members offered help to the needy, they as easily turned their backs to those who didn't fit a mold acceptable to them.

Her father preached against intolerance. Yet, he ignored William's prejudice. She stopped suddenly and grasped the rail of a fence nearby. *Could my children be born colored? Was it possible?* She had no idea what her mother looked like. *Was she light colored? Did she have coarse hair like Lovena's?* Her father must have thought of the possibility. Did he truly believe William, as the future Reverend Tapley, would grow in tolerance and accept a child with mixed blood?

Her inner questioning nearly caused her to walk past the stone pathway that led to the parsonage. She wanted to walk on, keep walking, rather than face what she must do. Talk to her father and find out why he was pressuring her into marrying William. Talk to Lovena and learn more about her mother.

She stared up at her home but instead of walking up the drive, she pressed against the trunk of a large oak tree that edged the property but hid her from the road. Clutching her stomach, the floodgate of tears she'd been suppressing through the streets opened. Dropping to her knees, sobs racked her body again. Tears of pity, tears of fear and confusion fell. Tears of rage at the unfairness and at her father's deceit and betrayal spilled

out until only choked sobs remained. She fisted her
hands toward heaven and cried out silently to God until
a wellspring of calm began to settle her. She sat back on
her haunches, pulled at her long skirt and dried her face
with the gathered cotton. She sat still with her eyes
closed until a measure of strength returned and caused
her to push herself up from the ground. Swallowing
hard, she brushed grass from her skirt and walked up
the drive toward the side porch. With each step, she
regained a semblance of composure, preparing herself
for a battle she didn't feel up to fighting, but her self-
pitying thoughts had to stop. She'd spent the last hour
allowing her pain, fears, and inner truths that had been
covered up by piety, crush her spirit.

Enough.

She climbed the side porch steps and paused before
opening the door, taking in a deep breath. When she
walked into the house, she searched out Lovena and
found her leaving her father's room with a tray in hand.

"Livie, you look terrible. You hurtin'. I can see it in
your eyes."

"Has Father eaten?" she asked, ignoring Lovena's
observance and pitying gaze.

"Got him to drink some broth and nibble at some

crackers. Not enough to keep a bird from swoonin'. How was the Johnson boy?"

"Not well, not well at all."

"Poor little one."

"His parents fear the worst. All we can do is pray." She reached for the door handle. "I'm going in to see my father."

Lovena gave her a wary look.

"I'll try not to upset him. Later, we must talk."

Lovena gave a resigned nod. "A letter arrived for you. Looks like it be from Mr. Tapley. I put it on your dresser.

"Thank you."

"And Ben stopped by, wantin' to see you. It's the second time he's come."

Olivia released the door knob. "What do you want me to do? Pretend I am who I thought I was a few days ago? Welcome his attentions?" Olivia knew she was being a shrew but anger was her constant companion. Right now it gave her strength. Without it, she feared she'd crumble as she did only minutes earlier. She turned away and opened her father's door, leaving Lovena standing in place.

Entering the darkened bedroom, she found her father

propped up against his pillows.

"Olivia, you've come."

She walked closer. Her father looked pale and drawn. A stab of compassion struck her but she firmed her jaw. "The Johnsons send their good wishes."

"How is their little boy?"

"He's fighting a spring cold."

Her father nodded grimly. "The child does not fight off illness easily."

She walked closer to his bedside and stood, arms crossed. "Why do you want me to marry William?"

Reverend Fuller heaved a deep sigh.

"I'm waiting."

"Your mother and I feared for your future, when you would marry and desire children."

"Which mother? Did my real mother have any say in my future?"

He lowered his eyes.

"And how was my marrying William going to shield me from the truth? You've seen his attitude toward Lovena. We both know others who feel the same way. I thought I carried no prejudice but now I wonder."

"How can you say that? I've taught you to accept all men as equal under God. You have demonstrated great tolerance of others regardless of differences."

"Tolerance, yes. Is that all we offer, tolerance? Do we truly feel equal? I wouldn't want to be just tolerated. Perhaps, if the truth is revealed to our congregation, I *shall* be tolerated."

"My dear, you are making more of the word than is necessary."

"I speak the truth. Why did you choose William to be my husband?"

"Please, sit by my bed."

She remained standing, her arms tightly folded to her waist.

"Olivia, William is intelligent, devout, respected. He's young. God will continue to work in his heart. You must understand."

"Understand what?"

His lip quivered. Did she see dread in his expression?

"William has no desire to father children."

Olivia's jaw dropped. She took a step back.

"A grave illness exists in his family line. He harbors great concerns about fathering children. If …your child was born with features…" He stopped appearing unable to go on.

"Negro features?" she blurted. "And that's why you

made this choice? Not because of his ministry or your high opinion of him? Because he doesn't want children?"

He nodded slowly. "My heart pained me, knowing how much you love children. I've been so afraid you'd learn the truth. Too many children are orphaned and need a loving family. I trusted that once you accepted William's decision, you'd consider adoption. I admit William can be too opinionated and arrogant, but I truly believe his service to the church will soften his rough edges. He'll make a good husband and you would be shielded from society's judgments and bigotry. We both know racism cannot be escaped."

"And if I became pregnant despite William's desires? There's no guarantee. Father, you are betting on futility in your plan for my life. Unless... Does William plan for us to live like brother and sister?"

"Please, I beg you to understand. I didn't know what else to do. I prayed for God's will daily, pleaded for an answer to my fears. When William pledged never to father a child, I felt as if my prayers were answered, especially when you both appeared to be interested in one another. Your marriage would be a perfect union, he a minister, you a minister's daughter brought up in the church to serve. I convinced myself that God brought William to my door."

He heaved in a shaky breath and exhaled. "Do you see how it all made sense? I suppose not. I was blinded by my fears and desires to see you protected. The world can be so cruel. I have begged God in his mercy to forgive me for my egregious sin and show me a way out." He reached out a hand to her. "Please forgive me. I cannot bear the censure I see in your eyes."

"Then I will excuse myself." She stepped back and walked from the room.

Olivia sat on her bed, holding William's letter in her hand. He must have mailed it in town before he left. She wouldn't have received it so soon otherwise. Her father's admissions still echoed in her mind. "Poor ignorant William, who would marry me and protect me from the truth without knowing what he was doing."

She ripped open the envelope.

My dearest Olivia,

> *As you are reading this, I shall be taking my final exams for the ministry. I pray this letter finds your father improving daily. At our parting, I was uncertain whether to be*

elated with hope or to be in despair. Although your father is delighted at the possibility of our marriage, I sensed your trepidation. Therefore, I wanted to write this to you before I must be focused on my studies.

I believe with all my heart you and I will have a blessed marriage. One God approves of and will bring both of us contentment. We have both been groomed to serve God and his church. Our devotion to the Lord and his children could only bring about spiritual blessings too numerous to count. No doubt in your prayer life, you have asked God's will for your life, just as I have. He has brought us together to find joy in each other and in our good works. Our hope is heaven and our earthly calling is to serve his church. How anxious I am to hear your answer and consider our future together! I shall return on Saturday. I pray you will accept my proposal and make me the happiest of men.

Yours in Christ,

William

SHE FOLDED THE letter and replaced it in its envelope, setting it aside. She felt nothing. He never spoke of love only the blessedness of their union. Was love to be tossed aside? Perhaps her father was right. Marriage to him would keep her on the same course she'd lived her entire life. She'd continue with her work at the church and help at the local school.

Of course she must give up the desire to have children and push aside the truth of her birth. Live a lie as her father did, live as if she'd never learned her mother was a colored servant. If she married William, she could ease her father's suffering and his guilt. William would profit from the marriage. Her father hoped he would take over his pulpit. She could adopt. Orphaned children needed good homes.

Her heart ached and tears threatened but she'd cried enough. *What of intimacy?* Her parents seldom demonstrated desire for each other in her presence, even slept in separate rooms. They served the church together, welcomed guests to the parsonage, worked side by side as was expected. Was it selfish of her to want a marriage with passion and intimacy? No, she could not bend to her father's wishes. She had no idea what to do with her new truth, her new identity, but she couldn't deny it.

Thoughts of Ben broke through the icy chill that had taken her heart hostage. She loved him. She thought of the way he helped Lovena, his kindness, his concern. Would he understand and accept her truth? Was it too much to ask? She didn't know how to let go of her desire for him.

She might best never marry. That was the only solution that made sense. No heartache for anyone except her.

Chapter Sixteen

"I DON'T KNOW, Livie. This trip only gonna add to your misery," Lovena muttered as they walked to the cemetery the next afternoon.

"I need to see her grave," Olivia said, ignoring the maid's warning. Since she'd found out the truth of her birth, she'd been living a nightmare she couldn't wake from. Her entire world was off balance, trust and faith in her father's integrity tossed away like hay on a threshing floor. Doubts flooded her mind. She hoped seeing the grave would make the present more real.

"Tell me more about Jimmy," she said, pushing away her confusion.

"He was sweet on your mama, like I said. When she went to work on another farm, he brought her to see you, always when your parents were off to meetin' on Sunday.

"He's still alive?"

"I think so. Last I knew he was married and with a couple of young boys."

"Maybe I can find out where he lives, talk to him."

"Don't know where he be livin' now."

Olivia eyed Lovena's cane. "Is your ankle bothering you? I should have waited a few more days."

"No, it be fine. It's good to be out walkin' though I'm not too pleased where we're goin'."

"We'll stop and rest if you need to."

"It ain't much farther."

Olivia slowed her steps. She'd keep a watchful eye on Lovena's gait and if it changed, she'd insist they stop to rest.

As they walked on in silence, Olivia continued to think about Jimmy's whereabouts when another question intruded and she blurted it out. "Was my mother the kind of woman who gave her body freely?"

"*No, child.*" Lovena slowed her steps. "Not Cissa. She was like you, just bloomin' into womanhood and noticin' the admirin' stares'a the menfolk. Had her eyes on Jimmy…" She stopped suddenly as if she realized she'd said too much.

Her abruptness caused Olivia to clutch her throat. "Did she consent to have relations with my father?"

Lovena's chin lifted but she didn't look at Olivia. "You askin' questions that ain't my business to answer. Your daddy has given you a good life, one your natural momma could never have given you. Adaptin' to the truth of your birth ain't easy, but don't cause yourself more sufferin'." She increased her stride as they approached the cemetery, saying no more.

Olivia pushed away more questions, ones she feared the answers to and ones Lovena obviously didn't want to answer. When they reached the wrought iron gate, she unlatched it.

"Wait," Lovena charged. "Hold this for me."

Olivia took the small bouquet of flowers the maid had gathered before leaving the parsonage. As Lovena rifled through one of her pockets, Olivia brushed her fingers across the petals. She'd been too steeped in her own misery to think about bringing flowers to the cemetery. She was grateful Lovena thought of it. She watched as the maid pulled out a small cloth bag.

"You be needin' this." Lovena handed the pouch to Olivia.

"Why?" she asked as the maid pushed the gate aside and marched on ahead.

"It be the African way. Narcissa's spirit been restless and it be important to figure out why she been stirrin' up trouble. I think maybe she want to bring about justice and forgiveness too. Talk to her now, in your mind. She been reachin' out to you. You need to tell her what you want. Pray and listen. When we get there, I'll tell you what to do with the bag.

Olivia pondered her words before obeying. Neither spoke as they walked toward the back section of the graveyard. Olivia paused when they passed tiny stones placed in remembrance of infants, too many of them, with symbols of peace or resurrection etched into the stones.

"It was because of me she died, wasn't it? Giving birth, I mean."

Lovena, who had walked on ahead a few feet, stopped and turned around, voicing an audible sigh. "Don't you go blamin' yourself. Too many women folk die in childbirth or shortly after. Lots'a babies too, or sickness take them even if they survive a few years. You seen it enough right here in this town. Death is a part a life. Ain't nobody's fault."

Olivia knew death was all too common, especially for little ones during a harsh winter. When she was old enough to accept the reality of death, her father allowed her to come with him when he officiated at funerals or to visit grieving families. Seeing mothers and widows dressed in black with faces covered in veils was all too common. Death was no discriminator of persons, regardless of age or circumstance.

Lovena pointed to a section of the cemetery that edged the property. "She be over there." She led the way, skirting around other monuments. Eventually, she stopped in front of a narrow stone that jutted about three feet from the ground with weeds growing around it.

Olivia heard her gasp. She watched as the maid used the stone to support her as she brought her knees to the ground.

"What is it?" Olivia stepped closer.

"The stone, it moved. Oh, *Lord*, it moved, just like it said."

Olivia looked from Lovena to the stone. She saw that a root stretching from a tree nearby had grown under the stone, causing the ground to heave. The stone was tilted from the force of nature, she thought, before she read the crudely carved inscription.

> *This monument is erected in memory of*
> *Narcissa Dunn*
> *Who died May 19, 1807*
> *In the 18 year of her age*
> *Beneath this stone*
> *deaths Prisoner lies*

This stone shall move

The Saint shall rise

What's now concealed

Beneath the dust

We hope will rise among the Just

Olivia pressed a hand to her heart. The stone *had* moved, a natural phenomenon. Yet, she understood Lovena's reaction. All her dreams, the strange happenings, the truth coming to light. Now the appearance of the slanted stone caused her imagination to wander into mysterious realms once more. She read the inscription again. Had her father chosen the touching epitaph? She reached out and rubbed her hand across Narcissa's name before kneeling and bowing her head.

They both remained silent. Lovena's lips moved, most likely in prayer. Olivia became lost in feelings she couldn't name. After a few minutes, Lovena sank back on her haunches. "It be an ancient African belief that if we honor our loved ones who have gone before us, they'll protect us and help us in our need."

Olivia watched as Lovena reached out an arm and knocked three times on the stone.

"I be asking Narcissa for permission for you to take

some dirt from her grave."

"Grave dirt?" Olivia's forehead creased in confusion. She was aware of Lovena's superstitious nature and, on occasion, the maid shared some of her distinctive traditions that grew out of her African culture. But harvesting grave dirt? It struck her that the culture with its unusual customs was her own.

"Now you use that bag I gave you and with your hands, dig into the ground right about here." Lovena pointed to an area a couple of feet from the front of the headstone. "Fill it with a good handful of dirt. I think that where her heart might be."

Olivia remained staring at Lovena.

"Do what I ask, Livie. I'll hold the flowers. Her grave dirt be something you can keep to stay connected to her spirit and to call on her when need be."

Olivia closed her eyes and took in a deep breath before following the instructions. She dug into the ground and shoved a handful of dirt into the cloth pouch before tying it up with the strings attached to it.

Lovena handed her the bouquet. "Now you lay these down where you took the dirt. These be your payment." When Olivia gave her another wary look, Lovena nodded assurance.

She laid the flowers down on the interrupted soil.

Lovena smiled before pressing on her cane to get to her feet. Olivia stood and reached out her arm to steady the older woman.

They stayed, staring down at the grave, both appearing lost in their own thoughts and prayers.

"We need to go home." Lovena handed Olivia a handkerchief to wipe her hands and brushed dirt from her own skirt. "Miss Emma got to get back home and make her dinner."

They'd asked a neighbor girl to stay at the parsonage in case the reverend needed anything. Their hope was he'd stay sleeping until they returned.

The two women walked in silence from the cemetery. Olivia tucked the bag of grave dirt into her skirt pocket, realizing she felt closer to the woman who birthed her. She could no longer think of her as simply a servant impregnated by her father. She'd died so close to Olivia's own age, her life cut short after bringing a life into the world. She deserved respect as a mother.

Tears threatened again. She wanted suddenly to give this woman's life meaning. She didn't want to deny her the gift of motherhood or hide the truth as her father desired her to do. Narcissa had held her in her arms and obviously nursed her from her own breasts. She'd given Lovena the gold cross to save for her, most likely her only possession of value.

For whatever reason, Narcissa chose to reveal herself in Olivia's dreams. She couldn't deny it. The mystery of it lived beyond this world, a mystery only God could explain. She thought of the words on the gravestone.

What's now concealed beneath the dust, we hope will rise among the just.

She drew her arms through Lovena's and walked on. Something had changed within her. The cold numbness that had replaced her heart's warmth seemed to have begun to thaw. Feelings were growing for the woman who birthed her. Her mother.

Perhaps, she'll visit me again. Olivia drew in a deep breath, exhaled, and patted the pocket that held the small pouch.

"LIVIE, I GOT things I gotta say about your father," Lovena said once they were back on the road to the parsonage.

"I refuse to talk about him, not now. My mother lies dead in that graveyard because of his lust. He was twice her age. You told me she wasn't a loose woman. And she was in love or at least attracted to another. She might be alive today, perhaps married with other children. Instead, I live because my father took advantage of her innocence. She deserves something from me. It is not to accept my father's lies or his plea that I forgive him. Not now or ever."

Lovena heard the anger spewing from Olivia's words. She pulled her arm away and walked over to one of the benches that bordered a small park they were passing by. She sat, pressing her hands to her knees before sending up a prayer for wisdom.

Olivia didn't sit. "I've pushed you too far today. I'm sorry."

"Don't you worry 'bout me. Sit and listen to what I have to say."

Olivia obeyed, but her body remained stiff and unyielding.

"I was workin' in the kitchen the night it happened."

Olivia pressed a hand to her breast. "One night?"

"Shush! Listen. He was on the porch drinkin'. He ain't never before or never after drunk like he done that night. No doubt he thought I was off to bed but I was worried about him. Never saw him like that. He was grumblin' to himself. I couldn't hear him from inside but he was in a mood. A mood your momma, the momma that brought you up, had a hand in. She was a cold woman. You knew that about her."

Olivia nodded. "I can't disagree with you. When I needed a hug or comfort, I came to you."

"They argued that night. It's not a big house. I couldn't help but hear many of their arguments. After too many miscarriages, she accepted that she'd never have children of her own. She left your father's bed. He poured himself into his work but he was an unhappy man. The church people viewed them as devoted to each other, but I knew otherwise." Lovena sighed before going on. It pained her to talk negatively about someone who was dead.

"A poor marriage is no excuse to take up with a servant," Olivia scowled.

Lovena pressed Olivia's hand but diverted her eyes. She needed to say what she had to say.

"I watched him go to the barn, but I never coulda imagined what he was thinkin'. That was the night he bedded Narcissa, the only night, not that it mattered. She got pregnant. There ain't no excuse for what your father did. Can't blame the alcohol or a cold wife. He lost all common sense that night and did something unforgivable in our eyes. But not in God's." She stopped. There was no reason to say more."

Olivia gave no response, her face a mask of shock and disbelief.

"The Lord calls us to forgive the unforgiveable. He tell us to 'forgive seventy times seven,' but without God's grace it be a hard thing to do. I can tell you that your father suffered after that night. He changed."

"And what of Narcissa? Should I feel more compassion for my father than the woman who bore me? She had to live with the shame of a pregnancy that she couldn't have wanted. Did she tell you what happened that night?"

"Narcissa worked out in the fields, helped in the garden. She did what she needed to do, that's all I'm gonna say." She could only imagine what must be going through the girl's mind.

"A minister of God took advantage of her and she protected him?"

"Yes, Livie. She had nowhere else to go and nothin' could be done. It's the nature for women to bear what we must, especially colored women. The world don't do much to fight for us. Narcissa and your daddy went on as if nothin' had happened. They both did what they had to do."

Olivia's stony expression nearly stopped Lovena from saying another word, but she went on. "When the mother you knew discovered the pregnancy, she assumed it was the stable boy that hung around Narcissa, Jimmy. She wanted to kick her off the property with nowhere to go. The only job Narcissa could have gotten was workin' out in the fields somewhere. Your father wouldn't hear of it. He may have suspected it could be his.

"I helped birth you when the time came and when I carried you outta the room, your daddy's face went pale as talcum powder. He expected a colored baby. There was no denying the truth once he saw you. I'm surprised the bones in your daddy's knees still hold him up. He spent so many hours on them repentin' before and after your birth.

"He couldn't disown his own child. He confessed the truth to his wife. Her anger was like a raging windstorm. She went on and on, marchin' about the house, cursin' and shovin' chairs over. She had good reason. But after a time, she grew real quiet. She stayed in her room for days. When she come out, she had the kind'a calm you feel in the air just before a storm.

That's when she demanded he take you and send Narcissa away. She was a pitiful woman, sorrowful and bitter over not bein' able to have her own children. She didn't know how to find any joy apart of her desire to bear a chile."

"And what happened to Narcissa?"

"Your daddy found her a job keepin' company with a kindly old woman who lived alone and needed extra hands. Unfortunately, Cissa's body just didn't heal right. She got real weak and in a few months, she was gone." Lovena waited for Olivia to ask more questions but she didn't. Instead, she remained staring out into the street.

"Your daddy told you to talk to me. Don't know if he expected me to tell you all that, but you have a right to know. It took me a long time to swallow down my anger, but I could see that he loved you and was grief-stricken for what he done. You gotta remember all the good things and measure them against the bad."

Olivia stood and walked to the edge of the road without a word. She waited for Lovena to follow. The maid understood. There was nothing more to say. They walked back to the house without a word said between them.

CHAPTER SEVENTEEN

OLIVIA PRAYED THAT her mother would come to her again, but she didn't dream that night. She'd barely slept with one thought over another demanding dominance. She'd heard her father preach on the importance of forgiveness hundreds of times, but she'd never had to forgive the unforgivable. How often had he said that a person who refuses to forgive and show mercy can suffer a worse fate than the one who needs pardoning? She'd accepted the tenet, believed it, but no one's sin had affected her so personally. By forgiving her father, wasn't she denying her true mother the respect she deserved? Was Narcissa's existence simply to be cast off without meaning while her father continued being loved and even revered? To keep his secret, he was willing to marry her off to a man she didn't love. Every moral lesson he'd taught her had been cast aside through deceit.

And what was she to do now with her future? She knew for certain she would never marry William. She could keep the secret, continue the lie, but she didn't know if she could lock the truth inside her heart like her father had done.

She prepared for the day and spent the morning doing necessary chores with only a passing word to Lovena. Dr. Hines visited in the afternoon and gave Olivia a report. He appeared unaware that she hadn't visited her father. He'd told her that her father was still weak but holding his own. That was all Olivia needed to hear. She wished him no harm, but she couldn't visit him or give him reprieve from a sickness of the soul. UnChristlike, she knew. Maybe someday her heart would soften but today she felt nothing but disgust and sorrow.

The remainder of the day was difficult with church members stopping by regularly to ask after their minister and to leave thoughtful gifts and food items. Men of the church spoke with Lovena about chores that needed to be done and offered assistance. Visitors spoke of times when her father's guidance brought them through a difficult situation. There was no doubt he was loved and appreciated for his service.

Her heart remained cold and unyielding. Yet, she welcomed the visitors, listened to their stories, and thanked them for their gifts. Some remarked that she looked tired and pale and urged her to rest. They naturally assumed it was worry over her father's health. She'd smile and express gratitude for their concern. They could never have imagined the thoughts that filled her mind or the agony that tugged at her heart. Her identity was shattered and she didn't know how to regain balance and move forward.

With little sleep the night before and an exhausting day, she fell into a deep sleep when she retired, but not a dreamless one.

Sweet child a mine.

Don't fear the day

The sun gonna shine

You gonna find your way

Hmm hmmmm hmm hmmm

Olivia opened her eyes. She'd heard the humming again and her mother's song came back to her. *Don't... fear the day...* Oh, if she could only remember more. Peacefulness covered her like a blanket. "You're still here," she whispered.

A steady rapping on her door shook her from the tenderness of the moment and replaced it with anger at the disturbance.

"Livie, wake up. The new minister's comin' this

mornin'. You best be up and dressed."

Was that what woke her? Had Lovena been knocking? If only she could have remained asleep a little longer. Maybe she would have seen her. She rubbed her eyes. The rapping continued.

"I'm awake. I'll be down soon enough."

"He said he be comin' bright and early."

"I hear you." Olivia pushed aside the covers still feeling disoriented. Speckles yawned and clawed the quilt. Reaching for her, she snuggled the cat in her arms. Speckles' purrs of appreciation comforted her.

Today was Saturday. The note from Reverend Slater arrived two days earlier concerning this morning's visit. As she rose from the bed, setting Speckles on the floor, she tried to remember more of her dream. "Did you sing that to me, Narcissa, when I was a baby?"

Don't fear the day, the sun gonna shine.

Olivia brought a hand to her lips. Where did those words come from? They'd passed through her mind like a soft breeze.

Lovena returned and knocked again.

With a frustrated sigh, Olivia opened the door. "What is it? I said I'd be down."

"I just went to check on your father. He wants to see

you."

"I've spoken to the doctor. That's all I can do." She feared seeing him. His condition might garner her pity. She wanted to give him none.

"It might help to see him."

"I can't. I'm not ready."

Lovena gave a defeated shrug of her shoulders. "Your heart is gonna tell you what to do. In time, you'll do the right thing."

"Is anything right anymore?"

Lovena didn't answer.

Don't fear the day…

"I'll be down in a few minutes to greet Reverend Slater."

THAT GIRL GOT so much sorrow in her eyes. How she gonna get through this, Lord? Lovena prayed as she dusted the furniture in the parlor.

Benjamin says he gonna come by and give me the diary. What am I gonna do with it? I don't know. Maybe I should tell him to burn it before it gets into the wrong hands. Don't feel right givin' it to the reverend. Cissa, what you want? Do you want Olivia to see it?

Each time she allowed a speck of hope Olivia might

have a future with Ben, she pushed it aside. *He knows about my Livie. He says her havin' a colored mama don't change his mind about her. What else he gonna say, 'specially to me bein' as dark as night? He got a lot to think about too.* With a deep sigh, she wiped down the last chair and returned to the kitchen.

She found Olivia standing by the window looking out toward the barn.

"Benjamin wants to see you," Lovena said as she set down her dusting cloth. "Maybe you should talk to him. I suspect he gonna be back soon."

"It's better if I don't see him. As it is, William is returning today. He expects an answer to his proposal."

"What you gonna say?"

"What should I say? Agree to marry him and carry on with the lies?"

Lovena walked to her side and reached out. Olivia went into her arms, resting her head on her shoulder. "I think you gonna follow the harder road, whatever that be. It ain't in you to take the easy way."

Olivia lifted her head and Lovena brushed away a tear. "You ain't no different inside or out. It's the people out there who cause the misery. They the ones who need to change. We're all victims in one way or another, whether we bein' abused or we bein' the abuser. Hatred, it's been brewin' its poison long before we was thought about. You gotta be strong and follow what's in your heart. If we slump our shoulders and give up believin' things gonna be made right some day, they win." She swept Olivia's curls behind her ears. "God gonna reward us, if not here then in heaven. He give us the might to survive the worst'a things, but he leavin' it up to us to do our own fixin'.."

Olivia rubbed a hand gently along Lovena's bare arm. "What if I had been born with darker skin? Would my father have taken me from my mother?"

"Oh, Livie."

"Would he have acknowledged me?" She touched Lovena's cheek before touching her own. I've come to see your skin as beautiful. I could have been born with darker skin. If I had, my life would have been so different, but you would have been there for me. Wouldn't you? You have been like a mother to me."

"I love you, chile. I woulda made sure you were taken care of."

"I believe you."

Lovena turned away, her eyes welling up. "I gotta get busy," she said with more brusqueness than she meant.

"You go wash your face. No tellin' how long Reverend Slater be with your daddy. The days still young. We may be gettin' more visitors stoppin' by to ask after him. Don't know what I'm gonna do with all the dishes and such that everybody's droppin' off."

When she turned around, she realized she was talking to an empty room. Olivia was gone.

"CHARLES, YOU LOOK like you've lost about twenty pounds. You need to get your appetite back and some color," Reverend Slater said with a smile as he pulled up a straight chair and sat by his old friend's bedside.

"I needed to lose a few." Reverend Fuller's voice didn't sound like his own but rather like a weak old codger.

"I must talk to your cook about adding some fat to your diet. I'll not allow you to become thinner than me. It's the one thing I've had over you. Never could put on an extra pound no matter what I eat."

Despite his guest's attempt at being jovial, Reverend Fuller saw the concern on his face. "Bah, with all the traveling you've done, when would you find time to eat a hardy meal? The last letter I received from you came from some tribal community in upstate New York. Has your preaching to the Native American tribes brought new converts?"

"I made some inroads, but younger men need to take over. I'm getting too old to keep traveling all those dusty roads."

"So you're ready to become a settled pastor?"

"I'm staying closer to home these days."

"Mark, how long have we known each other?"

"It's been long enough that I've forgotten." He rubbed his bearded chin. "Let's see, I'd been only a year out of Princeton and you had already been preaching for a few years and married. You were the settled one. I still remember the day I came by to visit and saw you with a squirming two-year-old in your arms. Speaking of Olivia, she's become a beautiful woman."

At the mention of his daughter, Reverend Fuller gazed at his bedroom door as he had done often over the past couple of days. Each time he'd heard her footsteps in the hall, he prayed she'd enter. He looked back at his friend. "Could the Lord be leading you to serve one congregation?"

"Never thought I'd want to stay in one place but my bones are getting weary from carriage rides. Perhaps that's a sign it's time to stay put. I gave up going by horseback to those remote areas a couple of years ago. I have been unmerciful to my aching back." He pressed a hand to his lower spine and stretched.

"I hope you'll make your stay here permanent. I won't be returning to the pulpit."

"Come now, this affliction will pass. You need a few weeks to regain your strength and I'm happy to help out. Your church is praying for your swift return. You just need to cut back on too many activities."

"I'm *not* returning to the pulpit, regardless if my health improves or not." His voice was shaky but determined.

"Your heart belongs to the church, Charles. When you regain strength, you'll feel differently. A man like you can't just sit around in front of the fire. You have too much yet to give."

Reverend Fuller winced, not with physical pain but a deeper ache in his soul. "I don't belong in the pulpit. Perhaps, I never have," he murmured, his voice low and cracking.

"What did you say?" Reverend Slater leaned closer. "I must have misheard or this ill health has affected your mind. We may not have always agreed, but you are probably the hardest working and humble pastor I've ever known. Your sermons are polished, instructive, and doctrinally sound. These young, inexperienced ministers filled with book learning but little working wisdom need lessons from you."

He put a gentle hand on his ill friend's arm. "You're depressed. Can't say I blame you. Lying in bed can do that to a man who is accustomed to busyness. Once you're well, return for a time until you can leave ready to relax into old age."

"I will not change my mind." Reverend Fuller's voice took on a finality that couldn't be missed. "And there's something else. It concerns the theology student I've been mentoring."

"William Tapley. You mentioned him on my last visit. Has he finished his training?"

"He's returning from New Haven later today. His final examinations were this past week. I installed him as my deacon just before my collapse."

"You must have great admiration for the young man. Could you see him as your successor? Your church may be best put in the hands of a capable and prayerful younger man. And, if what I hear is true, he's been courting Olivia. Is there a marriage in their future? She's been brought up in the church. The two will work well together in carrying on your legacy."

Reverend Fuller's thoughts returned to a previous conversation with Olivia. He'd refused to listen to her concerns about William despite the truth of her words. He had offered William his pulpit without praying about it and for all the wrong reasons.

"As William's mentor, and you as my closest friend, I must be forthcoming. William takes his studies seriously. He's intelligent and well versed in scripture. There are some areas, however, where he needs more advising before I would recommend him to pastor his own church."

"I'd be please to take over his mentorship while you convalesce. Can you tell me a little more? Since I'll be working with him, I'd appreciate your insight."

Reverend Fuller sighed. In his desire for William to marry Olivia, he'd chosen to overlook flaws in his character. "William is quite ambitious. He's young, inexperienced, and that must be taken into consideration, but he reveals some intolerance and…arrogance. I thought he might succeed me after my retirement. I may have been over anxious. He is not ready."

"Are you suggesting he may not have the necessary

gifts for ministry?"

"He needs to grow in humility and compassion. I trust you'll observe his behaviors and give him guidance. His ambitions may need to be reined in and prayers for a humble spirit given more emphasis. I admit I turned a blind eye to his immaturity and his character flaws."

"I refuse to accept that of you."

"I am not the worthy man you believe me to be."

At this, Reverend Slater guffawed. "Your humble spirit is doing you more harm than good right now. We must not be the one to extol our own virtues but self-deprecation can be pride turned inside out."

"It is not pride but loathing for my sins."

"I am at a loss to counsel you." Reverend Slater leaned back in his chair and observed his friend with a discerning eye. "I've never heard you talk this way and it worries me. Accept God's forgiveness for whatever you're holding on to that's causing such grief. I have never seen you do anything less than serve the church with your whole heart. God is your judge." He reached out his hand and rested it on his friend's arm. "Would it help you to talk to me about what's bothering you?"

"No." He no longer cared about his own image.

Bringing his sins into the light might bring him a measure of relief, but he could not reveal the truth for Olivia's sake. If it was to be made known, even inadvertently, he'd cause her more suffering.

"I feel very tired." He pressed his head into his pillow and stared up at the ceiling.

"I apologize. I have overstayed."

"No, no. Thank you for coming."

Reverend Slater stood and pushed back the chair. He pressed a hand to Reverend Fuller's forehead and said a silent prayer before stepping away from the bed. "I'll return in a few days with the hope you'll reconsider your decision about retirement."

"I won't, Mark. Expect my resignation letter."

"I'll pray for your recovery and for lightness of spirit," the minister said before going to the door and shutting it quietly behind him.

SHE HADN'T MEANT to listen in on their conversation. She'd been passing her father's slightly opened door, carrying laundry to her bedroom when she'd overheard her name mentioned. Stopping short, she listened before hurrying past when she heard Reverend Slater prepare to leave.

The minister had asked her father about rumors of a future marriage between her and William. Her father didn't answer the question but his comments about William left her stunned. He admitted William wasn't ready to take over a church. Had he also reconsidered his demand that she should marry him?

"God is your judge", Reverend Slater had told her father. His words remained with her as she finished her morning chores. She'd been taught not to make judgments against others but to leave it to God.

Forgiveness was another matter.

She could not forgive him and she couldn't wipe away the truth. She was a *Mulatto*, a word that had never passed her lips before. She feared the blackness of hate and cruelty that was the fate of the colored race, a race that was now her own. Despite his own hypocrisy, her father had taught her to stand up for truth and not back down. He'd taught her to see all men as equal under God. Those truths were ingrained in her.

Her love for Lovena was as deep as her love for the woman who she'd thought was her mother. She thought of her dreams, not just dreams but visitations, her mother's spirit standing at her bedside. If her mother could reach her through the mist of death and life, why hadn't she returned before, or had she been with her always?

Her father taught her that God works in strange ways and leaves man questioning enough to keep him on his knees. She winced at the memories of so many sage sayings her father professed.

"Mother, what am I to do?"

Listen to your heart.

The words came to her in an instant. She waited, closing her eyes and hoping for more.

The silence was broken by the sound of carriage wheels outside. She went to the window. William was stepping down from his carriage. Not now, she thought with a grimace.

Why put off the inevitable? She needed to face him. Glancing in the mirror, she straightened her cap and tucked in stray curls. She looked terrible and she didn't care. Her refusal might be clumsy but she had to get it over with, and he must take her words seriously.

CHAPTER EIGHTEEN

"WILLIAM, I DIDN'T expect you would be back this early in the day."

"My dear Olivia." He walked toward her and reached out his hand, but hers remained clasped behind her back. His expression reflected a moment of annoyance but he immediately covered the reaction with a slight upward curve of his lips. "I escaped all the revelry following exams. I was anxious to see you. How is the good reverend?"

"Recovery is slow. He has little appetite but the doctor remains hopeful."

"Thank the Lord. You must remain positive as well. I'd like to see him if I may, but first, could we sit for a time and talk?" He stretched his arm out toward the parlor couch.

She nodded, choosing a straight chair, aware that she'd annoyed him once again. "I hope your exams went well?" she asked, after he sat on the edge of the couch nearest to her chair.

"Well enough. I was sufficiently prepared and it's a

relief to have them all behind me. I look forward to my ordination and working with your father. I plan to stop at the Meeting House to meet his temporary replacement before going home. I want to assure him that I am available to help immediately."

"Reverend Slater. Father has great faith in him. They have been long time friends."

"Yes, your father has mentioned him in the past." He paused and twisted a ring around on his finger. "Enough about the business of the church." His voice grew softer. "Let's talk about our future. I realize you have been under great stress. Forgive me if my request is ill-timed, but I've spent sleepless nights wondering when you would accept me as your husband.

Olivia folded her hands in her lap and took a deep breath before looking directly into his eyes. "I am truly sorry, William. The past few days have been difficult, at times nearly unbearable. Regardless, I remain clear in my mind. My feelings for you are of friendship. I cannot accept your proposal."

"*What?*"

Olivia saw disbelief cross his face before anger distorted his expression.

"I… I admit I am stunned," he said after a long

silence. "I believe we get along quite well and friendship can lead to more. Why your father has given…"

"It's not up to my father to choose whom I am to marry." She stood abruptly, determined not to continue a futile conversation. "You wanted to see him?"

William rose slowly from his seat, adjusting his cuffs. He looked about the room appearing almost confused before turning his gaze back to her. "Is your father aware of your decision?"

Olivia took a step back. Had his eyes darkened? They appeared almost menacing to her. She lifted a defiant chin. "Why does that matter? I must decide my future."

"He has high regard for me and believes you and I…"

"May I bring you some tea, Mr. Tapley?" Lovena interrupted.

Olivia breathed a relieved sigh at seeing the maid standing in the doorway. She likely overheard and came to her rescue.

William's lips tightened in a grimace. "No. I'll be leaving after seeing Reverend Fuller."

"Lovena, please take William up to see Father." Without looking back, Olivia left the room.

"I need to check if he be up for another visitor. Best you wait here." Lovena gave a curt nod and left William standing alone in the parlor.

She returned a few minutes later. "He'll see you now."

William followed her up the stairs and to the minister's bedroom in silence.

"He gets tired real easy so don't stay too long," she said, before stepping aside from the closed door.

He nodded dismissively and walked into the room, shutting the door behind him.

"THANK YOU FOR seeing me. I'm pleased to see you're sitting up. You look comfortable."

"I look like a man who is nearing death."

"You must not say that."

"I'll hang on for a little longer, but I'm ready." He waved to a chair while observing William more closely. For a man who just completed his studies, he appeared subdued.

"I'll see you in the pulpit soon," William said, taking the seat near the minister's bed.

"My preaching days are over."

Had William's face brightened suddenly? The

minister realized what he was about to say would be even more difficult than he'd imagined.

"You may reconsider once your health improves."

"No, I told Reverend Slater today that I am retiring. You don't need to indulge me."

"I'm truly sorry to hear of your decision." William clasped his hands together and appeared doleful. "No doubt it was difficult. I pray you will remain my mentor when you're better. I have truly appreciated your wisdom and direction. Once I'm ordained, and with your guidance, I shall be sufficiently prepared to take over your pulpit. I'm sure Reverend Slater will want to return to his own ministry sooner than later."

The minister looked away, before turning pained eyes back to his visitor. "Much has happened in a short time, William. My daughter…" He paused, pressing his lips together.

"She has refused me."

The reverend lowered his eyes. "I expected she would."

"I am disappointed, of course, but Olivia and I can maintain a friendship and still work together in serving the church. You'll be happy to know I have graduated with honors and commendable recommendations."

As the minister searched for the right words, he observed William's proud smile and knew he was about to crush the man's hopes.

"My son, I have asked Reverend Slater to stay and take over my position. He has accepted. I need only to send in my resignation and my recommendation." The frailness in the minister's voice did not take away from the finality of his decision.

William hunched forward, the planes of his face hardening. "I don't understand. You led me to believe I was to be your successor."

"I know." The minister grimaced. "I sincerely apologize for misleading you."

"Misleading me? You talked of the parsonage as my future home. Was it only if I married your daughter?"

Reverend Fuller gazed at him with weary eyes. "It is with great sadness that I must tell you this. I was wrong in my attempt to plan my daughter's future and to push you toward a position you are not fully prepared for yet. I must ask your forgiveness. I've been forced to look within at my mistakes and face truths I've avoided. I encouraged you to court Olivia. I tried to force my daughter into a marriage unfortunately not of her choosing. I have also not been fair to you as your mentor. To assume leadership of a large congregation such as ours takes greater maturity. I was wrong to have led you to believe you were ready for such an immense responsibility. Reverend Slater has willingly agreed to continue your mentorship as you grow in your vocation. I must do what is best for the church."

William sat with his mouth dropped open as the minister spoke. He gave no response but as he appeared to come to terms with the news, his reddening face revealed suppressed rage.

"I am truly sorry," the minister said, not surprised at William's obvious disappointment as well as his anger. "I pray you might understand and…"

"*Understand*? I expected you would convince your daughter of the benefits of our marriage."

"I cannot force her to do my bidding."

William glared at the pastor for a long while before appearing more composed. He relaxed back in his chair, resting his elbows on its arms. "Reverend," he said between thinned lips, "I must assume Olivia doesn't know?"

The minister's brow furrowed at the unexpected question.

"I believe you had other reasons to encourage my

marriage to your daughter, reasons I suspect you have not wanted to reveal to her or to the church."

The minister twisted his shoulders toward William. "What…are you referring to?"

"Please understand, I am not inclined to reveal your secrets but I am quite disheartened." William pressed his palms to the arms of the chair and rose slowly. Standing tall, he looked down at the minister. "I'll leave you now. Perhaps you'll give more thought to your recommendation and realize my unselfish offer to marry Olivia. If our marriage is not to be, I must be able to hold my head up in the congregation. I'll not disappoint if I am named pastor of our church." His lips curved up slightly before turning and walking to the door.

"*Wait*. Why are you saying this? Where did you…" The minister sat up too abruptly, causing him to feel faint. He sunk back onto his pillows.

William turned slowly. "I took pity on you and your daughter. I was even willing to sacrifice my own scruples to marry her, despite her shameful parentage. And keep your secret."

Dread filled the minister, nearly taking away his breath. "Tell me what you know," he said, preparing himself for the worst.

"If you insist." William walked closer to the bed, resting his hands on its foot board. "My father arrived at the parsonage one winter day over nineteen years ago," he began in a hushed tone, as if he were relaying a secret known only to the two of them. "He heard angry voices in the yard near the porch and saw your wife scolding a Negro servant girl. He couldn't help but notice the girl was quite pregnant; your *wife* was not. Father noticed because of the frigid weather that day. He thought Mrs. Fuller must have rushed out of the house since she wore only a sweater and appeared chilled, clutching her arms tightly around her waist. Shortly after, you announced at church that your wife, who hadn't been seen through some of the coldest months, had birthed a child, a daughter. My father's thoughts returned to that day he'd visited the parsonage, only a few weeks earlier, and of the pregnant servant girl. She was an attractive, light-skinned Negro, father told me. He said she disappeared after Olivia's birth. Should I go on?"

The minister's fisted hands clutched the sides of his quilt but he said nothing.

"I'll continue. Olivia's coloring is obviously darker that yours or your wife's though her resemblance to you is evident, confirming my father's original suspicions. The day I told you of my decision not to father children, you commended me, and to my surprise, began to encourage me to court Olivia. I told my father. He is a decent man and most likely would never have told me the story of seeing your wife that day. But when I told my parents I might have to accept a position far from home, or worse, travel about making converts on Indian reservations, my mother was distraught. She'd already lost one son to a wretched illness and wanted me close to home. Father took me aside and encouraged me to consider the advantages of courting Olivia.

"When you urged me not to tell her of my decision concerning children until after we were married, any doubts about my father's suspicions were erased. Offspring can carry the features of a grandparent, my father believes, and he suspected that was your greatest fear. He urged me to propose, especially when you hinted at my taking over your position and making the parsonage my home. I admit I would not have chosen Olivia for a bride, but she's been raised white and demonstrates intelligence and worthy values. My father agreed that she'd make a good wife if I could overlook her beginnings and conceal it as you have done. Her service would be invaluable to me as the church's minister. I am not disappointed that Olivia refused me. I would hope, however, that you might reconsider your choice of a successor. You would not want your secret…exposed." William offered a reassuring smile and released the foot board, folding his arms across his chest.

"Olivia knows the truth," the minister said slowly and with surprising calm.

William's chin dropped.

"I confessed to her a few days ago. She's distraught. I pray you will understand and demonstrate compassion and discretion."

"Discretion?" William lifted his brow, appearing to recover from a momentary lack of self-assurance. "Like my father, I can keep a secret. Perhaps I should tell Olivia what I know. She might reconsider her refusal."

"What do you want from me?"

"Not to cause you added grief. I only ask for what you have promised me."

"I committed a grievous wrong in making such promises. I was desperate. I beg you as a Christian, a man of God, to accept my apology and remain silent. You are not ready to lead our congregation. But consider what greater damage could be done not only to Olivia but to the church if her origin was made public."

"I agree. The church would be greatly damaged if they learned the truth. I don't agree with your assessment of my abilities. Take some time to consider what I have told you." He paused. "You look tired and your voice has weakened. I'll return another day. Do not fear. I'll remain discreet for the time being. I feel confident you'll reconsider your previous decision. He stepped away from the bed. "Good day, Reverend."

He walked from the room, leaving the minister to grieve this new development and to ponder what needed to be done.

CHAPTER NINETEEN

BEN SWEPT THE carpentry shop floor, thinking about the past weeks with each sweep of the broom. A simple carpentry job had begun a journey he could never have imagined. He'd discovered a minister's scandalous past and read about a dead woman's story of heartache. If it hadn't been Olivia's story too, his find would have been an eye opener for sure, but someone else's tragedy that didn't concern him.

Except that he was in love with Olivia and he couldn't walk away.

Only if she told him to go. Only if she chose to marry William Tapley.

He needed to talk to her. With her father so ill, it wasn't right for him to ask anything of her now.

After all the sawdust was swept up, he stood the broom against the wall and walked outside. It was a crisp spring day and it felt good to breathe in the fresh air. He'd get cleaned up and ride over to the parsonage this afternoon. He'd kept Narcissa Dunn's diary long enough. Today he'd give it to Lovena.

Within an hour, he was on his way, the shabby journal tucked into the pocket of his coat. When he arrived at the parsonage, he saw Lovena at the woodpile. Dismounting nearby, he tied Liberty to the hitching post and walked to her side just as she lifted a log.

"Let me help you." He reached out and took it from her.

"I must'a been lost in my thoughts, I didn't hear you comin'."

"You were focused on dislodging this log. It's too heavy for you."

"The Lord ain't taken away my strength yet. The boy from the church usually comes and fills up my wood bin but he ain't showed up today."

"Go on." Ben waved to the porch. "I'll bring in some for you."

"Thank you. I'll be holdin' the door open."

Ben gathered logs and carried an armful up the porch steps and into the house. Once he'd stacked them in the bin, he walked out for more.

"I think that's enough for today," Lovena said, after Ben carried in a second armful."

"There's still room for more. Another couple of

armfuls should do it."

As he gathered the final load, he wondered if Olivia was home. He hadn't asked. He needed some time alone with Lovena to give her the diary. Olivia might be with her father or at the meetinghouse, he thought. She could even be with Tapley. That thought irritated him as he stomped up the porch steps and into the open door.

"What the…" Speckles howled as Ben stepped on the cat's tail and lost his footing. He tried to stop his fall while keeping a grasp on the load of logs he held. Two rolled off as one of his knees hit the floor. One of the logs rolled toward the cat. It scooted away as if it was being chased by a wild dog.

He pushed himself up and regained his balance just as Olivia rushed toward him.

"Are you hurt?"

Ben turned, slightly stunned but happy to see her. "I'm fine, just feeling a bit awkward to have you find me on my knees."

"I'm so sorry. Speckles was into mischief, chasing something. I was after her. I didn't know you were here."

Ben readjusted the few pieces of wood left in his arms and bent down to pick up one of the fallen logs.

"Why didn't you call for me, Lovena?" Olivia scolded. "I would have gathered the wood."

"You had other things to do."

"Oh, what's this?"

Ben's mouth fell open as Olivia bent down and picked up the diary that must have fallen from his pocket when he tripped.

Olivia spread her hand across the soiled cotton cover and fingered its shredded edges that revealed the leather beneath. "It's quite old, isn't it?"

Ben didn't know what to say. He held his hand out. Olivia looked at him oddly as she handed it to him. He couldn't blame her. What was he doing with a withered, old journal wrapped in flowered cloth?

"You best give it her, Ben," Lovena said quietly. "She don't need no more secrets."

Ben shot a glance at the maid.

Lovena walked to him and took the book from his hand. She handed it to Olivia. "It's your momma's book."

"I don't understand."

Ben drew a long breath. "I found it hidden in a wall when I was razing the rooms next to the barn."

Olivia looked closer at the book, opening it slowly to

its yellowed pages.

"It be Narcissa's." Lovena said, her voice strong and firm. "There ain't nothin' to hide from you anymore."

Olivia gasped, pressing the book to her breast. She stared at Lovena, then at Ben. "But you tore down those walls weeks ago. Have you kept it all this time?"

"I didn't know what to do with it." He had no excuse for holding on to it. Ben saw the questions in her eyes. He should never have read it. Hell, he should never have taken it home with him.

Lovena drew closer to Olivia and held out a gesturing hand. "We need to talk."

Olivia brushed her hand aside. "You knew he had this and you didn't tell me?"

"Livie, you and me can read it together."

No." Olivia shook her head, stepping back, her face etched in horror and disbelief before she rushed from the room.

Ben watched her disappear before turning to Lovena. "I'm sorry. I planned to give it to you today."

"Son, you meant no harm." She walked to the wood bin and lifted one of the newly placed logs and settled it into the fire. Reaching for another one, she did the same.

There seemed nothing more to say. "I should go." Ben walked to the door.

Lovena turned and looked at him kindly. "Things happen for a reason, Benjamin. Why she come in just at that moment? Why she the one who saw it lyin' there? There ain't no coincidences. Maybe she was meant to have it, not me, or the reverend."

He shook his head and walked out. The ache in his chest remained throughout the ride home and into the night.

LOVENA WAITED OVER an hour before going upstairs. The house had been eerily quiet. She'd stopped by the minister's room to find him sleeping. When she reached Olivia's door, she'd stood contemplating what to do. She heard no sound in the room. Unable to bear the silence any longer, she rapped on the door. There was no answer. She knocked again before opening it.

Olivia stood facing the door, her face stained with tears, the diary still in her hands. Lovena held her arms out and Livie walked into them. She held her as she had often done when Olivia was a small child, rubbing her back and letting her tears dampen her housedress until there was no more to shed.

"Come, let's sit." Lovena led her toward the bed. Olivia sat on the edge and Lovena took a seat in the chair next to it.

"He took advantage of her," Olivia whispered, sucking in a labored sob. "But I already knew, didn't I? I didn't want to believe it."

"There ain't no nice way to put it. Men, sometime, let that thing danglin' between their legs take power over common sense. Your daddy lost his mind that night. I ain't makin' any excuses for him. The only thing I can say is he ain't gone without sufferin' for his deed. And, for Narcissa, it's time she had some peace a mind. The Lord says to forgive."

Olivia shook her head. "I can't forgive him. He deserves to be punished, shamed as he shamed my mother!"

"'Vengeance is mine sayeth the Lord'. You know that. We ain't privy to the sufferin' sin has caused your father. When we forgive, it ain't got nothin' to do with what's between the Lord and him. It's freein' for our hearts. You don't wanna carry that kind a bitterness inside you. Your mama's book showed up for some reason. Maybe she want you to know where you come from. It's what you gonna do with it that matters now.

Olivia looked down at the diary and rubbed a tattered edge of the cloth covering, almost reverently. "When she spoke of me, her words were like warm milk. She called me Rosalee."

Lovena gave a sad smile. "She poured as much love into you as she could."

"She forgave him. She forgave him for the awful thing he did to her."

"Then she gonna be at rest. She be with the Lord and there ain't no better place to be."

Lovena reached out and rubbed the pad of her thumb gently across Olivia's damp cheek. "Time heals and who knows what God gonna do with this mess. He can take it all and twist it into a blessin'. You got to trust in Him. Take the time you need to let your grief have its way, but then you gotta fluff your hair back and lift that chin. You been givin' a good upbringin'. I know you gonna get through this."

"Right now I can't see beyond these fragile pages." Olivia pressed her hands against the book now closed in her lap. "I wish I could have known her."

"I think she's makin' sure you do with all these antics she been carryin' out."

"Why? Why have I been dreaming of her now?"

"I think she been wantin' to make things right. Your daddy may have been thinkin' he was doin' what was best. I think your momma wanted to put in her two cents. She need to be restin', Livie, and you need to be getting' on with your life. Now why don't you freshen up and go out and get some fresh air. You gotta take grief one handful at a time. Let it go through your fingers and brush it away until you ready to scoop up another handful. In time the vat gonna be empty and you be smilin' again."

"How did you become so wise?"

"What come out of my mouth don't come from anything I done. We all suffer in one way or another on this earth. When God's gotta take somethin' away, he replaces it with somethin' nobody can take from us. And when we let go of what ain't workin' anymore, he changes our insides. Once you get through this, you gonna see things through the eyes'a the soul in ways you ain't never imagined."

"Thank you," Olivia whispered, reaching out a hand to clasp Lovena's.

Lovena squeezed her hand before rising from her seat. "Go on now, wash your face, and get outta this dark room."

"I need to know." Olivia rubbed her hand across the diary's cover. "Did Ben read it?"

Lovena nodded, not sure how the girl was going to take the news. "He planned to give it to me today. Guess it was meant for you."

Olivia's mouth opened and closed. The maid could see the girl needed time to think about that.

"Do you want to read it?"

"I think your momma's story needs to be laid to rest. I don't need to read it. I was there."

"You can tell me more about her."

"I will when the time is right."

"Ben knows the truth. What must he think? Of my father? Of me? I can't believe he read it and never told me what he'd found."

"You give him some credit. You can't blame him for wonderin' about that old book hidden for all these years. He couldn't'a known what it would tell. Don't you be mad at him. If you want my opinion, I think he was the one meant to find it."

Olivia just stared at her, looking bewildered.

"When you be done workin' through all those thoughts churnin' 'round in your head and the mess a feelin's risin' and fallin' inside you, you need to talk to

Benjamin. He's in love with you. Why it's written all over his face every time he looks at you. I can't help but wonder if your momma had her own ideas about who you should marry."

Olivia's stunned expression brought a wide smile to the old maid's face before she gave the girl's hand a final squeeze and left the room.

CHAPTER TWENTY

"UNCLE SYL, WHAT'S gotten you so riled up?" Ben found his uncle muttering under his breath and pacing back and forth on the front porch the next morning.

"Damn Tapley. He thinks he can just push a letter under the door without having the decency to come in and face me."

"What is it now?"

"Here." His uncle picked up the crinkled paper he'd tossed on a porch rocker and handed it to his nephew.

Ben flattened the rumpled sheet and read it, his forehead furrowing in disbelief.

"The pompous buffoon orders a fancy bedroom set for his beloved son and just like that, cancels it. Half of the wood has been delivered already. Now I have to sit on the debt and hope another order comes in that can use it."

Ben stared at Mr. Tapley's words, his mind reeling with questions and possibilities.

"You hear what I'm saying, Ben? What's going on with you? You've been in a strange way lately."

"I'm sorry. It's hard to explain."

"Why don't you try? I may be able to help."

Ben grasped the porch railing and stared blindly out into the street. God, he needed advice, especially now, but where to begin? The wedding he'd feared must be off. Why else would Mr. Tapley cancel his wedding gift?

Uncle Syl sat back on one of the rockers and stared up at his nephew.

Ben turned, pulled up another rocker and joined him.

"Let's hear it, son."

"I found something when I was working at the Fullers, an old book hidden in a wall. I read it. Not sure if it was wise at the time but my curiosity won over common sense." When his uncle made no comment, he continued, telling him what he'd discovered. He knew his uncle well enough to know the revelations would go no further.

He confessed his own advances toward Olivia despite the well-known courtship between Tapley and the minister's daughter. His uncle didn't show surprise when Ben told him the feelings appeared to be mutual. Ben's admissions caused his uncle to raise his brows on occasion but he remained silent, listening as the story grew more complicated.

Ben couldn't stop talking. He'd stored up too much rage at Reverend Fuller and the unfair burden placed upon Olivia. He explained how he'd gone to the parsonage to give the book to the maid only to have created a situation where it ended up in Olivia's hands.

He left nothing out.

When he finished, he slumped back into the rocker and closed his eyes. When he felt his uncle's hand on his arm, he opened them and looked into the older man's face. He saw compassion and understanding.

"Ben, I admit I have a world of questions fighting for first place in my mind but none of them are important. What's important to me is that you've done a lot of soul searching. You know what you want and you just need a nudge to go after it. It's not going to be easy but I believe you and the girl belong together. If she accepts you, you could both be facing a rough road ahead. It will depend on the decisions you make together for your future. I'm proud of who you are. The girl is going to need someone on her side if the truth is made known, someone who can stand up to injustice. You need to go and see her father and plead your case." He paused before smiling at his nephew. "I believe you're going to marry the young lady. God be with the both of you."

"Thank you."

Uncle Sylvester picked up the crumbled paper his nephew had discarded. He pulled matches out of his pocket, lit the paper on fire, and tossed it on the ground to smolder. "I think I'm going to be able to put all that wood to good use for a nice wedding present."

BEN RAPPED THE knocker at the front door of the parsonage. Lovena opened and stared in surprise at seeing Benjamin dressed up in a suit. "Why don't you look handsome. You goin' to a weddin' or a funeral?"

"I'm here to see Reverend Fuller."

"Oh, Lordy."

"I could use His help."

Lovena stepped aside. "Come on in. You know he's not farin' well. He can't abide a visitor more than a few minutes. Doctor's orders. And he don't need to be gettin' upset."

"I am not here to cause a problem but I need to see him. Is Olivia here?"

"She's out back workin' in the garden. I pushed her out the door. She needed some sunshine."

"Good."

"Wait here, Benjamin, while I go and see if he's up for a visitor."

She returned five minutes later.

"He'll see you." She led him up the stairs and stepped aside when they reached the minister's open bedroom door. "Remember now. Don't rile him," she said before walking away.

Ben walked into the room, not knowing what to expect. He hoped his surprise at the minister's aged appearance wasn't obvious. He waited to be recognized.

"Benjamin Pratt."

"I appreciate you seeing me."

"Take a seat." Reverend Fuller waved a pale hand toward a nearby chair.

"No, thank you. I need only a few minutes of your time."

"As you wish. You have finished the barn repairs?"

"Yes, it should make it through a few more winters."

"I looked it over before I… before I became ill. You did a fine job. How is your uncle?"

"He is well." Ben hadn't expected to carry on even a brief conversation. The minister's voice was soft but he appeared alert.

"Has the church given you enough compensation for

your efforts? I assume that is not why you have come."

"There is no issue with payment."

The minister nodded, looking Ben directly in the eyes. He said no more.

Ben clasped his hands. He hadn't known how the minister would greet him. He'd been so determined to get it over with, but now that he was standing before him, his mind was taking a step back. He remained surprised he was being received with some graciousness. Maybe he should have approached Olivia first. What if it wasn't what she wanted?

"I suspect from the look on your face, young man, you aren't here to see how I'm doing."

Ben stood straighter, pushing away his wavering thoughts. "I've come to ask for your daughter's hand in marriage." He expected a reaction, perhaps an expression of disbelief, even anger. Instead, a shudder came from the open bedroom door. Ben twisted around to see Olivia standing there, splayed fingers of one hand covering her open mouth, the other holding Narcissa's diary.

The minister broke the silence. "Much needs to be talked about." He was staring at his daughter.

"I don't believe, sir, there is a great deal to discuss,"

Ben said, looking at him before turning his eyes back to Olivia. "I love your daughter and I also know the truth of her birth."

"You told him." Reverend Fuller's words didn't carry surprise but resignation.

Olivia stepped into the room. "No, my mother did."

Ben watched the minister's eyes grow wide.

She raised the worn book she held. "Ben found my mother's diary hidden in the wall of her room. The room where you…" She closed her eyes, wincing.

Ben walked over to reach out to her but Olivia held him off. "I know everything, Father, and I know of my true mother's love and her forgiving heart. She forgave you. She must have been a God-fearing woman. I will try to do the same."

Reverend Fuller's eyes filled with tears, a sob escaped his throat. Ben drew Olivia to him and this time, she went willingly into his arms. They turned toward each other, rather than watch her father's brokenness.

When the minister regained some composure, he looked up at Ben. "Do you love my daughter?"

"I love her with all my heart and with all I have to give."

"And you love him?" He gazed at Olivia.

"Yes," she whispered, looking into Ben's eyes.

The minister's lips quivered before a smile broke through. "If Olivia desires this marriage, you have my humble blessing and the feeble prayers I can offer."

Ben looked at Olivia, the question in his eyes. Despite her trembling chin, she smiled and he knew her answer.

"May God be with both of you."

Ben and Olivia turned from each other to the minister, a man who only a few weeks before looked stately and dignified. He appeared very old, his once robust body shrunken beneath his covers.

With Ben's hand in hers, Olivia walked to the fireplace. Taking one last look at the soiled and frayed flowered cover of Narcissa's diary, she tossed it into the flames.

CHAPTER TWENTY-ONE

"I NEED PAPER and pen."

"You need to rest," Lovena admonished, after removing the minister's dinner tray that evening. "If you expect to get stronger, you gonna need to eat more than bread crumbs and a sip of my soup."

"All I've done is rest. I'll be getting all I want when my body is in the earth."

"Don't you talk like that."

He grasped her arm as she plumped up his pillows. "I well know my time is getting short, Lovena. Thank you for all you have done for my family, and for me."

Lovena saw gratitude and remorse in his expression. "You ain't goin' nowhere tonight so you don't need to be thankin' me like it's your last opportunity."

He smiled. "You have talked to Olivia. She's told you?"

"You mean about givin' your blessin' to her and Benjamin? It's about time. The two of them gonna work things out come what may. 'All things work to the good to those who love the Lord.'" Lovena lifted her eyes up toward the ceiling. *Narcissa you got your way. Never mind you scared me half to death.*

"You're preaching to me, Lovena?"

"Only repeatin' what you been preachin' about for as long as I can remember."

"I don't deserve the peace I'm feeling right now."

"You let God decide," she scolded as she set his small writing desk across his lap.

"The weight I've carried in my heart all these years has finally begun to lift. No, I don't deserve it but I thank God for his mercy."

"Amen," Lovena sang out.

The minister smiled. "Has anyone from the church stopped by to help with outside chores?"

"Mr. Simon's in the barn takin' care of the horses."

"Good, ask him if he'll deliver a couple of messages. I'd like him to stop by the church and ask Reverend Slater to come see me in the morning, and I want to see William Tapley later tomorrow afternoon."

Lovena looked down at the writing desk. "Will you be writing them notes?"

"No, just tell Mr. Simon to deliver the messages. I have other business I need to take care of now."

Lovena nodded. After filling his water glass, she left the room.

What was that all about? It was the first time in days she'd seen him animated.

When she went downstairs and out the door, she found Olivia and Ben sitting on the porch swing wrapped in each other's arms.

"Where are you going?" Olivia asked.

"I have a message for Mr. Simon. Don't mind my business. You got plenty of your own." She winked at them as she walked down the porch steps.

"I WAS PLEASED to hear from you," William said the next afternoon. "It's good to see you out of bed and in a chair."

Reverend Fuller didn't miss the look of anticipation on William's face or his attempt at pleasantness that appeared far from genuine. The realization that William knew his secret had been devastating. The young man was far more enterprising than he could have imagined and a schemer too. Yet, he couldn't cast judgment. He had been as devious. What a fool to think he could control his daughter's future and worse, to believe he was justified in doing it. He still feared for her future but he needed to trust God.

"Have a seat, William."

"Am I to hear good news?" He pulled up a chair closer to the minister's armchair. "I admit I am not proud of the measures I felt forced to use at our last meeting. Please know I am still willing to marry Olivia and protect her from truths that would devastate her. If she remains inflexible and refuses my offer, we can still work together amiably. I consider myself a tolerant man."

The minister sat patiently, watching and listening as William spouted off as if he'd been a victim of circumstances and willing to humble himself now that he believed he was to gain what he wanted.

"Olivia will be marrying Benjamin Pratt."

"*Pratt*? She rejected my proposal for him?"

The reverend saw disgust cross William's face.

"And what of my position in the church?"

"I have not changed my mind. Again, I must ask your forgiveness for giving you false hope and putting my own needs before the church. Your threat in exposing my sin and in doing so, hurting my daughter, confirmed I have made the right decision."

William's face contorted into anger. "Why am I

here?"

"I'd hoped I would see in front of me a contrite young man. I hadn't expected you to condone my wrongdoing. For my daughter's sake and for your soul, I have prayed you would have reconsidered your threat and returned with a more charitable spirit. I see that is not to be."

The minister reached for a sealed envelope, he'd placed on a side table. "This letter is addressed to Reverend Slater and the congregation. It is a full confession and a plea to demonstrate loving kindness to my daughter. She is not responsible for my grievous sins. I have also admitted that I do not confess out of a need to purge my soul or to beg for mercy. Instead, I acknowledge that I am forced to do so to appease my former student who has threatened to expose me unless I offer him my pulpit."

"*No!*" William pushed up from his seat. "My reputation, my standing in the church will be ruined!"

"True," the minister said calmly, not surprised at the young man's rage. "If I give this letter to Reverend Slater, your future as a minister or deacon in our congregation or any other in this area will definitely be compromised. You may have to travel a good distance for a position. Perhaps become an itinerant preacher."

"You will not give it to him then?"

"Not if you reconsider your demand. I'll do my best to pretend our previous conversation never happened."

William sunk back into the chair, his expression shifting from fear, to anger, and to a modicum of acceptance. "You leave me no choice. I will remain silent."

"Your concession comes with obvious animosity rather than humility. I admit it worries me. I fear I may leave this earth without feeling secure over our agreement. Therefore, I'll place this letter in trusted hands, to be made public if you, or your father, decide to expose my past sins after I am gone.

William opened his mouth to speak but appeared to reconsider.

"Reverend Slater is close to my own age, William. If you prove yourself under his guidance, you might yet gain my pulpit or one equally respected. In the meantime, I pray you will seek the Lord's guidance in your spiritual growth. And before you assume I am protecting myself, I assure you I am not. A man must feel honorable in his own heart. I have spent too many years with a burdened soul of my own making. What others think of my actions, good or bad, carry less weight now. I desire rightness with God and mercy for my wretched soul."

He put his hand on the sealed envelope. "This is my meager attempt to protect my daughter from a cruel and intolerant world. If the truth is to come to light, and it may eventually, let it be my daughter's decision and in the way that feels right to her. Allow it to be in her hands, not yours."

Wearing a defeated expression, William nodded. He stood, hesitating, before walking from the room. Reverend Fuller thought he saw a hint of shame on his former pupil's face. He hoped it was true.

CHAPTER TWENTY-TWO

One month later

OLIVIA ROSE FROM her sitting position on her bed. She'd been listening to the birds out her window and enjoying the warmth from the sunlight that filtered through the curtains. She'd felt her mother's presence during the night and sensed she was at peace. Would she return? Olivia wondered, or was it time for her to leave and be with the angels. She opened the lid of the small wooden box beside her and rested her hand on the small bag that held the soil taken from her mother's grave. She would hold on to the traditions Lovena taught her, and treasure everything that brought her closer to the mother who birthed her. She wanted Narcissa to remain close, but if lingering kept her from the joys of heaven, Olivia needed to let go.

Her father's condition improved little over the past month and she knew his time was limited. Their relationship could never return to what it once was, but she would hold onto the goodness she knew was in him and appreciate the devoted father he had been to her.

Today, she and Ben were to be married, a small ceremony in the parlor of the parsonage with Reverend Slater officiating. Olivia could hardly believe all that had occurred and led her to this moment. If Ben had never come into her life, if he hadn't found her mother's diary; if she'd never learned the truth— So many ifs, yet none of them mattered because a greater power had been at work. She would never doubt God's hand in her life.

Ben understood her concern for the future and her need to embrace her heritage. There would be no lies or secrets between them. Truth had found its way through deception and brought a profound awareness of life she'd never experienced. She was no longer afraid or angry or in despair. God was in control. Ben loved her and, well, she couldn't even begin to express the love in her heart for him. The thought of becoming Ben's wife and being in her husband's arms tonight, just the two of them, learning more about each other, becoming one, made everything beautiful this morning.

A familiar knock at her bedroom door brought her out of her reflections.

"Livie, you need help gettin' ready?"

Olivia smiled, rose from her bed, and opened the

door. "I would love to have you help me dress for my wedding day.

Lovena beamed. "Well then, let's get you all prettied up."

UNCLE SYLVESTER STOOD proudly by his nephew's side as Olivia entered the parlor. She wore a simply designed but elegant ivory silk wedding gown with delicate lace trimming that had been worn by her father's mother. A lace veil fell to her shoulders. She carried a small bouquet of roses. Ben, looking handsome and happy, stood tall wearing a navy blue suit, a starched white shirt, and white cravat.

Their eyes met before they both turned to stand before Reverend Slater. The ceremony took little time and soon they were sharing their first kiss as man and wife. They turned around to applause from the little group. Reverend Fuller and Lovena were both dabbing their eyes and Ben's uncle wore a broad smile.

Due to Reverend Fuller's fragile condition, they had decided to have the intimate ceremony in the parsonage so he could attend. Church members, however, would not be deterred when it came to a reception for the couple. While her father returned to his bed, the small group went off to the Meeting House for an afternoon feast planned by the women of the congregation.

It was nearly ten o'clock in the evening before Ben and Olivia arrived at the Griswold Inn in Essex. It was too dark to enjoy the view of the Connecticut River, but they weren't interested in the lovely Essex scenery. Ben jumped from the carriage and held out his hand to help Olivia step down. As the carriage driver collected their baggage, Ben took his wife's arm and led her into the inn and once registered, carried her over the threshold of a small but elegantly decorated room. Their three-night stay was a gift from the congregation. Ben's uncle rented a luxury carriage for their trip and Lovena prepared a basket of wine, sandwiches, fruit, and desserts, everything they would need so they wouldn't have to go far from their room at the inn.

On the third morning after their arrival, they walked down to the water and sat on a bench looking out at the boats tied to the wooden jetty.

Ben drew Olivia close. "I love you," he whispered. "Living in my uncle's house will not be as grand as it's been these last few days, but one day we will have our own home, one I've built. I promise you." Uncle Sylvester had insisted on moving into Ben's room above the workshop and refused to take any arguments from the couple. He would still have his office and share in their mealtimes. Lovena made the decision to stay at the parsonage with Reverend Fuller.

"As long as we're together it doesn't matter where we live," Olivia said, cuddling closer to her husband. Her body still tingled from their love making an hour before. Ben refused to consider taking precautions although Olivia tried to draw him into the conversation about children. She thought of their earlier conversation as they sat quietly looking at the water.

"Ben, you insist on avoiding the reality of what our future might hold," she had told him.

Ben had placed a finger gently to her lips. "I'm not avoiding anything. We both know our path may not be easy. We can only pray hearts change."

"Even if our children are born without a trace of their Negro ancestry, I don't know if I can hide behind my color. I no longer live outside a disparaged race. You refuse to discuss the ramifications."

"Let's not worry over things we have no control over. Our children will know their heritage."

Yes, Olivia thought. *There will be no secrets.*

They rose from the bench and stood for a moment

looking out at the Connecticut River. The waters that had been flowing peacefully earlier were stirred up when a steamboat passed by. Troubled waves slapped the sides of smaller boats anchored or tied to the jetty, causing them to rock back and forth. One slammed against the wooden pier, causing a seagull that had been resting on one of the pylons to fly off, screeching as it flew away.

Olivia and Ben turned their backs to the agitated river. They walked back to the inn to spend their last few hours in each other's arms before returning home to their new life together.

AUTHOR'S NOTE: OF FAITH UNDER FIRE

During a walk in a cemetery, I came upon an old monument with the inscription I mentioned in this story. The stone was indeed moved by tree roots that had grown under it and inspired me to write book one of the Redemption series, *Of Faith Under Fire*.

What follows is an excerpt from Book Two in the Redemption Series.

Hope UnShackled

Author's Message

Although this is a work of fiction, it presents harsh realities of life in New England in the pre-Civil War period; more specifically, the devastating effects of the Fugitive Slave Law of 1850, and the amazing work of the Underground Railroad. Although the fugitive Elijah is fictional, I encourage readers to research the true account of a fugitive slave's escape from the steamship,

Hero, on the Connecticut River in 1850. This actual historical event was the inspiration for this novel.

PREFACE

Elijah's foot tore loose from his remaining shoe. He couldn't remember when he'd lost the other one, only that it was buried in muck somewhere along his escape route. Bending to slip his foot back into the shabby shoe, he ignored the bloodied cuts and scratches visible through his torn shirt sleeves, and the jagged tears in his pant legs caused by the thick tangles of brush, brambles, and thorn bushes he'd run through in his escape. Even the burning pain from the ugly gash below his knee when he fell on a sharp, protruding rock, hidden by leaves, didn't stop his progress. Silence and speed was all that mattered.

None of his injuries could compare to the pain he'd suffered from whip lashes that scored his torso and upper arms, or the invisible pain from the loss of his family that seared his heart deeper than the brands that had been burnt into his shoulder and buttocks. It was these memories that gave him the courage to run and erased any fear of death.

Since escaping from the steamship, he'd been working on as it navigated the brisk waters of the

Connecticut River, he'd come upon smoother paths to travel, but ignored them. Better to make his way through unforgiving brush until he came closer to his destination.

His owner had discovered his whereabouts and hired slave catchers to find him. The underground agent on the ship had warned him, having overheard talk of the slave catchers waiting at the Hartford docks, ready with chains to take him back. The underground network that had been his salvation to this point, had proved its dedication.

He'd been following the river, just as the underground agent directed him, and already traveled more than twenty miles, he figured. He hadn't sensed anyone following, but the sudden sound of voices caused him to freeze in place, afraid one step might crack a branch and draw attention to him. Fear lodged in his throat, his heart still pounding from his swift trudge through the thicket. Through the brush, he watched two white men pulling a small boat out of the water. He'd been told many New Englanders were anti-slavery sympathizers, but there was no way of knowing if these men were friend or foe.

He knelt, trying to suppress his heavy breathing from

his abrupt halt behind the sparse tangles of fallen limbs. He waited until the men finished dragging the fishing boat off, before daring to go on, further inland this time, where better cover could be found.

He ran on like a doomed man escaping the gallows, just as he'd done months earlier on a dark, cloudy night, leaving behind the red clay of North Carolina and leaving behind the grave of his beloved wife, Belle. His young daughter, Emiline, had been sold off at the slave market further south. The master bragged about the good price she'd brought and laughed at his pleading when he tried to find out where she'd been taken. Too many young ones, born of slaves, were wrenched from the arms of their mothers and taken away to be sold for profit.

He would never go back. He'd die first.

Despite the sweat dripping from his brow, his shoulders quivered from a sudden chill that ran up his back now that evening brought colder temperatures. He'd been running since dawn. His destination had to be close.

He'd stopped only to catch his breath when his hurried movements left his throat parched and his chest aching. In late afternoon, he'd come upon a farm with a crop of tomatoes, either green or near rotting, but still on the vine. Despite eating the tomatoes and some berries he'd found along the way, his stomach growled with hunger.

He crouched on his haunches and pulled out the map the agent had given him and studied it. The crudely sketched signposts were meant to lead him to a station, a safe house. The agent told him a closer one was filled, and he'd have to travel these extra miles to another one.

He'd already found some of the signposts shown on the map—cracked flower pots, rags attached to trees, clusters of rocks oddly placed. If he'd been following the right path from the previous signpost, he'd find another one soon.

Sucking in a deep, ragged breath and releasing it, he looked down at his shoeless foot crusted with mud and black from filth. He wrapped his fingers around the bare bloodied toes, squeezing them and adding pressure to ease the constant ache, before he rose from his squatting position. Wiping away sweat that dripped into his eyes, he trudged on.

As he eyed tree branches above him, searching for the next sign, he stumbled over a gnarled tree root protruding from an old oak. Searing pain shot through him when his cut shin, crusted with dried blood, hit the ground, but he stifled a groan. Breaking a near tumble with bent arms, his forehead sunk into mud. He wiped the silt from his face and hair with his sleeve, pushed himself up and went on, limping now. The one shoe he still wore was drenched in mud, the sole open like a gaping mouth. He considered leaving the shoe behind, but even its meager covering helped when rocks impeded his path.

A half-mile or so later, he spotted the signpost he'd been looking for, a red printed rag tied to a tree limb. A salty tear rolled down his cheek to his lips. He wiped it away. He wasn't lost. He considered reaching up and untying the rag to wrap around his bleeding foot, but another runaway might one day search for the same sign.

He walked on, too tired to run. Another few miles, he thought.

In darkness now, with only the moon and stars to lead him, he held onto renewed hope. He was alive, still breathing, and free. The New England frost hadn't set in yet, but autumn nights were growing colder. His torn clothing would give little protection. Yet, that fragment of red cloth lifted his spirits and gave him another measure of strength to go on.

Pushing away occasional doubts that invaded his thoughts, he whispered a prayer that he was still following the right path. Then he saw it, a rusted lantern attached to a fence post, just as the agent described it.

He pressed his back against a tree trunk, his knees nearly collapsing beneath him as the weight of his journey and the unforgiving aches in his limbs could no longer be denied. Burying his face in his hands, he gathered scattered thoughts that pulled and propelled him throughout his journey. He steadied his breath, garnering what little strength he had left to face whatever was before him. Using his sleeve to wipe the salty sweat from his cheeks, he lifted his eyes to the dark sky. The quarter-moon gave little light for the path ahead, but he needed no more to push him forward.

Had he found the right place? Was this Mr. Michael Jamieson's land? The agent said that Jamieson was an abolitionist leader and would help him. If he'd been misdirected or followed signs in error, then what? Would it be a compassionate stranger, or someone who would delight in capturing a runaway slave?

CHAPTER ONE

Connecticut, Autumn, 1850

"AW, LIVIE, BLACK don't become you. Mr. Benjamin's been gone over two years now. Before the Lord calls me home, I want to see you in pretty dresses again."

Olivia frowned at Lovena, her elderly maid and dearest friend, who rocked slowly in her usual chair on the back porch. "I came out for some morning sunshine, not to hear the same lecture. And stop talking about leaving me for heaven's doors."

"The Lord's been good to me. How many people do you know living past seventy around here?"

"You have been uncertain of your age throughout my lifetime."

"I hear my old body creak and see my wrinkled hands, never mind my hair getting thinner." Lovena put a hand to the flowered scarf wrapped around her white wooly hair. "But you are ignoring the subject. You need to push aside grieving the best you can and get on with living. Your boys and your girl, they need to see you moving on with your life."

Olivia winced as she stood at the porch rails looking across the long yard at her tall sons who were chopping wood near the barn. She was trying, really trying. Her days were filled with busyness, but nothing filled the emptiness that lived in her since her husband's death.

"I heard Mr. Benjamin in those last days, Livie. He didn't want you spending your life in sorrow after his death. He had someone picked out for you, if I recall, though my mind loses bits and pieces of the past."

"I don't want to talk about that." She remembered, too well, Ben's plea for her to remarry.

"He was looking out for your happiness. If he's not at peace in heaven, it's because you won't let go."

Olivia pressed a hand to her heart. That possibility never entered her thoughts. If her preacher father was still alive, he'd probably give her a similar sermon.

To calm the surge of anxiety Lovena's words aroused, she drew in slow, easy breaths, before turning to face her. "I've found a measure of peace living in my memories." Lovena's compassionate gaze revealed her understanding, but even as Olivia spoke the words, she realized the futility of going on as she'd been doing. Everything reminded her of Ben. He'd just turned forty-five when his body couldn't fight off the pneumonia. Memories of their twenty-two years together, the joys they shared, and the sorrows, kept him alive. But, lately, memories weren't enough to fill her darkest hours. Needs crept in and tugged at her resolve to remain Ben's wife always, body and soul.

"Could it be because you fear letting go when you don't know what the future holds for you?"

As always, Lovena struck a chord of truth within her. Her attachment to everything that held a memory of Ben wasn't helping her sons or her daughter move on. With a weary shake of her head, she settled into a nearby rocker, one of the many her husband had carved. Ben had built their farmhouse and most of the furniture while teaching his sons carpentry skills. Their oldest son, Jeremy, inherited his father's gift of working with wood, and he'd already obtained a few customers of his own.

If he's not at peace in heaven, it's because you won't let go. She couldn't brush off the weight of Lovena's words. Sensing the maid's patient presence waiting on her, she forced a smile. "I have begun to make changes."

"Well, that's good to hear." Lovena gave her a full-cheeked grin.

Olivia frowned, knowing her next words would sadden her beloved, elderly maid, who'd been with her since her birth. "At last night's meeting, I told Michael Jamieson I could no longer harbor runaways." Her breathing caught at seeing a pained expression cloud Lovena's features before her lips tightened into a set line of acceptance. Although Lovena had always been a free negro, she knew well the horrors the enslaved of her race endured. Her effort to suppress conflicting feelings mirrored her own. But what else could she do? Family turmoil had become a daily occurrence. She needed to make changes.

"Aah, that is a *big* step," Lovena said, giving a grim nod of understanding. "You've done so much for runaways over the years."

"Please know that shutting down the safe house is the hardest decision I've ever made. My sons, especially Jonah's recent rebellion, leaves me little choice. Ever since he read the government's concessions to the South in the new Slave Act, he refuses to listen to any of my arguments to continue. Jeremy is less hostile in his opposition, but he recognizes the greater dangers we face."

"I never thought you'd keep it going after Mr. Benjamin passed. It's been hard for you without him to lean on, and I've heard your boys urging you to quit."

"With the stronger penalties enacted for harboring runaways, they worry for my safety. I realize, too, my sons could be held liable. They are young men now, no longer able to hide behind my skirts. Ben and I accepted the dangers, but what if my sons were arrested, even imprisoned for my willingness to break the harsher laws the government has put in place? My decision may not be forever, but until they find their way, I believe it's the right thing to do."

"I haven't missed Jonah's tirades. I hear him arguing with you. That young man buckled under Mr. Benjamin's firm hand but, lately, he's been a handful. Don't know what's gotten into him. Anger drips out of him like a leaky spigot. It's hard to believe he's nineteen already, and with an older brother like Jeremy who's trying too hard to be the man of the family, it isn't easy for him."

"Jeremy is so much like Benjamin. He worries too much about me when he should be thinking of his own future."

"He's troubled in a different way, and I can't put my

finger on it." Lovena gave a sad shake of her head. "Lord knows, the safe house has been a life saver for many, but you're doing what is best for now. You have other worries that need tending. And it's not just your children's prickly moods that create tension. You've been uptight and edgy."

Olivia hadn't realized her own restlessness had been so obvious. She gazed up at the oak slats in the porch roof as the rockers creaked against the floorboards. She didn't want to admit she longed for normalcy, even tranquility, rather than the unexpected that marked all underground workers—secret, scribbled notes hurriedly passed on from one agent to another, often frantic preparations, sudden arrivals in the dead of night, and worst of all, hearing news of a runaway captured, despite the underground's efforts.

Lately, other longings kept her awake at night, ones more personal. As much as she wanted her memories with Ben to be enough for a lifetime, she was lonely.

"Things will get better in time, you'll see."

Her companion's comforting words pulled her from musing on a certain someone she'd tried too often to push from her mind. "Thank you for your support, Lovena, always. Your advice cuts deep, but is seldom wrong."

"I'm glad I'm still good for something. I'm not much help around the house anymore."

"I need your wisdom and friendship most of all." She reached out for Lovena's workworn hands when she saw the old maid's eyes brimming with tears. How hard it is for this woman who has served her entire life to accept rest and care from others, Olivia thought. When Lovena became unable to keep up with heavier chores, she had offered to leave, but she wasn't going anywhere. She had been more of a mother to her than the woman who raised her.

"What are you thinking about, Livie?"

"Hmm... My mother."

"I'll be. What made you think of Narcissa now?"

"Perhaps it's the roses. Their sweet scent carries with the breeze this morning." She looked out at the fragrant rose bushes that lined the fence along the stone drive. A few clusters of crimson roses still clung to their stems. Soon they would fade and dress the ground with shriveled petals. Roses always brought memories of her birth mother who died a few months after her birth, a woman who'd visited her only in dreams and spoke silently through her diary found years after her death.

"If it wasn't for my mother's eerie interference, I might never have gotten involved with the Underground Railroad."

"Not surprising to me that Narcissa reached beyond the grave to speak her mind, but I always believed in such things." Lovena squeezed Olivia's hand before reaching for her cane. "There is no reason to be going back to the past again. You're putting up another defense against facing your future." She pushed herself up from the rocker. "I need to check on the meat I've been stewing. Time to add some vegetables."

Lovena had been gone only a few minutes when the porch door swung open and Rosalee stepped out.

"I've finished my chores, Mother. May I go to Sarah's now?"

"Yes, but be back by three to help with dinner." She smiled at her daughter who had her father's sandy-colored hair, hazel eyes, and the same sprinkle of freckles on her nose.

Rosalee rolled her eyes as if she'd heard the same words many times before. "Sarah's pups are almost ten weeks old. Her mother is after her to give them away soon. When can I bring mine home?"

"I'll talk to Sarah's mother. Have you picked out one

you like?" She'd given into her daughter's pleas for a dog weeks ago.

"Oh, yes. He's the smallest one of the litter, but he's the sweetest."

"He will be your responsibility."

"I know. I can't wait to bring him home, Mama." She kissed her mother on the cheek and took off down the porch steps.

"Say hello to Mrs. Griffin," Olivia called out as she watched her run across the lawn toward their neighbor's farm.

Lovena, who stood in the doorway listening, gave a hearty chuckle. "She may be sixteen but when she calls you *Mama*, she's the sweet child she is and not the one that tries to act like she's all grown up."

"She's becoming a young woman. I wish my mother could see her."

"Narcissa would be proud. She's most likely looking down from heaven wearing a broad smile."

"I believe she is." Lovena had known Olivia's birth mother before she died and had shared many stories about her. "Enough talk of the past." Olivia gave a self-reprimanding frown and rose from her seat. "I have errands to do in town, but first I am going up to change."

"Change?" Lovena eyed the dreary black dress Olivia wore as she opened the screen door and stepped into the house."

"I think I'll wear that pretty green calico you have left hanging for days on my closet door." As she walked through the kitchen and up the stairs, she heard Lovena's cheerful laughter and felt better than she had in a long while.

A FEW DAYS later, Olivia pulled ripened beets out of the dirt in her the kitchen garden that bordered the rear of the house and porch. Setting them in a basket, she was startled by the heavy crackling of leaves nearby. Still crouching, she twisted her neck toward the noise.

"Mr. Stiles." She rose, lifted the basket of vegetables and brushed dirt off her long apron. "I didn't hear you arrive."

"You were working hard tugging at those root vegetables. I didn't want to disturb you, and it was my pleasure watching you. I heard you shed those dismal, dark colors."

She didn't miss the way the neighboring farmer eyed her up and down. Though she'd kept her trim figure, she was forty-two and past the age for the look the man gave her.

"What can I do for you?"

"One of the legs cracked on my bed. I came to see if your sons could fix it."

She wasn't surprised by the repair. Mr. Stiles obviously enjoyed food. His sack coat was pulled taut over a large belly and its buttons were close to popping off.

"Jeremy is back in the wood shop. You're welcome to go and speak with him."

"I'd much rather spend time with you, Mrs. Pratt. You've been alone a long time. I'm sure it's been difficult. We all have needs."

Had he just winked at her?

Stiles took a step closer. "I was wondering, the County Fair's coming up soon, and the Harvest Dance. I don't dance myself, but the women always put on a nice spread. I'd like to take you along."

He reached out and laid a hand on her arm. She shrugged it off and took a step back. "I am not interested, Mr. Stiles."

"We've been neighbors for years. It's time you called me Edgar." His smile broadened, revealing yellowed, chipped teeth.

She swallowed in disgust.

"I see Jeremy's brushing down his horse outside the wood shop," Lovena called out in a raised voice from the porch above the garden. "Isn't he the reason you're here, Mr. Stiles?"

The man shot an irritated glance at the maid leaning on the porch rail, glaring at him. He turned back to Olivia. "Another time?" Tipping his worn felt hat, he walked off.

"The *nerve* of the man," Olivia muttered once she'd joined Lovena on the porch.

"You're an attractive woman. He wanted to find out if you're interested."

"In *what*? How dare he suggest that I might have needs."

"Some men think a woman who's been alone a long time is missing the act."

"I've got a good mind to pull out those black dresses again."

"Oh, no, you won't. I packed them away. You need to get accustomed to being admired. You have natural beauty you can't hide. The man's right about one thing. You have been alone a long time, and you have too much to offer to stay that way. There are old fools like Mr. Stiles, but there's some good men left around too. Why don't you just be open to what the good Lord has for you, whatever it might be?"

"I have chores to do." Grumbling, she pulled open the kitchen door and waited for Lovena to enter. Once inside, she realized she'd been ungrateful. "I appreciate that you came to my rescue."

"It's nothing. Mr. Ben didn't like him either, and I don't think you've seen the last of him. Anyway, I have a message for you from Mr. Daniels."

She gave her a quizzical look. "When did he come?"

"Just before Mr. Stiles rode up. They missed each other by a couple of minutes. Good thing. I was coming out to tell you."

"I didn't hear either of them arrive."

"You were most likely digging deep in your harvesting and in your thoughts. I was sweeping the front porch when Mr. Daniels rode up. He gave me the message and rode on. I asked him if he wanted to talk to you, but he was in a hurry, said he had a lot of people to see. You were the first stop."

"What is the message?"

"Mr. Jamieson's holding an emergency meeting

tonight at seven o' clock. The Daniels will come by in their carriage a little after six to pick you up, like they've done in the past. He said he understands if you choose not to go, but seeing you're on the way, they'll stop by just in case.

Olivia nodded. The Daniels were aware of her decision to stop the safe house. It was kind of them to stop by on their way, regardless, and offer a ride.

"You know what an emergency meeting usually means. Maybe it's best you don't go," Lovena said.

"It may not be about a fugitive needing shelter and if it is, I can offer to help in other ways. I will not go against my word. The safe house is closed."

"Uh, huh." Lovena's lips twisted into a doubting smirk.

Olivia didn't miss it. Her maid was well aware of her despair over her decision. "I made a promise to my sons, Lovena. And who knows, there may be other important news Michael believes can't wait. I won't miss the meeting."

LATER THAT EVENING, Olivia waited on the front porch for Mr. and Mrs. Daniels, fellow underground railroad agents who lived a few miles down the road. When they arrived, Mr. Daniels helped her into his carriage where his wife, Mildred, sat, before climbing up onto his seat and urging the horses on.

"I appreciate the ride," Olivia said, sitting across from Mildred, a petite woman, a few years older than Olivia, who greeted her with a welcoming smile.

"You're right on the way, my dear."

"Are your guests still with you?" They both liked to refer to the runaways they harbored as guests rather than fugitives.

"Yes, the older man, Joseph, is still ailing. We think in another week or two he'll be strong enough to be on his way. The journey was too much for him at his age. He wanted his son to run off without him, but the boy refused to go. We'll keep them until the man regains some strength."

"Bless you. I suppose Michael has told you of my decision?"

"Yes, it's understandable. I wouldn't be able to continue our safe house if I lost my husband. I've admired your bravery, especially raising three children alone."

"More likely, too stubborn to stop, rather than a measure of bravery. I debated whether to attend tonight, but I'm hoping I can be of help in some way."

"Whatever you can offer will be appreciated."

"I know, but we've lost safe houses all over New England since the changes to the Fugitive Slave Act. Now I've added to the numbers."

"You have done your share, Olivia. With the harsher punishments and the hefty fines, agents fear being caught. They must think of their families. Hard working farmers fear being unable to pay their mortgage if they're jailed. Shop keepers can't afford to spend six months in jail or pay a $1000 fine. They could lose their farms or their businesses. These slave catchers have no decency, and the law credits their actions."

"The law is on their side," Olivia said, frowning.

"The Union wants to appease slave holders. It's a savage compromise. Some slave catchers will even kidnap a freed Black to replace a runaway they didn't catch. They'll rip up their freedom papers. If the poor soul tries to go to court, it does no good," Mildred said with a discouraged shake of her head.

"Not when the courts won't allow African Americans to speak in open court. Prejudiced white neighbors don't want to speak for them either. Without proof of their freedom, judges must obey the law and the slave catchers profit. It's shameful." Olivia bit into her bottom lip, as a knot of anger settled in her throat.

She was doing what was best for her family, but at the same time, her heart held threads of guilt for no longer keeping a haven available for a desperate runaway. Perhaps she should have stayed home tonight.

"I can't imagine the horror of being a free man only to be captured and enslaved. To these hunters, anyone with brown skin could bring profit. Canada seems the only safe place for them now. Despite our efforts, Walter and I become so disheartened. It's difficult to see an end to the savagery," Mildred sighed.

The rumble of wagons passing by, drew the women's attention as they entered town. After a short distance, Mr. Daniels drove the carriage up a stone path lined with evergreens that led to Michael Jamieson's stately Georgian style home. He drove around to the back of the house. Another carriage and a couple of wagons were parked behind each other. A few horses were tied to nearby rails, signifying that other members had already arrived.

Once inside the large, dimly lit parlor, Michael Jamieson's daughter, Amy, offered the dozen or so guests lemonade. It was an unseasonably warm night for early October, and the cool drink was welcome.

As a few members conversed, Michael Jamieson drew a chair up to where Olivia sat on one of the two tapestry sofas. "How are you?"

"I am doing well." She smiled at the man who'd been a good friend to her and Ben. Michael had been a constant visitor throughout Ben's illness, sitting by his sickbed and telling stories that brought laughter into their grieving home. Michael's dark, wavy hair was receding now with streaks of gray. Lines had deepened on his face, but he was still a handsome man. Seeing him, Olivia was reminded that Ben, as he lay dying, had encouraged her to consider Michael as a future husband. She'd been angry at Ben for even suggesting that she remarry. Now her discomfort came more from confusing thoughts and feelings than from Ben's plea.

"I missed you at the last meeting, Olivia. I understand and, perhaps, this wasn't the best meeting for you tonight. I'll be asking... Well, I'm glad that you came. By the way, you look lovely."

"Thank you." Olivia's cheeks warmed at his compliment. The genuine flattery she saw in Michael's gray-blue eyes, and the sincerity of his words, caused her to feel something she thought had long since died within her. Maybe shedding her blacks had cracked opened the door of her heart.

"I have some good news from Canada. Henry arrived safely."

"Thank the Lord." Olivia remembered the young runaway well. She'd harbored him for a couple of weeks. Too often news wasn't as good. Some runaways never make it to the border, die on the way, or are captured. Others are never heard from, leaving those who aided them to wonder about their fate.

"He was weary, the letter said, too thin, but he made it. He's been given refuge until he finds work and a place to live permanently."

"He left us last spring. He's had a long journey."

"He found work along the way and few problems. He was a fortunate one. I knew you'd want to hear." Michael eyes remained on hers a few moments longer before he gazed around at the gathering of men and women. "It looks like everyone has arrived. It's time to begin."

He stood and walked over to the fireplace, standing before its opening that was surrounded by gray marble and flanked by simply carved columns. Candles, set in tall brass holders, flickered behind him on the mantle. A large, antique gold-framed picture of a fox hunt decorated the wall above the hearth. He presented a stately appearance, Olivia thought, though he wore no suit coat, only a dark vest over a plain cream-colored linen shirt.

"I thank all of you for coming at such short notice," he said with earnest at the small group of farmers, shopkeepers, and women dedicated to the abolitionist cause. "I had hoped for better attendance, but it is a trying time." He paused when his daughter waved good-bye and disappeared down the hall that led to the front door. She lived nearby and often came to help her widowed father set up for meetings before returning to her husband, Robert, and their two small children.

When he heard the door close, he continued. "Let me explain the predicament. A runaway, working on the steamship *Hero,* escaped off the ship down river near East Haddam yesterday. Our network warned him that slave catchers were waiting for him at the Hartford dock. An agent directed him here. He is in my root cellar, as I speak."

With the last remark, a few in the audience gave audible groans. Michael, a respected town lawyer, was well known as a leader of the abolitionist movement and, therefore, had both friends and enemies in the legal system.

"No doubt the agent who gave him a map to my home was unaware of the recent scrutiny I've received from authorities," Michael continued. "He needs immediate shelter before we can plan the next leg of his journey. As all of you know, some stations have been removed from the list because of the Fugitive Slave Law's new mandates."

A couple of the men in the audience grumbled and others nodded with solemn faces. Olivia felt a sting of despair that she was one of them. She had made the right decision for her family, hadn't she? Safe houses were desperately needed. More and more brave souls under the yoke of slavery, hearing of the work of the Underground Railroad, were fleeing their masters. Many never make it North before being captured, but those who did, believe they will find freedom in the Northern states. Unfortunately, it has become a false hope for many because of changes in the laws meant to appease the South. Canada had become the new sanctuary.

Olivia pushed her doubt aside and focused on Michael's words.

"The man, Elijah, came to my back door late last night, ragged and shoeless, with bloodied wounds from his journey. It appears no one saw him arrive, but he is not safe under my roof. If one of you could shelter him, I'll move him out as soon as I can find another house along the route to Farmington."

Whispers flew through the room. Soon members stood, acknowledging the fugitive wasn't safe in Michael's home, but one by one, or as couples, they refused to harbor him. Some had distant relatives visiting or were traveling soon themselves. Two men admitted the new heftier penalties and the danger of imprisonment, left them with no choice but to refuse. They couldn't support their families if they were tossed into prison for breaking the law. Their wives offered to help with clothing needs and produce from their harvests. Two men offered to set up or check warning signals and route markers or carry messages, common needs in all the anti-slavery organizations.

Olivia clutched her shawl more tightly against her breast as if it would stop her heart from its rapid pounding. Warring thoughts clashed. There was a desperate need and she'd never refused before. She thought of Jonah's outburst a few days earlier. Her younger son's behavior lately was troubling, but he refused to talk about anything except the new law's sanctions and her agreement to stop harboring fugitives. She'd even admitted to herself that she welcomed change. *A normal life, an end to grief, a chance to build a future free from anxiety and secrecy.*

Was she being selfish to pray that someone else would stand up and offer? They all knew it was dangerous for Michael to harbor a fugitive. His house would be the first to be searched if he came into question. His knowledge of the workings of Connecticut's Underground Railroad and his contributions to the anti-slavery cause were immeasurable. If he was arrested, the entire movement in the area would be endangered.

Mutterings continued around the room, but soon the group began to disperse. Olivia remained seated while Michael shook hands and thanked those who offered aid in other areas. As the room cleared, he delayed Walter and Mildred Daniels. Olivia remained seated, listening as he asked them about the health of the older man in their keeping.

When their discussion ended. Mildred Daniels nodded to Olivia, acknowledging they were ready to leave. She stood and came forward.

"I'll take him. Can he be transported tonight?"

ABOUT THE AUTHOR

A veteran English teacher, Elaine presently teaches public speaking part time at a CT community college. She is a member of the Historical Novel Society, CT Romance Writers, Women's Fiction Writers Association, and a PAN member at Romance Writers of America. As a lover of the ocean and its energizing beauty, she happily resides on the Connecticut shoreline with her golfing husband, Drew, and delights in being a wife, mother, and grandmother.